© 2022 Robert

The Badlands Bounty is a work of fic represent the likeness of actual events or persons.

Sign up to Receive Free Books and $0.99 New Releases[1]

For every new book release, I randomly select 200 mailing list subscribers to receive a free advance Kindle copy. All other subscribers will receive a special offer to purchase the book for only $0.99 on the day of release before the price goes up to $3.99. This is not a newsletter. You will only be contacted about free books and $0.99 discounts on New Releases. Thanks again for your support!

---

1. http://www.enterechoeffect.com/

Dedication

To the encouragers in my life, thank you.

Chapter 1

Since his arrival at the Ionith docks, Harcan's initial impressions of planet EL-73 had lived up to its reputation.

It was a shithole. There were only scattered patches of civilization between vast stretches of uncharted, swampy terrain crawling with dangerous lifeforms. To boot, it smelled like a giant landfill.

But through the mess of tangled trees, marsh, and stench, Harcan had found the bar he was searching for, hidden from the prying eyes of the Republic authorities. The sketchy watering hole was a known haven for rogues and scoundrels, just like him.

Harcan noticed the grumpy old bartender in front of him. He was short and stocky, with a buzzed high-and-tight haircut. He wore a white button-up shirt—and a black vest that was at least a size too small. His rounded face carried a lot of water and was spotted up like he was wearing blush. To Harcan, he looked about a hamburger away from a heart attack.

A bead of sweat ran down his pasty forehead as he took a swig of liquid courage, sizing up Harcan's abnormally large frame through the cloud of cigarette smoke.

He shook his finger and grinned. "A little birdy whispered something in my ear about you, mutant. We don't get many of your kind on this side of the galaxy, but I do hear *plenty* of rumors," he hinted.

"*Oh?* Like what?" Harcan asked with his deep, throaty voice. He stared through his shot glass while swirling it around on the damp wood bar.

"They say the scientists on artificial structure EL-59 were ordered to create *attractions* for their Halloween festivities years back. Monsters to terrorize their population. Supposedly, the fat cat Republic senators are bloodthirsty bastards, and they like to gamble on the survivors from their high-rise penthouses," the tipsy barman stated.

3

"Sounds like a tall tale if you ask me," Harcan growled.

The bartender sneered. "Funny that you mention that. What are you? Seven feet tall?" the bartender probed.

Harcan hesitated. "Thereabouts. Everyone rounds up an inch, don't they?"

The barman raised his bushy white eyebrows. "Rumor has it, one of the monsters escaped, and it resembled a *giant* black werewolf near seven feet, with fangs, claws, and rippling muscles. And if that weren't enough, they described a white streak of fur above the left eye, *just* like yours," he pegged with a smirk. He raised his voice, seemingly enticing the drunk mercenaries at the end of the bar to join in on his hunch.

The bartender stood proudly, pulling his vest over his bulging belly. "Now, I'm no betting man, but if I was, I'd bet the farm you're the big black furry freak they were talking about," he concluded. The grizzly mercenaries snickered at the barman's comment.

Harcan raised his glass in the air as the laughter quelled. "*Touché.* It seems there's no fooling you, old man. You're looking at genetic engineering at its absolute finest."

The barman took another shot and gazed ahead with a long face. "Well, I'll be damned. I guess this confirms our fears. Our Republic leaders have spiraled completely out of control."

"I hate to break it to you, but it's been that way for a long time," Harcan mumbled.

"That doesn't make me feel any better. I've worked this deadbeat job for twenty-eight years now. No retirement or pension, while those senators sit pretty on EL-59. Rich, powerful, living the high life of luxury on an artificial structure. They've got the time and money to come up with ridiculous festivities and create a werewolf? For *one* Halloween party? That's just *filthy* rich, ain't it, boys?" he asked, looking down the way at the mercenaries.

"I'll drink to that! Money to burn!" one of the scruffy mercenaries slurred, raising his beer.

"It was *four*," Harcan growled.

"What's that?" the bartender asked, lowering his eyebrows.

Harcan stood up from his stool, and the vinyl seat cushion exhaled in relief from his 600-pound frame of fast-twitch muscle fibers. "I did *four* Halloween parties, *four* years in captivity in EL-59's simulations." Harcan pulled his custom-made silver trench coat forward and buttoned it up slowly, taking his sweet time.

Harcan narrowed his deep amber eyes at the bartender. The yellow, almond-shaped eyes were exaggerated by his midnight-black, almost blue fur. The thick hair around Harcan's head flared out wildly like a lion's mane, intensifying his already massive stature.

"What's my tab?" Harcan curled his lip on one side, flashing a canine.

"Ah. Eighteen credits," the barman replied, cupping his hands as Harcan trickled the Republic coins over.

"Sixteen, seventeen... and *eighteen*," Harcan counted. The barman closed in his stumpy fingers, shifting his eyes up at Harcan as he towered over him. He turned around in front of the cash register, dumping the coins inside.

"And my shotgun, fork it over," Harcan demanded.

"Of course." The bartender's turkey neck jiggled as he struggled to heave Harcan's forty-pound weapon up on the bar.

"*Ugh.* Good grief. I guess you don't worry about anyone stealing that damn thing. No one else could lug it around," the bartender joked as Harcan snatched it off the bar with ease.

"Much obliged," Harcan said, tipping an invisible cap.

The group of six mercenaries seated to his right were staring, and for good reason. Harcan was armed to the teeth, literally. His weapon of choice: a two-petawatt laser shotgun. Its pitchfork-tipped barrel could fire three simultaneous beams at the speed of light.

One of the mercenaries glanced over his shoulder at Harcan. "So, uh, where ya headed there, *boy*—I mean, bounty hunter?" he slurred in a thick, backwoods accent.

"Not far," Harcan growled, turning up the last bit of vodka.

The merc nodded. "We heard rumblings that the Wolfman might be prowling in the area. Rumor has it you brought in the Blue Baron bounty 'bout a week ago? He was wanted in fourteen systems for nearly sixty murders. Dangerous, elusive fella, like a ghost." He sneered.

"Even more so now," Harcan joked as his eyes drifted through the mercs. One of them heckled at his comment, and the room turned awkwardly silent.

The merc cleared his throat. "Musta been a tough job, even for the Wolfman. I can't seem to remember the reward on the Baron's head, but oughta been a pretty penny," the redneck pried. He smiled, flashing a set of pearly white perfection—except for the single missing tooth in the middle.

"Enough for my room, board, and the tab." Harcan put down his glass.

The thin, weaselly looking merc with patchy facial hair raised his eyebrows. "We both know the Blue Baron paid out more 'nat, but I respect your privacy. Anyhow, you don't need to worry about us, big guy. We're smugglers mostly, and *way* too drunk for any problems," he spoke up.

"I was counting on it." With a quick flick of the wrist, Harcan aimed his shotgun at them from the hip.

"Whoa! What—the—fuck?" One of them threw his hands up.

Another merc stood up slowly with bulging eyes. He put his trembling hands in front of him. "H-hold on now, we're all blue-collar mercenaries here, surely we can work *something* out? We don't mean no trouble," he pleaded.

"Ain't no trouble," Harcan muttered. He pulled the trigger, melting five of the six mercs with one shot. The wide array of beams plunged grapefruit-sized holes clean through them as a red mist wisped into the air, scorching the table's legs behind them as it crumbled over in flames.

"No! Take it outside!" The bartender ducked down behind the bar, inadvertently raking a bottle of liquor with him as it shattered on the floor.

The only surviving merc dove on the deck and crawled behind the bar as Harcan circled around. The spurs on Harcan's black boots clacked as he mercilessly fired into the inlet. Bright flashes strobed as holes pierced through the bar, all the while the wooden gate door swiveled back and forth on its hinge, squeaking loudly.

Silenced ensued as smoke trailed up from behind the bar.

"You alright back there, *boy*?" Harcan mocked in an exaggerated backwoods accent while checking his laser shotgun.

"H-he's dead. *Dead!*" the bartender cried out.

"Hm." Harcan peeked around, observing the merc's seared, blackened chest cavity. The flurry of laser javelins had riddled his torso through and through, steam pouring up from the body.

The bartender's hands shook as he wiped his sweaty forehead with a handkerchief. "The docks have always been n-neutral ground for mercenaries. I've gone nearly thirty years without a shooting in my bar."

Harcan shrugged. "Streaks are meant to be broken, old man. It turns out your smuggler patrons here double crossed the wrong folks. *My* clients," he replied.

Harcan made his way toward the corpse behind the bar. He reached inside his long coat and pulled out a handheld device, holding it up to the target's face. He peeled open the corpse's eyelids. "Looks like a dead ringer."

PROCESSING...

PLEASE MAINTAIN SCANNER POSITION...

RETINAL AND FACIAL IDENTITY CONFIRMED: ARCON CORRALIM

MISSION STATUS: COMPLETED. TARGET DECEASED.

YOUR ACCOUNT WILL BE AWARDED 3600 CREDITS BY THE END OF THE CURRENT PLANETARY NIGHT CYCLE. THANK YOU.

"No, thank *you*," Harcan muttered, plopping back down on the barstool. He fired up a cigarette. Truth be told, Harcan wasn't officially licensed for this line of work. He was running all his gigs through a bounty hunter's identification that was sent to kill him years ago. It was a failed attempt that granted Harcan access to all the tools of the trade. It allowed him to fly under the radar of the Republic authorities and make some coin.

Harcan held out his pack of cigarettes to the traumatized barman. "You want one?" he asked.

The bartender nervously peeked over at the scorched bodies littered about. "No," he answered, burying his face into his hands. Harcan took in a long draw from his cig. He puffed out a cloud that covered the bartender's dazed face.

Harcan stabbed his cigarette toward the bartender. "You know, before I started raising hell in here, you had an *awfully* big mouth on you. You're a snarky, meddlesome old fart. I'm surprised someone of your age wasn't educated in the art of *shutting the fuck up*. You've at least heard of it?"

The barman's bottom lip trembled. "I didn't mean nothing by it. I was just 'funning around. You know how it is on these outer worlds. The bounty hunters and mercs come in here with the long faces, and I try and c-cheer them up, that's all. We just try and have a g-good time," the bartender stuttered.

Harcan smiled, outstretching his arms. "We're having a great time now, aren't we? Pour me another shot!" he snarled, showing his canines.

"R-right away." He poured the alcohol, spilling some of it on the bar.

"Pour straight!" Harcan roared.

"I'm sorry. It's my nerves. They get to me." The bartender held the bottle with both hands.

Harcan glared at the bartender. "If I get wind that you said *anything*, I'll be back. We both know you're the only witness. Leave a *full* bottle of vodka on the bar and get your sweaty, frumpy ass outta my face before I change my mind," he warned.

The bartender put the bottle on the bar and quickly darted out of sight, nearly tripping over his own feet. Harcan put out his cig on the bar and flicked the butt onto one of the corpses.

Harcan shook his head. He knew it didn't make sense to leave the bartender alive, but he did anyway. "Gettin' soft," he muttered.

Harcan snatched up the bottle of vodka and downed half of it. He wiped his mouth and glanced at his wristwatch. "Hey, Ellie, do you copy? Is the ship ready?" he asked.

"*Yeah*. It's been ready." A young girl's voice erupted through the speaker on his watch.

"Good. I'm headed your way. Keep a lookout for anything suspicious," he ordered.

"Did you claim the bounty?" she asked.

"Course I did," he answered.

"Well, let's go. I'm not getting any younger," she hurried.

Harcan scoffed as he marched through the saloon doors and onto the wooden dock outside. The old planks creaked beneath his enormous frame.

He was surrounded by a lush, dark-green swamp with murky water. It was a humid night with a thick green fog covering the area. The noxious, dank smell rushed into his hypersensitive nostrils, causing him to scrunch up his snout. "Every last one of these outer worlds smells like a toilet," he mumbled.

As he made his way back to his ship, he noticed the swamp was teeming with exotic, brightly colored alien life at this hour. Most of the lifeforms he could see resembled small reptilians. They glided from tree to tree using wing-like flaps of skin under the front legs.

The shrieking creatures seem alerted by Harcan's presence, as their high-pitched, earsplitting screams intensified. They jumped back and forth on the tree limbs, shaking them violently.

Harcan downed the other half of his vodka. He reared back and tossed the empty bottle at one of the trees, shattering it. "Now shut the hell up!" he roared. Most of the critters were silenced as they scattered into the dense foliage.

One remained. It squirreled around the trunk of an old tree before taking flight directly above Harcan. "What the—"

He raised his shotgun as the creature defecated, raining down a slimy string of yellow feces from above, narrowly missing him.

He snarled, firing his shotgun at the creature as it escaped into the opposite tree line. He continued firing, and several dozen trees toppled over as his fearsome weapon melted through the tree trunks. Burning bark and tree limbs sizzled as they crashed into the swampy waters.

Harcan turned and marched toward his Roland-class freighter at the end of the dock. The crude, tube-shaped craft's vertical thrusters emitted a faint blue flame at idle.

As he neared the ship, the rear liftgate slowly lowered as Ellie waved at him from inside.

Harcan gestured toward the water. "Hey, you wanna take a swim before we go?" There were dozens of slimy, eel-like creatures weaving around the wooden dock posts below.

Ellie leaned forward, peering into the murky waters. She looked up at him and faked a smile. "You first," she answered.

Ellie was a four-foot-tall synthetic with shoulder-length curly brown hair. She had freckles all over her round face with big hazel eyes. Her appearance was convincingly human, and she could pass as a young Shirley Temple at a glance. Harcan lit up another cigarette. He took two draws and flicked it into the water, watching as it fizzled out.

Ellie snapped her fingers. "Hey, why are you taking your sweet ass time? You know the rules. We can't stick around after claiming a bounty," she demanded with her hands on her hips.

"Maybe I'm wounded," he said.

She looked him up and down. "No, you're not."

He laughed. "But what if I was? What if I'd died in there?" he asked.

She rolled her eyes. "I'd probably freeze your corpse and snack on the leftovers for weeks. Until I found another gig, that is," she responded.

"You don't eat meat," he commented, turning his body away from her to take a piss.

"No. But since you're drunk, and saturated in alcohol, it might buffer the awful taste," she replied. It began to drizzle.

"That reminds me, I could use another drink," Harcan said as he stumbled up to his ship's rear gate, hunkering low through the circular cabin. The rain pitter-pattered on the metallic freighter as Ellie sealed the gate. Harcan placed his shotgun on the magnetic rack to his right, just inside the door.

"You just *had* to get wet, didn't you?" she asked.

"Here we go with the wet dog jokes," he replied. He arched an eyebrow as Ellie began skipping around the ship excitedly.

He shook his head, following her with his eyes. "In humans, there's a psychological term for these wild mood swings, but I can't recall the term. Maybe your software adopted a clinical disorder along the way?"

"How much?" She changed the subject, batting her eyes up at him with a smile. "How much did we make this time?"

He rolled his eyes. "Thirty-six hundred."

"Not bad. I get twenty percent, right?" she asked.

"That's always been your cut. Nothing's changed." Harcan sat down, stretching his furry legs out on a bunk bed. He stared ahead as the rain spotted up the bubble-shaped windshield in the cockpit.

Ellie stared at Harcan. "I lost communication with you in the bar."

"Really?" Harcan asked, pretending to be surprised.

"Yeah. I heard the bartender asking you some personal questions, then *conveniently* I lost communication before your response," she said.

"Strange," he mumbled. He figured the less she knew about him, the better.

Ellie shifted her eyes at Harcan. "*Any-way*, where to now?" she asked, plopping down in the pilot's seat. A thick cushion on the chair raised her high enough to see the instrument panel. She spun around in the swivel chair a few times before locking it down.

Harcan yawned. "Go to Republic Port 47. I need to withdraw funds so I can pay my annoying little helper," he replied.

"Woo-hoooo!" she cheered, pumping her fist into the air.

Harcan's ears perked up like a dog alerted to a blaring siren. He covered them with his paws. "You make those high-pitched noises as if my hearing isn't hundreds of times more sensitive than yours," he reminded.

"I'm excited. I've almost saved enough for an upgrade. I've got my eye on a new adult-series model." She crossed her arms.

"How delightful. My own little android, growing up before my very eyes," he replied with a sarcastic tone as he stowed his boots under the bed.

Ellie sighed. "Can you stop referring to me like I'm some run-of-the-mill android? There's little parallel between myself and them, and you know it. I'm a *transcendent*. My consciousness was mapped after a human's and transferred to a synthetic chassis. That makes me *much* different. Not sure why I have to keep reminding you of that," she said.

"Maybe you should try telling me things when I'm sober," Harcan slurred.

"Which is never," Ellie mumbled. She spun around in her chair as a holographic display appeared in front of her. She guided her finger upward on the purple star map as the ship lifted off quickly, blasting through the thick haze of the murky swamp as they soared upward.

"Autopilot, rendezvous at Republic Port 47," she ordered as Harcan began to snore loudly. The turbulence caused his enormous body to jostle around in the bunk as they broke through the green, hazy atmosphere. They zipped past a group of colossal transport freighters hovering in the upper clouds.

Harcan wasn't sold on the idea of transcendents. Their artificial intelligence was designed to mimic a deceased human's intellect and personality traits. Not only was the technology controversial, he doubted the transcendents could pass as their human counterparts. In his view, there were too many small nuances to sentient beings, making them near impossible to replicate effectively.

As they reached space, a weighted tether deployed as the ship began to roll. Ellie unbuckled from her seat, tiptoeing toward Harcan's bunk. She stopped, observing his slow, deep breaths. Ellie leaned in, reaching inside his coat pockets cautiously. She felt around as Harcan began to drool. Ellie looked down, gulping as she noticed his dinner plate sized paw. It was twice the size of her head, with each claw longer than her entire hand.

Suddenly, Harcan's eyes opened, glaring right at her. "Find what you were looking for?" he asked with a growl.

She jumped back with bulging eyes, showing Harcan her palms. "No-no, it's just—I was checking if you had any leftover change. I didn't want it to fall out of your pockets and get lost."

Harcan leaned up slowly. He dropped his head in disappointment, closing his eyes as he sighed. "You thought I was withholding credits from you? You really think I'm *that* cheap?" he snarled, lowering his eyebrows.

Ellie looked away. "Well, it's just—I know you like to gamble, and your communicator went offline. You were in that bar for a *long* time. My time is valuable too, you know."

Harcan shook his head, but held his stare at her. "Hm. So you were going to take twenty percent of my poker winnings?" He arched an eyebrow.

"Anything you earn on *my* time, I get twenty percent of it. That was our deal. Humans I've worked for in the past usually try and stiff me. I'm used to it," she stated.

He chuckled. "Do I look human to you?"

"No, but half your DNA *is* human," she replied.

"And your programming is designed to simulate human behavior, so I guess that means neither of us can be completely trusted?" Harcan asked.

"To be fair, I've never done anything like this before," she added.

"*Hey.* Hand me my shotgun, you little shit." Harcan pointed behind her.

Ellie bit her lip. "Uh. *What?*" She did a double take toward the formidable weapon.

"Calm down. If I wanted you decommissioned, it'd be over with by now." He grinned.

"Reassuring, I guess." She spun toward the rack and stood up on her tippy toes, lifting the massive weapon from the magnetic grate. It skidded across, creating a screeching sound.

Harcan's ears twitched, and he scrunched up his thick black snout. "Be careful with it," he warned.

"I'm trying. I hate this damn thing! It's so heavy!" she complained.

"I thought you were supposed to be strong for your size?" he joked.

"I am. Ugh, *here.* Things like that are just another reason why I want a taller body!" She rolled her eyes, dumping it over into his lap.

He pointed the barrel away from her, aiming it at the rear gate. He pulled back on a slide just above the trigger, splitting the weapon into two sections. This exposed a honeycomb-shaped compartment inside near the trigger.

"See that? Those pentagon-shaped holes?" He tilted the weapon for her to have a look.

"Yeah," she said, crossing her feet as she backed away.

"The lasers are powered here. Batteries go in those slots. Each one of them costs me two hundred credits. They last about ninety days on average, depending on how busy we are," he explained.

"I had no idea you spent that much just on ammo," she stated.

"That's not even counting parts and maintenance. I do it myself, but it's still expensive and time consuming," he said.

"I get it. This is all a big investment," she commented.

"You're damn right it is. That's part of the reason I'm the best. I pay for the best, and I don't go cheap on my stuff. When I can afford it, I'll be making repairs to this ship. I may drink, curse, and gamble, but when it comes to my equipment, I don't half-ass it," he stated.

"Gotcha. *Odd*, but, whatever," she muttered.

"Which brings me to my point—what did you tell me when we first met, over on that mining planet, EL-102?" he asked.

She glanced up at the ceiling. "I gave you my labor rates, twenty percent. I told you I'd work year-round."

"Before that, Ellie. What was the first thing out of your mouth?" He arched an eyebrow, looping his index finger counterclockwise.

"*Oh*. I mentioned that I was the best hacker sidekick on this side of the galaxy. I told you about my military-grade software, and you checked my credentials. Then you hired me on the spot," she replied.

"And have I ever given you a reason *not* to trust me since then?" he asked.

"No," she said, putting her arms behind her back. She began slowly tapping her foot.

Harcan nodded and leaned toward her, glaring into her synthetic caramel-hazel–colored eyes. "Then don't give me a reason not to trust you either. It should work both ways. When my equipment starts malfunctioning, I *replace* it," he said, snapping his shotgun back together aggressively. Ellie flinched and took a half step back as it clicked loudly.

"Follow?" he growled.

"Y-yep. Uh-huh. Got it," she said with wide eyes.

Harcan grinned and placed his weapon on the rack. "Now, how long until we reach Port 47?" he asked plainly.

Ellie cleared her throat. "Three hours, maybe less," she replied.

"Good, I'm going to shut *one* of my eyes. Wake me up before we get there," he ordered.

"Smartass," Ellie mumbled. She waddled back toward the cockpit and sat down. She stared at the deck, twirling her thumbs. "Harcan," she said.

"Yeah?"

"Can I ask who's our next bounty?" she asked, shifting her eyes away from him.

"They call him the *Imp of Corrolion.*"

Ellie spun around, staring at Harcan as he shifted his weight around on the bunk. "You've got to be shitting me. I can't believe you would even consider it. That's one of the most dangerous bounties in the galaxy."

"One of the most rewarding, too," Harcan replied, yawning.

Chapter 2

Republic Port 47 was an installation on a moon with almost no atmosphere. Harcan woke up groggy and with a slight hangover. He glanced at the pair of red-yellow stars on the black horizon. One was slightly larger than the other. Behind him, a giant blue-green gas giant loomed in the skyline with swirling clouds and cyclonic storms throughout.

"You've been here before?" Ellie asked.

"Once or twice," he replied.

"Wanna tell me why we're here? We're fully stocked on supplies," she asked.

"You'll see."

The moon colony was nestled between two large mountain formations. Port 47 consisted of four twelve-story buildings, each connected by covered walkways. Around the structures were dozens of hologram projectors. Very few of them were in working order these days, displaying advertisements for various attractions.

The colony was once a powerhouse trading port decades ago. Now, it had been reduced to a galactic rest stop with an assortment of sketchy characters: merchants, smugglers, mutants, androids, bounty hunters—even a few scattered Republic authorities.

The vibe was blue collar and gloomy, a place past its prime. Everyone seemed to be focused on getting what they needed and leaving.

While the chances of recognition were low on this side of the galaxy, Harcan thought it was best to lay low. He usually steered clear of high-traffic areas and wore a hood over his head.

Harcan and Ellie made their way from the space docks out onto the covered walkways. Harcan peered down, overlooking an enclosed commons area with merchants, bars, and cruddy food joints. He panned left and right as he stopped in front of the Republic credit dispenser. "*Hey*, Ellie. Keep an eye out." He nodded.

"Sure," she responded, humming to herself as Harcan scanned his wristwatch near the dispenser.

REPUBLIC CREDITS ADDED TO WALLET: 101,700

THANK YOU.

Ellie's eyes widened as the holographic screen projected the balance. "Whoa. Why are we carrying so many credits?" she questioned.

"Because the Imp bounty requires thirty thousand credits just to enter EL-174's atmosphere. It's heavily policed by orbital troopers and pirates," he answered, turning toward her.

"But what about the rest? That still leaves over seventy thousand credits. That's not smart to be carrying around," she warned. Harcan ignored her question, continuing to check his recent transactions.

Ellie put her hands on her hips. "And why the hell is the Imp way out on EL-174? That planet is nothing but ice," she asked.

Harcan glanced at her, raising an eyebrow. "Because he's *hiding*, Ellie. That's what fugitives do, remember? They go to remote worlds and hope we can't find them," he answered.

Ellie sighed. "Smartass. I know *that*, but—"

"*Hey*. How much did you say that new adult android model was, the chassis you've been wanting?" Harcan interrupted.

"Um. It's a top-of-the-line adult-series model, Harcan. Fifty-five thousand credits. Why do you ask?" She narrowed her eyes.

Harcan grabbed her hand, pressing a button on the side of his wristwatch that beamed light onto hers.

CREDITS TRANSFER

INPUT: 60,000

CONFIRM TRANSFER TO NON-LIFEFORM? YES

PASSCODE: 7810

CONFIRM? YES

"There you go. That's enough for the new adult model you want, plus a little more from the last bounty, for good measure." He nodded.

She narrowed her eyes at him. "I don't know what to say—*wait*. This sounds an awful lot like goodbye, Harcan. Are you giving me a parting gift?" Her arm dropped lifelessly after the transfer was completed.

"Something like that. I thought you'd be happy," he answered, looking away.

"Well, I'm not. After I upgrade my chassis, I'll be broke with no job," she responded.

Harcan took in a deep breath. "This would have happened sooner or later, Ellie. We had a decent run together. There's plenty of bounty hunters 'round here who need hackers, smugglers too—I'm sure they'll be needing a sidekick with your skillset." He turned his back on her and took several steps.

"*Hey!* Just like that, you're *ditching* me?" She shook her head. He walked down the glass walkway and stopped, looking at the two stars in the distance.

Ellie caught up and stood beside him. "Can you at least tell me *why*? I deserve that much, don't I?" she asked.

Harcan pulled out a cig and fired it up. He took a long drag and exhaled, filling the space around them with smoke.

"You know there's no smoking here. It's posted everywhere," she warned. Harcan gazed forward without a word.

"Is this because I checked your coat for credits? I thought that was settled. It won't happen again," she insisted.

Harcan raised his dark, bushy eyebrows. "That has nothing to do with it. This is something new I've decided."

"I don't understand why you wouldn't need a partner for your most dangerous mission yet. It makes no sense. Are you drunk? Is that it?" she demanded.

"Not yet," he replied. Harcan glanced toward a row of neon-lit bars down on his left. Several prostitutes were standing outside in skimpy attire, along with a half dozen shady characters huddled together in the adjacent alley.

Ellie sighed and shook her head. "If you don't have enough respect to tell me the truth after the shit we've been through—good riddance! Your head wasn't filled with many brain cells in the first place, and you've killed off the rest of them with your addiction," she scolded.

He did a double take at her. "Why are you still standing here? You got your money, you made your point, now *go*!" he roared, leaning close to her. He snarled, flashing his canines.

Ellie's eyes lit up. "You know what? I think I just figured this out," she muttered.

Harcan narrowed his eyes at her as she began to walk away. She stopped, glancing over her shoulder at him. "You're impatient."

Harcan tilted his head. His pointy ears perked up briefly before flopping over. "*Impatient?*" he asked.

She pointed at him. "You're choosing these increasingly dangerous missions for a reason, Harcan. Same reason you're drinking and smoking more than ever. But apparently, none of it is killing you fast enough, is it? This whole thing is a suicide mission. That's why you're ditching me. You're going after the Imp bounty *alone* because you know this is your last rodeo," Ellie stated.

Harcan dropped his head and sighed as Ellie stormed off. He flicked his cigarette butt off the walkway, gazing through it as it slowly fizzled out on the ground. "Maybe it's better to burn out than to fade away," he muttered.

He noticed several smugglers walking below. They were wearing long leather cloaks with tinted glass helmets that obscured their faces. One of them stepped on his cigarette butt, stomping it out.

"Excuse me," a robotic voice erupted behind Harcan on the walkway. Its tone was loud and obnoxious. Harcan turned around and noticed an older, dull-green humanoid android facing him. He glanced behind it and caught a glimpse of Ellie disappearing out of view as she descended a set of steps. He gritted his teeth in anger as the android blocked his view.

"*Sir.* Excuse me," the old robot repeated. It was an ancient model with a boxy torso. The rubbery skin over the face was almost featureless, like a mannequin. Harcan observed it had been mixed and matched with various parts. The arms were different sizes, and the legs seemed to be a generation apart. He noticed a few laser scorches on its shoulders, arms, and torso.

"What the hell are you supposed to be?" Harcan stood up tall, towering over the android.

The robot looked up at Harcan. "Greetings. I am Zet-Fourteen. You might be unaware, but smoking in this area *is* prohibited. The fine for this violation is four thousand Republic credits," the android informed him. As it spoke, a horizontal white light blinked near the mouth area.

Harcan shrugged and glanced down at his paws. "Are your optics fried? I'm not smoking," he responded.

"Ah. But you *were*. I recorded you in the act, from a distance," the android answered proudly.

"You were spying on me?" Harcan demanded.

"I'm willing to delete the video file of your criminal activity, for a price. Otherwise, I would be forced to transmit the data to the local Republic authorities," it explained.

"Fuck off." Harcan poked the android's torso armor with the tip of his claw, nudging it backward. "You're not even an official Republic bot. You're a bottom feeder, a scammer," Harcan taunted, looking it up and down.

"Sir, my price is fair to prevent a costly and potentially time-consuming infraction with Republic authorities. I can offer you a limited-time three-hundred-credit discount to erase your unlawful act," it haggled.

Harcan walked away. "Get outta my face."

"Two thousand credits, please. This is my *final* offer," it insisted, following close behind Harcan.

Harcan glared over his shoulder at the bot as it continued pestering him down the walkway. It dashed forward and stood in front of him, blocking his path. "Sir. *Please.* Pay the fine and—"

Harcan growled, grabbing the android by the neck. He picked it up with one hand, lifting its feet off the ground. Harcan closed his other paw and bashed the top of its head, hammering it like a nail. The android's arms snapped off at the elbows as it attempted to shield its face. "Cease y-your attack immediately. I *am* Republic property!" the android pleaded with a distorted voice.

Its optics popped out its head as Harcan turned and tossed the android thirty meters down the walkway. The robot shattered into a thousand pieces on impact. Its metal head popped off when it clacked against the ground and bounced several times before rolling out of sight.

Dozens of people on the walkway below stopped what they were doing, taking notice of the commotion.

"You!" a male voice behind Harcan erupted.

"What now?" Harcan mumbled. He turned around and noticed an average-sized humanoid with deep blue skin. There were scars all up and down his forearms and neck. He had no nose or ears. He was wearing a pair of oversized circular goggles that were tinted red. He wore a shiny white vinyl jumpsuit that was snug in all the wrong places.

"You destroyed my android," the strange figure stated.

Harcan looked him up and down. "What are you, the robot's pimp?" Harcan joked.

"Something like that," he replied.

Harcan glanced back at the android's debris. "Well, here's a piece of business advice—don't scam six-hundred-pound werewolves with short tempers," he replied. Harcan leaned toward the stranger and raised his upper lip. His canines were less than an inch from the unusual humanoid's face.

The stranger lifted his glasses, revealing a set of glossy black eyes that reflected a nearby purple neon billboard.

"You don't frighten me." The blue humanoid smiled, showing off a mouth full of triangular, shark-like teeth.

Harcan's head whipped toward the sound of stampeding footsteps behind him. Ten Republic guards were running at Harcan in formation. They were a serious-looking bunch, armored in head-to-toe gunmetal plating, black masks, and sporting heavy laser rifles.

"What the hell is all this?" Harcan demanded.

"You've destroyed Republic property," the mysterious fellow replied.

"A platoon of soldiers called in over that piece-of-junk android? I did you a favor by scrapping that old shitbox." Harcan pointed at the android's debris.

The stranger chuckled under his breath as another formation of Republic guards approached from the opposite direction. Now, Harcan was boxed in from both sides. He looked over the handrail of the bridge. "Shit." It was too far of a jump. He turned, reaching for his shotgun under his coat.

"No!" The blue humanoid threw up his hands at Harcan. "Don't do that, Harcan. You'll lose, eventually," he warned.

Harcan had a puzzled look on his face. "How the hell do you know my name?" he asked.

"There's not much I don't know," the stranger replied.

The guards surrounded Harcan as the blue humanoid circled him. "My name is Tarron. I am an aide to the Republic senator for this district. I'm not sure if you've been keeping up with current events,

Harcan, but in the last forty-eight hours, the Republic is on the brink of a civil war."

Harcan crossed his arms, leaning back on the handrail. He shrugged. "What's that got to do with me?"

Tarron put his hands behind his back and glared at Harcan. "*Everything*. We've uncovered a ring of corruption on EL-59."

Harcan looked away. "You're a little late on the scene, detective."

"Not really. We've known about the senators' ring of cruel entertainment for years. I know you were genetically engineered as a part of their Halloween festivities, the killings, and—"

Harcan snarled and charged Tarron, grabbing him under the arms. He hoisted him into the air and held him over the bridge. "You *knew* about it, but you didn't put a stop to it? *Huh?*" Harcan roared, spitting in Tarron's face. The guards raised their weapons at Harcan, but Tarron waved them off.

"Wait. Wait. *Wait.*" Tarron's glasses fell off as he kicked his legs, looking down. His eyes bulged. "Harcan. *Listen* to me. We're on the same side. The leadership on EL-59, they're our enemies, too," Tarron pleaded.

"So, *now* you wanna do the right thing? After mass murder, brainwashing, and torture?" Harcan growled, squeezing Tarron's neck. A flashback rushed into his mind.

He recalled the EL-59 psyops and intelligence agents torturing him with electric shock sessions. The purpose was to generate hate in Harcan's mind for humanity. He vividly recalled the burnt smell of his singed fur—punishment for not meeting his daily killing quota.

Sometimes, slaughtering the survivors wasn't easy either. Harcan was challenged by organized human militias that formed on the installation. Armed survivors could carry anything from spears to laser rifles, depending on the simulation's various time periods. Harcan was trained by the EL-59 staff in military tactics, flanking maneuvers, deception, and concealment to combat this.

He needed to be versed in a wide variety of environments too. EL-59 had artificial biomes: forests, swamps, urban areas, and mountains. These themed battlegrounds served as Halloween festivities such as *Escape from the Twilight Woods*, *Full Moon Manor*, *Night of the Wolfman*, or the *Metro Massacre*.

The senators watched the action unfold from the comfort of their high-rise penthouses, shielded behind giant bulletproof viewing glass. Or they watched from the hundreds of hidden cameras placed throughout the simulations.

Tarron locked eyes with Harcan. "Help us put an end to EL-59, Harcan," he whispered, struggling to speak. Harcan slowly pulled Tarron away from the ledge. He sat him down and released his grip around his neck.

Harcan laughed. "What makes you think I'd go back to that shithole when I barely escaped with my life?" he asked.

Tarron caught his breath. "The death games are still going on EL-59, Harcan. They've replaced you with new mutants, and thousands of humans are being forced to survive. We both know they don't have a choice," he stated.

Harcan turned his back on Tarron. "Not my problem, and even if I wanted to go, I don't see how I'm supposed to help."

Tarron cleared his throat. "We have a plan. Our idea is to make it look like you were recaptured. We have an agent posing as a bounty hunter. Once his ship approaches EL-59, they'll send a drone inside his freighter to confirm its contents. Then they'll lower their shields, and that's when we strike," Tarron said with authority, clenching his fist.

"And you're gonna save the day, just like that?" Harcan asked suspiciously.

"We're going to remove the senators from power and relocate the victims to a safe zone. If we don't do something before the civil war breaks out, the population on EL-59 will be used as bargaining chips, hostages. We'll do all the work, Harcan. We just need you to help us get our foot in the door," Tarron said.

Harcan gritted his teeth. "And what's my reward if I risk my hide on this mission?"

"*Reward?*" Tarron asked.

Harcan lowered his eyebrows. "You really thought I'd go back to EL-59, for revenge? That was your hope?" he asked, shaking his head.

"Well, we hoped so, yes. But I have *other* incentives," Tarron hinted, as he stepped forward, projecting a blue hologram in front of him. Harcan's head dropped as the hologram flickered, displaying a young girl.

"We've been looking for your partner, *Ellie*, for some time. We recovered her, just now, walking alone. She's wanted in two systems for stealing a freighter and killing a former coworker," Tarron informed him.

"*I* ordered her to steal that freighter," he muttered, touching his chest.

"No matter, intelligence reports pin the crimes on her. There is significant evidence for a conviction. You *do* know the penalty when an android commits these crimes?" Tarron questioned, holding up his index finger.

Harcan glanced away. "Dismantled," he answered under his breath.

"Exactly. Now, we both know Ellie's more than *just* your sidekick. If you want to keep your little super-hacker friend from being pulled apart for scrap, I suggest you muster up some good ol'fashioned vengeance for your old pals on EL-59. Otherwise, we'll have to enforce the law," Tarron threatened. His jagged fangs gleamed in the neon light as he smiled.

Harcan growled. "You sack of shit. You took that wide angle with the moral high ground about stopping Republic corruption, then smack me in the face with blackmail? I oughta rip you in half right here. Matta fact, you think your soldier boys here in their shiny new armor are quick enough to stop me before I turn you inside out? Because I don't," Harcan warned, flashing his canines.

Tarron stepped toward Harcan. "That's it, *channel* your aggression, that's what we need. The problem is, you're directing it toward the wrong person. Let me ask you something. Who do you think protected you while you worked as a bounty hunter under someone else's identification? Who do you think paid Marx to smuggle you out of EL-59, Harcan?" Tarron posed.

Harcan's eyes widened. Tarron knew the name of the guard that helped him escape. Marx snuck Harcan out using a trash bin full of decomposing bodies.

Tarron pointed at his chest. "We're the *Initiative*, a secret organization within the Republic bent on bringing down corruption. We've been building our case against the senators for years, and now is our time to strike. Even our freighter pilot, Yassita, risked her life to get you off EL-59. If Republic authorities would have searched the trash compactor on her ship and found you, Yassita would have been killed for treason."

Harcan looked away. It was impossible that Tarron knew those specifics. The memories of his escape that he'd buried deep down suddenly surfaced. He remembered the rotting smell of corpses in the trash bin as he was mashed between them. He recalled being covered by the blood of those he'd killed.

During the experience, one of his victims awoke from the heap of bodies, pleading for help like a mortal would. Before he died, his cries revealed the other side of the story: the population was also manipulated into conflict against Harcan for the sake of entertainment. That was the moment that Harcan discovered the citizens he murdered were never his enemies.

It was all a form of manipulation, and for a time, this realization drove Harcan to the brink of madness.

Tarron showed Harcan his palms. "You should consider that we've helped you for a long time, Harcan. Think about Ellie before you make your decision. You refuse to help, not only is *your* fate sealed but so is hers."

Harcan grumbled as Ellie was pushed through the ranks of the Republic soldiers. Her hands were bound as she stared up at Harcan. "I swear, I leave you for five fucking minutes, and look what you've managed to get us into," she stated as one of the Republic guards aimed a rifle at her back.

Harcan looked left and right. He sighed. "Assuming I'd consider this, what happens next?" he asked.

Tarron raised his index finger. "The other half of the job comes into play."

"Other half?" Harcan asked.

"Yes. The vampire, Orchid. Do you keep in touch with your fellow escapee from EL-59?" Tarron questioned.

"Not even Birthday cards," Harcan replied.

Tarron grinned. "We know that Orchid is on Pison, and she's alive. We'll need *you* to convince her to come to EL-59 also."

Harcan shook his head and chuckled. "I don't think you know her very well."

"No, but *you* do," Tarron replied.

"Why the hell is she on Pison, anyway? That planet is a furnace," Harcan muttered to himself.

Tarron shrugged. "Stranger things have happened, I suppose. How did a genetically engineered werewolf team up with a criminal android hacker? One who's stolen illegal military software dozens of times just to stay ahead of the technological curve?" Tarron challenged, glancing down at Ellie. "That's also a crime by the way," he added.

"We needed an edge, and every bounty hunter needs a hacker," Harcan responded.

"Look. If you can convince Orchid to go to EL-59, you win Ellie's freedom. I'll have her record expunged. Do we have a deal?" he offered Harcan, outstretching his arms.

Ellie batted her eyes at Harcan. "Oh, *please*, Mr. Wolfman, only you can save me!" she said in an overdramatic damsel-in-distress voice. She rolled her eyes and looked away, crossing her arms with a frown.

Harcan looked at Ellie. "Fine. I'll do it, but I'm taking back the bonus I gave you," he stated.

"I'll earn it back." She smiled ear to ear as the guard unbound her shackles. She ran forward, hugging Harcan just above his knees as she kicked her leg back. "Yay, back together again! More drunken adventures!" she proclaimed.

Harcan growled under his breath as Tarron raised an eyebrow at the pair.

Tarron pointed at Harcan and cleared his throat. "Listen up. If either of you deviates from orders—Ellie's done. We've encrypted her with a virus that can corrupt her system in seconds, destroying her. Don't try me, Harcan. Go to Pison and pay your old friend Orchid a visit. Convince her to come to EL-59. Then get in touch with me. *Here*," he said, tossing Harcan a small chip. "I've uploaded Orchid's location and our communication frequency. Download it to your watch so we can stay in touch."

Harcan sighed. "I still don't know how I'm supposed to persuade Orchid to help me do this," he said.

Tarron smiled. "Try blackmail. The same way I convinced you with Ellie. Explain to Orchid that if she doesn't help us, I'll order my intelligence services ceased. We'll stop protecting you both, and your location data will be discovered in days. You could also motivate her by using the moral-high-ground angle. Explain how you're providing a *service to the galaxy*. That sounds pleasant, doesn't it?" he asked, tucking his hand under his chin.

Tarron and the Republic guards turned away from Harcan. Tarron stopped in his tracks about thirty meters away. "Oh, and Harcan, have some decency and take a damn bath!" he shouted. Harcan flipped him off.

"I tried to tell you. Your fur reeks." Ellie looked up at Harcan, staring into his amber eyes. "You just had to stand out in the rain last night and get wet, didn't you?"

Harcan pointed at her. "We've got bigger problems. Listen to me—"

"*No.* You listen. Those Republic guards would have killed you if I didn't calm them down," she stated.

Harcan laughed. "I highly doubt that, Ellie. You're a fugitive in two systems. Tarron told me that if we didn't help them, they would scrap you down for spare parts."

"*Oh?* Then that sounds a lot like you're doing this whole mission for me?" she asked, smiling from ear to ear.

Harcan looked at her with a blank stare. "Just get my ship ready before I change my mind. We're going to Pison."

Harcan leaned against the railing on the walkway, watching as Tarron and his soldiers marched away. Harcan snarled in frustration. While it was good to know that someone was making an effort to dismantle the Republic, why the hell had it taken this long?

The more Harcan thought about it, the more he considered his stance hypocritical. He was someone who intimately understood the wickedness of the Republic senate, yet he did nothing. It was only now, with his back against the wall, that he had to do the right thing.

Chapter 3

Harcan began his descent onto a barren ship dock in the middle of nowhere. The landing pad was shaped like a four-leaf clover. Upon closer inspection, Harcan noticed one of the docks had been damaged by an explosion of some sort. There was a large hole in the center and shards of twisted steel dangled beneath it, creaking in the wind. Under the demolished landing pad, he observed a pile of rubble on the ground, complete with the wreckage of a freighter not unlike his own.

"See that?" Harcan asked.

Ellie roamed around the cockpit, staring out of the glass like a wide-eyed kid on a scenic vacation. She looked down. "Looks like the dock was damaged, possibly an attack from a long time ago," she replied.

"*Yeah*. Keep your eyes peeled. Hopefully, we won't be here long," he said, initiating the autopilot landing sequence.

Ellie glanced out into the distance. Pison was mostly a barren, desert planet with rolling dunes. Over the last several centuries, its temperature had climbed slowly, deeming certain regions inhabitable due to extreme heat. In the east, a massive tan-yellow storm was brewing. Harcan took notice of the red lightning strikes in the center of it.

"Wow. You weren't kidding. This place *is* a dumpster fire," she commented.

"Fire being the keyword. It's nearly fifty-five degrees Celsius." Harcan glanced at the holographic readout on his cockpit.

"I see now why we didn't take any bounties on this planet," she replied.

"Tarron's intel says Orchid is close to these coordinates. Let's see what we can find out before that storm heads our way," Harcan said.

"Sure."

A weathered humanoid android wearing a cowboy hat and a tan duster lumbered toward them as they landed. It pulled its cowboy hat in front of its face as the ship's thrusters blasted it with sand and dust. Ellie lowered the rear gate, and they exited the freighter.

The heat hit Harcan. "Whew, how do you put up with this heat?" Harcan asked the android, pulling at his collar.

"He's an android, in case you didn't notice," Ellie whispered.

"I did. I'm just making conversation," Harcan responded, lowering his voice.

Harcan observed the unknown android's brown plastic skin. He had been damaged by the planet's star, charring him black in places. Harcan noticed a large, rusted six-shooter pistol on his hip.

The android waved. "Howdy, folks. Parking is fourteen Republic credits for every two hours," he said with a country-western accent, extending his left hand, which transformed into a scanner.

"*Fourteen?* That's a steep price." Harcan arched an eyebrow.

The cowboy looked away. "I don't make the rates, partner. Just doing my job," he replied.

Harcan sighed and aimed his wristwatch at the scanner anyway. He swiped it as he looked around. "*There,*" Harcan muttered, completing the transaction.

"Much obliged," the android said with a twang.

The android suspiciously followed them with his dull yellow optics as Harcan and Ellie walked toward the dock's exit.

"You don't want to ask that cowboy if he knows anything?" Ellie lowered her voice, looking over her shoulder.

Harcan glanced at her. "You didn't see his eyes, did you? That scrutinizing gaze?" Harcan asked.

"No, but I couldn't help but notice he is an ancient CBT9 model. Those androids are usually found in junk piles, nonoperational," she replied.

Harcan chuckled. "He's likely a spotter, Ellie. It's the perfect position to spy on newcomers. It's not always what you ask; it's *who* you ask. And that ol' cowboy would likely learn more from our questions than we would."

"I guess that makes sense now that I think about it," she said.

"Hence the reason you usually stay behind on the ship," he replied. Ellie rolled her eyes at Harcan as they made their way down four floors using a wobbly metal staircase mounted to the elevated landing pad.

"Think this stairwell is safe?" Ellie asked with wide eyes.

Harcan shrugged. "Probably not."

Ellie looked down. "Great."

Seven hundred meters to the east was a meteor crater over a kilometer in diameter. There were six dump trucks the size of small houses exiting the mine. The bed of each mammoth vehicle was overflowing with minerals, leaving a thick cloud of dust that trailed behind them. Protruding from inside the quarry were four large cranes. Harcan could hear the distant sounds of jackhammers and construction going on.

Near the landing dock, there was a large rectangular restaurant with a checkerboard black-and-white pattern on the outside.

"That diner is likely the best place for intelligence gathering," Harcan assessed, noticing the foot traffic flowing to and from.

"Looks like a cozy joint," Ellie said. They were looking down at the roof of the building while descending. Harcan noticed solar panels overlapping one another. There was a white chair on the eastern corner of the roof. Someone in a dark blue cloak was sitting in it, using a pair of binoculars aimed toward the quarry.

As they neared the bottom of the stairwell, someone leaned against the wall near the diner's entrance. He was holding a hard hat as he peered toward the crater. "I-I'm not going back," he mumbled to himself. Harcan noticed the man had gills on his neck and webbed fingers, possibly a genetic experimentation victim.

As Harcan reached for the door, the mutant stumbled and began slurring something unrecognizable. Ellie looked up at Harcan. "Looks like they serve alcohol, *and* mutants are welcome. Your kinda place, right?"

Harcan ignored her drunkard jab, swinging open the double doors to a jukebox blaring some old tune about a hound dog. The frigid air conditioning penetrated Harcan's thick fur instantly, kissing against his sweaty, coarse hide as he pulled at his coat collar.

The floors and walls were all checkerboards, just like the exterior. All around the edge of the interior were booths with turquoise-colored vinyl seats. In the middle of the diner was an island bar with two dozen stools surrounding it.

Most of the bar seats were full, and only a couple of the booths were open.

A tsunami of scents flooded Harcan's senses: vanilla, strawberry, chocolate ice cream, grease, and raw and cooked meat. He even caught whiffs of soiled clothes, body odor, and bad breath as he scrunched up his nose.

"What's wrong?" Ellie asked.

"It's not the most pleasant-smelling joint," he replied.

Ellie shook her head. "It used to boggle my synthetic mind that you have this hypersensitive sense of smell, *except* when it comes to yourself. But I found it's a common thing called olfactory adaption. You're literally oblivious to your own monster musk because of overexposure."

Suddenly, a tall, shapely emerald-eyed waitress with bronze skin approached, carrying a tray full of food. She was wearing a red-and-white-striped uniform, with red high heels and a miniskirt so short that it nearly showed her butt.

Harcan checked her out as she stopped in front of them. She put her hand on her hip, smacking her chewing gum as she sized up the unusual pair. "Table for three?" she asked, looking Harcan up and down.

Harcan chuckled. "How 'bout a booth for four?"

She smiled at him. "Well, go on and find a seat for yourself. I'll be right with ya, hunny," the attractive waitress said as she carried away a large tray of food.

As she turned around, Harcan took notice of the back of her neck. There was a patch of circuitry running down to her spine.

Ellie met eyes with Harcan as they proceeded to the right side of the diner to an open booth. "Every single waitress in this place is an android," she stated, glancing up at Harcan.

"I see that," he replied. She panned around the diner wide-eyed.

The vibe of the room was boisterous and loud, like a prison cafeteria without guards. Harcan observed nearly all the customers were male and wearing the same light-blue coveralls with white hard hats. He saw a mutant sitting by himself toward the back with thick, fire-red body hair. His oversized ape-like head and long, thick hands were wrapped in blood-soaked bandages.

As they walked through the room, the attention shifted toward them. The rowdy scene quelled momentarily as every set of eyes seemed to follow the pair.

Ellie stepped close to Harcan, looking up at him. "Can I be honest with you about something?"

"Yeah."

"I'm kinda nervous," she whispered. Ellie clenched Harcan's massive paw and placed it on her shoulder. "I don't like the way they're looking at me," she added.

Harcan did a double take at her. For the first time, she looked genuinely afraid as she faked a smile. "We're fine, Ellie. Let's sit over here so I can keep an eye on my freighter from the window," he assured.

The stares slowly dissipated as they were seated, and Ellie's nerves seemed to calm. She interlocked her fingers and took in a deep breath, staring up at him. Harcan pushed the table toward her so that he could fit inside the booth on the opposite side. He immediately fired up a cigarette.

The red-haired mutant in the back of the room stood up. Harcan noticed his posture was contorted, and he walked with a limp. He veered toward them, walking by Harcan's table.

He never once looked at them. Harcan noticed the bandage on his head was leaking a cream-colored fluid that dripped on the floor as he walked out. He shambled away from the diner into the middle of the dunes alone.

"Wonder what happened to that mutant?" Ellie asked.

"No idea. But if I had to guess, I'd say he was beaten and robbed blind. Most mutants I've seen on the outer worlds are often born with physical or mental handicaps, making them prime targets," he responded.

"You're not even the least bit concerned when you see another mutant in need? It doesn't bother you?" She leaned forward.

Harcan locked eyes with her. "I didn't say that, Ellie. For all we know, he brought his troubles on himself. But we don't have time to play detective and sort out his story," he replied.

Neither of them said a word for a few minutes as she looked around, observing the crowd in deep thought.

"You know, *this* diner reminds me of somewhere I've been before," Ellie spoke up, narrowing her eyes.

"Where?" he asked. He took in a long draw, blowing his smoke away from the booth.

"Remember when I told you about the human couple? The ones that special ordered me to replace their daughter that died?" she asked.

"Of course," he replied.

"Well, the human parents took me out to eat at a local diner on the small moon colony where they lived. It wasn't like this place aesthetically, but the crowd and the stares take me back," she recalled, biting her lip.

"Were the onlookers suspicious you weren't human?" Harcan asked. He turned his body sideways in the booth, propping up one of his legs on the seat.

Ellie looked around the room. "Yeah. Now that I look back, it might not have been so bad, but the parents tried to pass me off as their *real* daughter. But it was so awkward, and it made no sense. I was the same size as the little girl when she died—eight years previously. All her friends had grown up. Two of them even approached her parents to say hello. But they all had this cautious, unsettling look about them, like they'd seen a ghost."

"Did they ever say anything?" Harcan asked.

"Not really. They usually greeted us politely and left in a hurry."

Harcan took another drag of his cig. "And the parents, how did they handle the community's rejection?" he questioned.

Ellie shook her head. "They just tried to smooth it over by concocting this elaborate story about their terminally ill daughter. The lie involved this backstory that they froze her body and waited until more advanced medical procedures were available. That's how they justified the lapse in time."

"Did people believe it?" he asked, arching an eyebrow.

"I don't think so. I had to rehearse the account with my '*parents*' so that there were no discrepancies in our stories, but it gets even worse," Ellie hinted, looking away.

"Doesn't seem like it could get much worse," he said.

"Oh, it did. The parents started to believe their own lies," Ellie said. Harcan looked at her in disbelief.

"That's how it began to fall apart. After a while, instead of continuing to train me to be more like their daughter, they formed this belief that I *was* her. And then, this expectation formed slowly, to the point I had to recall the slightest details about their daughter's past. I just couldn't measure up to the lies they told themselves. I wasn't real, and there were too many nuances I couldn't recall. The whole thing exhausted everyone," she explained.

"Even you," he said.

"*Especially* me. And the longer I stayed, the more I could see their pain. It's sad, but I wanted to make them happy, Harcan. I tried. I wanted to be a part of that fucked-up dynamic, can you believe that?" she asked.

"Yeah, I can." Harcan glanced away. He recalled a brief time when he enjoyed his role on EL-59 as the hunter, the terrorizing Wolfman. It was a dark time that he never wanted to revisit.

Harcan cleared his throat. "How did you finally break away from the parents?" he asked, shifting his thoughts back to Ellie.

Ellie looked down at her hands. "It's strange. There was this voice deep inside me. It was beating like a drum over several days. It got louder and louder and said, '*You will never make them happy,*'" she replied.

Harcan held his cigarette away from the booth and flicked his ashes onto the floor. He thought about what she said for several moments. "And just like that, it was over?"

"Yeah." Ellie leaned back in her seat. "To be fair, I did learn a lot about human behavior in those weeks, but playing along in a web of lies... that just wasn't for me," she said.

Ellie put her elbows on the table. "You know, I sometimes wonder, though—they say we transcendents are the essence of the ones we seek to replace. Could it be that their daughter was crying out from deep inside me somehow, ushering her parents forward so that they could truly heal from their loss?" she wondered.

"That's deep," he said.

"It's not impossible, right?" she replied, shrugging.

Harcan stared at the burning head on the end of his cig. "I tend not to entertain those sorts of thoughts. Supernatural shit doesn't fly with me. Maybe I'm a bit biased, as a figment of human folklore brought to life through science."

"Fair enough," she said.

"But, I am curious, how did you escape your parent's home?" he questioned.

"There was a cargo runner that frequented the docks where we lived. He was an android. I used to sneak out and talk to him. He taught me how to remove the tracking device inside my chassis so that they could never find me. He asked me to come with him. From there, I jumped around to different planets and bosses, upgrading my software and—"

"Getting into trouble," Harcan interrupted with a grin.

She chuckled. "Yeah, that too. Even *some* things I might not ever talk about." Her smile quickly flattened out as she gazed through him.

Harcan wondered what else she had experienced. He wasn't the only one with a shadowy past, and just because Ellie was an android, it didn't make her experiences any less genuine. Maybe her emotions *were* just a simulation or clone of a sentient being's, but it all felt authentic to her, to the point she still carried the baggage.

Harcan could relate to carrying burdens.

One question remained in Harcan's mind: what kept her going now? What purpose did she have other than finding an adult body? There had to be more.

Ellie sighed in relief. "That felt good to talk about. So, who could tell us more about our contact? Could *Orchid* be one of these servers?" Ellie asked, looking around.

"Doubt it. She's not really the servant type, if you know what I mean," Harcan replied.

"Oh. Maybe the bartender knows something?" Ellie questioned, observing the overweight middle-aged male bartender with a hunched back.

Harcan sized him up. He was wearing an all-white uniform with a soda jerk hat. His unkempt sweaty hair and bushy eyebrows were unnaturally jet black, probably dyed. He sported an arrogant scowl on his face as he poured a rum and root beer into a frosted clear mug. He seemed to hate his job. He reached beneath him and scooped over a generous lump of vanilla ice cream into the mug. Soda spilled out of the glass and onto the bar.

"Yum! That ice cream looks good," Ellie proclaimed, beaming with joy. She kicked her legs back and forth excitedly, twirling her curly brown locks with her index finger as she started humming.

"Root and rum up!" the bartender shouted, sliding the frosted mug halfway down the bar to a consumer.

"Let's ask our waitress first. She's coming this way," Harcan said, watching as she approached them.

Suddenly, a handsome young man in the booth next to them stopped the waitress. It was packed full of miners. "Hey! *You!*" the young man shouted at the waitress with a condescending tone.

"Yeah?" she asked, smacking her chewing gum. The miner pointed behind her and she turned around to have a look. He licked his lips and smacked her on her butt. She rolled her eyes and turned toward them as his buddies burst out in laughter.

"Oh shit. Here we go," Harcan muttered.

The waitress held up her index finger and shook her head. "Now, now, you boys are new, aren't cha?" she asked, looking them over.

The young man who assaulted her perked up with a goofy smile. "Yep. Just transferred from EL-08 last week," he said.

The jukebox stopped as the crowd's attention shifted to the waitress. She pointed down at her crotch as a long slender object slowly pushed up her skirt. The young miner's eyebrows raised as he looked down at it.

"Well? You still like me?" she asked.

"All the same to me, I go *both* ways," he replied confidently.

"Both ways? Does that include *down*?" she asked.

"Huh?" he asked.

The waitress lifted up her skirt to reveal a six-shooter pistol mounted to her crotch. The weapon fired, blowing a hole between his eyes. The impact snapped his head back as his hard hat fell to the floor and his body slumped over. Blood splattered his coworkers as they got up, looking down at their shirts covered in blood and brain matter.

"Holy shit," Ellie said excitedly, staring at Harcan.

He shrugged. "The man said he went both ways. Apparently, *down* wasn't one of them," Harcan joked. The waitress bent forward with an inhuman range of motion, nearly touching the barrel of the weapon with her lips, blowing away the smoke with a seductive puckering of the lips.

"I gotta get me one of those," Ellie muttered.

The shocked coworkers rushed to the exit, nearly falling over one another without looking back.

The waitress put her hand on her hip. "Remember, boys, sexually assaulting sentient beings, androids included, is punishable by death. Y'all come back now!" She waved with a smile as they hurried out. The jukebox fired back up in the middle of a rock song. "—*she blew the boys away, it was then they'd seen.*"

The crowd continued about its business as if nothing happened.

Harcan wiped a speck of blood from his coat as two cleaner drones rushed toward the incident. One of them was shaped like a large hockey puck with a spongey underside. It had a container on top that could hold at least two liters of fluid.

The other robot was about the size of an adult German shepherd but shaped like a spider with ten spiny metal legs. It turned its rear toward the corpse and shot out a plastic sheet that covered it. The spider droid wrapped the corpse with blurring speed, cocooning it completely. It yanked the body from the booth aggressively and dragged it to the back of the diner.

"I've been to a bunch of shitholes in my day. Never seen anything like that before," Harcan mumbled.

"Me either," Ellie replied.

The circular drone began spinning like a top as it swirled around the floor, sucking up the blood splatter into the container. It hopped up onto the table and finished the job before zooming back to the kitchen.

The waitress tiptoed around the booth and stood over Ellie and Harcan. "I bet y'all are hungry now, ain't cha? Can I bring ya something to drink first?" She batted her eyes.

Ellie stared at her crotch as the pistol lowered. "I'll just take a cock soda—I mean, *club* soda," she corrected herself, closing her eyes as she bit her lip.

Harcan smiled. "I think I'll have one of those root beer floats, double rum, but with chocolate," he ordered.

The waitress grinned. "Sure thang. Anything else?"

Harcan nodded. "Yeah, there is. I'm looking for a female you might know."

"Well, we got plenty of those, just don't touch without asking first," she stated, chuckling.

"I see that. But I'm looking for someone specific; she's actually a mutant. Her name is Orchid," Harcan revealed.

The waitress smacked her chewing gum and narrowed her eyes at Harcan. "Can you say that name one more time, *hunny*? I might have some buildup in my ears," she insisted, digging in her ears with her middle finger.

Harcan leaned closer. "Or-chid. *Orchid.*" He raised his voice.

The waitress laughed and glanced over her shoulder. "You're looking for trouble, ain't cha? Didn't you just see what happened to the last troublemaker?" she warned. All the waitresses in the joint stopped what they were doing and slowly encircled Harcan and Ellie.

"Wait. What is this?" Harcan questioned.

The waitresses' skirts slowly lifted from the crotch area in unison. A dozen gun barrels were pointed at them.

"Well," Harcan mumbled, putting up his hands.

"Hold on. We're not here to cause *any* problems," Ellie asserted.

The waitress leaned on the table and stared at Harcan. "Ever been *surrounded* by crotch cannons, hunny?" she asked him, smacking her gum loudly next to his ears.

"Nope. It's my first time. Maybe you can tell me what happens next," Harcan answered with a grin.

The waitress raised an eyebrow and shook her finger at him. "You're a real smartass, ain't cha? Well, all those muscles and teeth don't frighten us, big boy. Stand up. Both of you," the waitress ordered with haste.

"Let's go!" she shouted, gesturing back to the kitchen. Harcan and Ellie proceeded through saloon-style double doors.

The temperature elevated as steam from the grills rushed into their faces. Harcan looked to his right and noticed a wide hallway with two large steel grills on each side. There was a tall, lanky male cook with a gaunt face standing over one of the grills flipping burgers. He had a cigar in his mouth and wore an all-white uniform covered in grease stains and sweat.

He turned and looked at Harcan before noticing the waitress. "Hey! *Jean!* Get that *damn* mutant outta my kitchen!" he shouted, stabbing his spatula at Harcan. "You ever heard of sanitation? No one wants *hair* in their damn burgers!" he yelled, as ashes from his cigar trickled onto the patty melts beneath him.

"Shut it, Carl! We're not going through your kitchen!" the waitress fired back, and pointed to the left. She nudged Harcan in the back of his leg with her cock pistol. "Go on, fuzzball," she directed.

Harcan turned left with Ellie in tow. They headed into a corridor with tall freezers on both sides. "I hope you know what you're doing." Ellie glared up at Harcan.

"Everything's under control," he replied casually. The truth was, he was beginning to question himself. It had been several years since he'd last seen Orchid.

Beyond the freezers was a dimly lit brick corridor with grimy lime walls. The spider droid that cocooned the dead patron earlier passed by them casually. It scampered through the kitchen, its legs clacking against the tile floor.

The cook spun around and kicked at the droid, narrowly missing it. "You're not supposed to be here either!" he shouted, dropping his spatula on the floor. He picked it up and wiped it on his pant leg, continuing to flip burgers.

Just as they were about to exit the freezer area and enter the shadowy portion of the corridor, Harcan turned around, showing the waitress his palms. "Look. There's something you should know." He glanced down at her pistol, now aimed at his lower stomach.

"I don't recall telling you to stop moving, did I, mutant?" the waitress challenged.

"Well, no. But I want you to know that Orchid is an old friend of mine," he stated, grinning.

Ellie yanked her thumb over her shoulder at Harcan. "Yup. They've been friends for *years*. He always talks about her. Orchid this and Orchid that, it's annoying," she lied, smiling from ear to ear as she leaned against Harcan's leg.

The waitress smacked her gum and raised an eyebrow. She slowly pointed down the hall. "We'll see 'bout that, but if you don't turn around and keep walking, *you'll* be the next thing on Carl's grill. I reckon we could flame broil at least a few hundred hamburgers outta that meaty frame of yours," she estimated, looking Harcan up and down.

Harcan turned around. "Suit yourself, but Orchid's not gonna be happy about the way you're treating her ol' pal," he warned. He and

Ellie moved down the increasingly dark hallway. There was a plain steel door on the right.

As Harcan neared it, the door retracted from the floor automatically with incredible force. The screeching metal caused Harcan to cover his ears for a moment. "Ahhhh."

The waitress nodded. "Go on now, get inside, you and the dollface."

"Dollface?" she whispered, rolling her eyes.

Harcan stuck his paw under the door and pulled back, testing the door. He eased forward, staring up at the razor-thin metallic door that could seemingly chop him in half.

"I don't like the looks of that," Ellie mumbled.

"Kinda reminds me of a guillotine," Harcan commented, looking back at the waitress.

The waitress chuckled. "If I wanted you dead, I sure as hell wouldn't do it this way. It'd be too much of a mess," she joked, blowing a massive bubble with her chewing gum. She popped it with her fingernail, and it spattered against her lips. "Get my drift?" she asked.

"Yeah." Suddenly, Harcan snatched Ellie into his arms. "Whoa!" Ellie shouted as he dashed through the doorway with blurring speed, cradling her in his arms.

Just inside the door was a stairwell to a sublevel. "Keep it moving," the waitress gestured.

They descended several steps into a long, gray, curved corridor. The passageway was a stark contrast to the diner and kitchen. To Harcan, it felt more like a newly constructed underground bunker. The metallic, glossy walls were more modern than the diner, yet very plain, pristine, and purpose built.

The smell of ammonia filled Harcan's nostrils as he observed two droids scrubbing the shiny, spotless floor. Their circular bodies hummed as they glided along the deck. The floors had large tile squares, each with a unique black handprint in each one's center. Ellie raised an eyebrow. "What the hell is that about?" she asked.

"No idea," he muttered.

Ellie stepped close to Harcan as they walked parallel through the corridor. "Suddenly the diner doesn't seem so bad, huh?" she asked.

As they proceeded through the basement, the temperature dropped drastically. Harcan could see his breath. On both sides of them, there were steel metal doors with circular windows. Each door was spaced apart every thirty paces.

"I can't see inside. What's that meaty smell?" Ellie asked, walking on her tippy toes.

Harcan looked through the foggy glass window. There were dozens of frozen bodies hanging from racks.

"*Humans.* Dozens of them," he answered plainly. He recognized the smell even before he saw them. Ellie slowly shifted her eyes up at him as Harcan slowed his pace.

Inside the freezer to his left, he noticed the dead patron that sexually assaulted the waitress. His body was on a stainless-steel table as two androids in lab coats unraveled the plastic cocoon around his body.

Harcan glanced over his shoulder at the waitress. "What kinda operation are y'all running down here?" he asked.

"The kind that turns a profit. Now, no more questions," she responded.

"Hm," Harcan grumbled suspiciously.

There was a guard checkpoint fifty paces ahead of them. Four androids in dull-yellow trench coats stood next to a door, armed with laser rifles. Their plastic skin was the same color as their coats, reminding Harcan of the sand dunes outside. Other than their glowing red-yellow eyes, they were quite generic looking. Harcan observed that one of them was missing its lower jaw.

The waitress walked around in front of Harcan and stood in front of the guards. "Is the queen inside?" she asked them.

The sentries looked at each other. "Shouldn't you be waiting tables, Jean?" one of the android sentries replied with a snarky tone.

The waitress pointed back at Harcan. "This mutant knew the queen's name. Her *real* name. That's enough to cause concern," she alerted them. Harcan noticed her country accent from before was suddenly absent.

The android with the missing jaw stepped forward and pulled out a small white box from his coat. Harcan observed a tiny neon-blue moth crawling out of it. It stopped, flapping its shiny metallic wings.

"What's that?" Ellie asked.

"Don't move. Let the drone scan you." The android pressed a button on the device and the moth took flight, circling Harcan and Ellie rapidly. A 3D hologram appeared atop the device as the moth mapped them from head to toe. As the moth reached Harcan's lower torso, it flew near his coat. The moth glowed red, pulsating like a firefly.

The androids drew their weapons on Harcan. "*He's armed!*" the jawless android shouted, marching toward Harcan.

"Hey. All you had to do was ask," Harcan challenged with a grin. One of the guards lifted Harcan's coat with the barrel of his rifle and removed his shotgun.

The jawless android glared at the waitress. "You brought an *armed* mutant right to our queen's doorstep?"

Suddenly, the door behind the guards flung open. A screaming man covered in blood lunged through the open door and fell at Harcan's feet. He panted heavily, curled up in a ball. "Keep her away!" he pleaded.

Harcan noticed two puncture wounds on his neck. "Looks like we're in the right place," he mumbled, moving his boot as blood trickled near it.

The injured man was wearing miner's coveralls, just like the workers in the diner.

Through the door, another figure emerged. It was a tall female with an hourglass shape. She wore a tight black spandex outfit with matching high heel boots. On her right shoulder was a maroon cape.

She stood in the doorway, partially concealed inside the dimly lit room. Her big, oval-shaped electric-blue eyes flashed as she looked at the injured man on the floor. She slowly panned up toward Harcan with a blank stare.

"Hello, Orchid," Harcan said, outstretching his arms.

She shook her head while staring at Harcan. "Now, this *is* a surprise. I thought you'd be dead by now," she said in a seductive voice.

Harcan shrugged. "Sorry to disappoint."

Orchid chuckled, revealing a set of pearly white teeth and a pair of long canine fangs. "I'm not disappointed, Harcan. I'm astonished that we both survived the aftermath, the trauma endured during our previous lives."

Harcan looked down at the vodka flask in his pocket. "I've found the ancient remedies of Russian culture to be incredibly helpful for post-traumatic situations."

"Really?" Orchid asked.

"Not really," Ellie mumbled, glaring up at Harcan.

Harcan cleared his throat as Orchid marched through the door confidently, wiping the blood from her bottom lip. Ellie's eyes widened at the genetically engineered vampire's striking appearance. She had flawless chocolate-black skin and long white hair that framed her perfectly symmetrical heart-shaped face.

She was Harcan's other half on EL-59, but unlike his primal, brutal appearance, she looked like she could walk off the pages of a high-fashion magazine.

Orchid was like the samurai's sheathed katana blade—deceptive and dangerous, while Harcan was more the barbarian's lumbering battle-ax, powerful and on full display.

Around Orchid's neck was a gold choker with a broken chain hanging from it. Upon closer inspection, Harcan noticed it was the same collar shackle they wore as prisoners on EL-59, but hers had been dipped in gold.

Orchid looked down at the bleeding man near Harcan's feet. "You've interrupted my dinner, Harcan. As you know, I prefer them *alive*," she said.

Harcan took a step back as Orchid dove atop the man, ripping into his shoulder and neck with her oversized fangs. He screamed in agony as his arms trembled and blood sprayed Harcan's feet.

"H-help me!" the man begged Harcan, reaching out for his boot.

Orchid glanced up at Harcan, pinning the pleading man to the floor with both her arms. "I'm curious—how did you find me?" she asked nonchalantly, looking up at Harcan as blood-soaked tendons and ligaments dangled from her mouth like spaghetti.

"It's complicated," he answered, as Ellie closed her eyes at the grisly sight.

"*Gross,*" she said.

"I'm guessing you need something, Harcan? Or else you wouldn't be here," Orchid stated.

Harcan raised an eyebrow as she plunged her steak-knife-sized fangs back into his throat. "If this is a bad time, Orchid, we'll wait until you're done," he replied.

Orchid held up her index finger while sucking on his neck. The man began to shrivel up like a prune as Orchid groaned in satisfaction. Within a dozen seconds, her victim stopped moving with a final jolt from the legs.

The android guards looked at one another as Orchid stood up slowly. She drifted side to side awkwardly, like a plump mosquito having more than its fill.

Orchid placed her bloody hand on the wall, regaining her balance. "Forgive me, I get a little lightheaded when I feed too fast," she mumbled, belching loudly.

Harcan cleared his throat. "Is there anywhere we can talk, in private?" he asked, glancing at the guards behind her.

Orchid covered her mouth like she was nauseous. "I think so," she answered. She bent down, outstretching her arms at Ellie. "But first, who is this little *person* you've brought along?" Orchid smiled.

Ellie lowered her eyebrows. "My name's Ellie, and I'm a big person, actually, just in a small package."

"*Oh*. Excuse me. How adorable," Orchid whispered.

"I'm wanted for *murder*. There's nothing adorable about me," Ellie warned, scrunching up her nose with a serious face. Harcan and Orchid looked at one another and suddenly burst into laughter. Even the android guards joined in on the fun.

"It's not funny!" Ellie shouted at Harcan. She punched his kneecap with little effect.

Orchid put her hand on her chest, catching her breath. "Ah. I needed a good laugh. Thanks for that," she applauded.

"Listen, Ellie. *All* androids, big or small, are treated with the utmost respect inside my establishment," she added.

Ellie crossed her arms and rolled her eyes.

Orchid slowly circled Harcan, staring at him. "Hm. Something's off about you, Wolfman. I noticed it immediately. Your blood, it smells *different*," she said, leaning in as she sniffed his back.

"Oh, it's always like that. I bet you're just smelling the higher blood alcohol levels," Ellie guessed.

Orchid raised her index finger. Her long nails were painted maroon, the same color as her cape. "I think you're right," she replied, walking back to the door she came from. A spider droid scampered past her and began wrapping the corpse at Harcan's feet in plastic.

Orchid took notice of the android holding Harcan's oversized shotgun. "Is that Wolfman's weapon?" she asked.

"Yes ma'am," the guard replied.

"Give it back to him—*now*," Orchid ordered.

The androids looked at one another in confusion. "But, my queen—"

"*Do it*. If Harcan was here with bad intentions, you'd be scattered across this corridor in a hundred pieces already," Orchid said with confidence. The android hesitantly returned Harcan's shotgun.

Orchid gestured her waitress back down the hall. "Oh, and thank you for bringing them to me, but I need all waitresses at the restaurant. Rush hour is in a half hour," she ordered.

Ellie winked at the waitress. "See ya later, *dollface*," she taunted, waving goodbye. The android waitress narrowed her eyes at Ellie, spinning around without a word.

Harcan watched as a spider droid bundled up the man's corpse in a plastic cocoon and carried it off. "I see nothing goes to waste around here," he commented.

"What do you mean?" Orchid smirked.

"I'm guessing those juicy burgers sold in your diner aren't made from *animal* flesh," he said.

"You always were a quick study, weren't you?" she replied.

He pointed at his nose. "The smell gave them away."

Ellie glanced at Harcan before staring at Orchid. "Wait a minute. You feed your customers human meat? From the freezers?"

Orchid crossed her arms. "Only after it's cooked and seasoned. No one can tell the difference anyway. Besides, it's nutritious and there's no law against it," she answered.

Ellie stuck out her tongue and pointed inside her mouth. "Ugh. That's disgusting. They could literally be eating one of their friends and not even know it."

Harcan chuckled. "I never figured you for the business type, Orchid," he said.

"And I never saw you as a drunk," Orchid replied.

"You just drained a full-grown man of every ounce of blood in his body and turned him into a prune. I think you're the one with the *drinking* problem," he told her.

"Perhaps." Orchid whipped around, flipping her long thick white hair. She looked over her shoulder and lasered Harcan with her glowing blue eyes. "Vodka, vampirism, we all have our burdens, don't we? The difference is, I'm genetically engineered to desire human blood. What's your excuse?"

"Happy hour specials," Harcan replied, shrugging his cannon ball-sized shoulders.

Orchid waved Harcan and Ellie toward the door. "Guards. They're coming inside with me," she ordered.

"What?" The armed android guards looked at one another in confusion. "Ma'am? Are you certain?" one of the sentries asked.

"Yes, let them through," Orchid replied plainly. Harcan and Ellie met eyes as two of Orchid's guards escorted them through the door.

"Whoa," Ellie said excitedly. Inside was a spacious, lavishly furnished quarters with leather couches and dark hardwood floors. The highlight of the room was a high, cone-shaped glass ceiling in the middle.

"Do you like it?" Orchid asked, running her claws across the granite wall.

"Not bad," Harcan replied. He was extremely impressed, but he didn't want to give her too much credit; after all, they were bred to compete with one another.

"So, what is it you do in here, other than gorge and brood over your human harvest?" Harcan asked.

Orchid raised her eyebrows. "Bookkeeping from the restaurant takes up most of my time. But you caught me on my break."

Above, a convincing hologram projected a cloudy full moon night. Harcan stopped, staring up at the moon in awe. His big amber eyes widened.

"Don't, Harcan," Orchid warned.

"Don't what?" Ellie asked.

Harcan felt an uncontrollable urge overwhelm him. Harcan's lips snarled up, and the hairs on his back stiffened. He dug his claws into the dark cherry hardwood floor beneath him. He growled and fell on all fours as he began howling up at the moon.

Ellie gave him a baffled look. "*Stop that.* You're embarrassing us. Get off the floor and quit making that awful sound," she hurried.

Harcan's howl became increasingly louder as Ellie backed away from him.

Orchid rushed to the opposite side of the room and flipped a switch, converting the moonlight hologram sky to a pleasant, sun-filled afternoon. Harcan immediately stopped howling and collapsed onto his elbows, panting heavily.

After a few seconds, he looked around as if he were woken up from a trance. Not since EL-59 had Harcan been subjected to the call of the night.

"Tell me you didn't do that on purpose," Harcan muttered, staring at Orchid. His shallow, short breaths flared out his nostrils.

"Hell no. I was setting the mood for a moonlit dinner until you and your halfling interrupted. Remember?" Orchid reminded him. "I should have altered the hologram before you came in. It slipped my mind," she said. Harcan stood up slowly as Ellie helped him to his feet to regain his composure.

"I'm confused. We've seen plenty of moons before, *real* moons. I don't ever remember you doing that," Ellie confronted.

"Ever seen Earth's moon?" Orchid asked.

"No one has that I know," she replied.

Orchid pointed up a spiraled stairwell in the middle of the room that ascended to the ceiling's peak. "During the Halloween months, the elitists on EL-59 projected this moon as a massive hologram. Harcan has wolf DNA, so he's just doing what came natural."

Ellie stared at Harcan with a puzzled look on her face.

Orchid smirked. "Harcan hasn't told you much about himself, has he?" she asked rhetorically.

"I guess not," Ellie replied.

"We had several featured attractions on EL-59. The moon usually set the mood," Orchid recalled, glancing away. "Of course, Harcan was our Wolfman, and I was the Vampire Queen. We were part of various set pieces called the *cull*. The elitists offered commoners a chance to stay at artificial structure EL-59 at an affordable cost. They were protected, fed, and sheltered. But the terrifying downside was the month of October games. *Many* perished," she explained.

"That doesn't sound like a game," Ellie commented.

"They called it the monster bash. Harcan and I had one job—reduce the population. We were rivals, competing to kill the most residents. Cameras were placed in every nook and cranny while the aristocrats watched the population flee in terror, or, unite and fight. Quite the interesting case study into human behavior, I would assume. Unfortunately, gambling was the main draw for the elitists. Senators came from all over the Republic to bet on different bands of survivors," Orchid explained, falling back onto a large black leather couch as she kicked her feet up on the armrest.

"Hold on. Let me get this straight. You two *murdered* civilians on a fucking game show just to make room for the following year?" Ellie demanded as Harcan stood up. He stumbled toward the staircase, leaning against it.

"Essentially, yes. It wasn't exactly a game show, and we didn't kill for fun. It was our job. Both of us were manipulated into thinking the civilian population was evil," Orchid answered.

"They tortured and lied to us," Harcan growled with his back to Ellie. She stared through him for a few moments.

"The problem was, EL-59 eventually ran out of space. It's a rotating cylinder that orbits Jupiter, and it only houses around twenty-thousand residents. I guess they figured, what better way to cure boredom than population control?" Orchid replied casually.

"You know, it's disturbing how indifferent you seem about all this. I'm the one that's supposed to be the stone-cold robot," Ellie observed.

Orchid narrowed her eyes at Ellie. "What an awful thing to say. That's not true at all. If there's one thing I hate, it's the wealthy benefiting at the expense of the less fortunate," Orchid replied.

"Tell me. How did so many 'less fortunate' people end up on EL-59 in the first place?" Ellie probed.

"Most habitable planets are either overtaxed or overcrowded. Many are looking for another option. The starting price for a residence on EL-59 was a one-time fee of fifteen thousand credits, and they weren't taxed. This was an enticing scam for many lower income families. They were put on a waiting list nearly five million strong, I've heard," Orchid answered.

Ellie paced back and forth. "So the *monsters* kill off the population, then EL-59 profits when new residents arrive to fill the vacancies. Then, the cycle repeats. That's how they maintained revenue year after year."

"Bingo, and that's not even the saddest part. Obviously, no one who pays for a residency on EL-59 knows about the death games in October, or they would never come in the first place. But when they do arrive, and discover the terrible truth, they're trapped," Orchid replied.

"Those motherfuckers," Ellie said, shaking her head. She nodded at Harcan. "No wonder he drinks."

"I'm curious, Harcan, have you heard the latest news about our old stomping grounds?" Orchid asked Harcan.

"Poor choice of words, but what about it?" he asked.

"Well, the rumor mill has been churning. The latest bombshell is that the Republic and our former masters are replacing EL-59," she revealed.

"Huh?" Harcan asked, whipping his head toward her.

"EL-59 is too small to meet the demand. EL-60 is their newest money-making monstrosity. Get this—the new artificial structure is said to house over two million residents," she revealed.

"Holy shit," Ellie muttered.

Harcan looked away. "How do you know all this?" he asked.

Orchid raised her eyebrows. "I get miners from the quarry and smugglers from all across the galaxy. They all have the same story—EL-60 is being built as we speak."

Harcan slumped his head, thinking about the unfortunate souls who would eventually be swindled into a residency on EL-60, only to die a horrific death for the sake of entertainment and greed.

Ellie leaned against the spiral staircase. "Before we go any further... One thing doesn't make sense to me."

"What's that?" Orchid grinned.

"Well, you and my pal Harcan here escaped EL-59 together?" she asked.

"That's right," Orchid replied.

"And you oppose the horrors on EL-59?" Ellie questioned.

"Of course. What's your point, little android?"

"My point is, all you've done since you've escaped EL-59 is trade one slaughterhouse for another. Your restaurant is a blood bank. It's a madhouse if you ask me," Ellie answered.

Orchid stood up slowly, glaring at Ellie. "Watch your tongue. I'll have you know that every miner in that quarry is a hardened criminal. They're the worst the galaxy has to offer, sentenced to come here and live out the remainder of their lives doing hard labor. They're prisoners."

"Then why are they allowed to venture to your diner unattended? I didn't see any guard escorts," Ellie challenged.

Orchid grinned. "You're full of questions, aren't you? As of a few years ago, all miners had trackers surgically implanted inside them. If they move beyond a certain radius, it sends a shock to their heart, killing them," she replied.

"Oh," Ellie said.

"And most every offense in this region is punishable by death when it pertains to convicted felons. Look, I didn't create the laws. I just make the most of it in my own way," Orchid said.

Harcan looked at her. "Yeah. Like Ellie said, we saw your collection of frozen slurpy treats in the freezers," he said.

Orchid clenched her fist to her chest. "You understand that EL-59 cursed me with this bloodthirst, and I'm doing the best I can to take advantage of the situation. I *need* their blood to live. You don't," she reminded.

Orchid was right. Even though Harcan had his share of emotional baggage and addictions, he wasn't required to kill to survive.

Harcan shook his head. "Orchid, we're not here to pester you."

"Then *why* are you here?" she asked without hesitation.

"I have an offer. An opposing faction within the Republic is on the rise that aims to take down EL-59's leaders. They want our help," Harcan revealed.

Orchid lifted her eyebrows. "Say that again?"

"The Republic is in a state of peril, Orchid. A group called the Initiative wants to prosecute and disband the senate. But even if the war started tomorrow, EL-59 has thousands of civilian hostages to use as bargaining chips. Our mission is to aid the Initiative's assault force by breaching the EL-59 with a surprise attack," Harcan explained.

Orchid laughed. "*Impossible.* I can't believe you would even consider this! We barely escaped with our lives, and you want to go *back*?" She spun away from him, swooshing her cape as she turned.

Tell her the rest, Ellie mouthed.

Harcan cleared his throat. "Orchid, I know this sounds crazy. I didn't believe it at first. The Initiative has a bounty hunter that's going to deliver us, posing as prisoners. It'll look official. We don't have to enter the structure. We just wait for the shields to drop, then the Initiative will launch their attack. That's it," he said.

Orchid sighed. "I can't help you," she said plainly.

Ellie threw up her hands and confronted Orchid. "You just told us EL-60 is under construction. Think about all the lives both of you could save if you pull this off! We could be talking *millions* of people over the course of a couple of generations."

Orchid turned toward them. "Harcan, how the hell do you know this isn't an elaborate trap to corral us for recapture? Huh? This story could be fabricated so that you would find me and—"

"I would have never found you, Orchid, if not for the Initiative. They knew both our locations. If they wanted us recaptured, it would have already been done by now," Harcan interrupted.

Orchid looked away and let out a deep breath. "Even if everything you say is true, I have my own problems, my own responsibilities here. I can't leave."

"What, besides stashing your freezers full of human popsicles?" Ellie muttered.

Harcan stepped close to her. "Orchid, the Initiative orchestrated our escape."

"How do you know this?" Orchid asked.

Harcan locked eyes with Orchid. "These people knew everything about me. They even helped conceal my identity while I worked as a bounty hunter, and they've been protecting you as well," he responded.

Orchid lowered her eyebrows and leaned back, glancing at Ellie. "Bounty hunter?"

"Bounty *hunters*. Plural," Ellie corrected.

Orchid laughed. "Now that I think about it, I guess there has to be some truth to it all if you haven't been recaptured by now. You're an odd-looking pair that sticks out in a crowd."

Ellie stood tall. "The Republic might have helped us stay hidden, but they can't take anything away from our success rate. We maintained a ninety-seven percent capture-or-kill rating," she boasted.

"We're getting off topic," Harcan muttered.

Orchid crossed her arms, looking the duo up and down. "Actually, we're *not* getting off topic if that's true. Skilled bounty hunters are difficult to find. This could work out quite well if you want my help on EL-59."

Harcan shifted his eyes at Orchid. "What? Are you suggesting we trade favors?"

Orchid held out her hands flat like a pair of tipping scales. "Isn't that how everything works? Maybe you can help me clean up a mess here, *then* I can go to EL-59," she hinted.

Harcan shook his head. "Ugh. Let me guess, someone in your freezers is important, and you've made enemies with powerful people," Harcan estimated.

Orchid paced back and forth. "Not a bad guess, but no. Despite how my day-to-day operations appear to *you*, there is a bright spot in all of this. You and I both know what it's like to be manipulated, Harcan. We understand what it feels like to be viewed as less than human, *slaves*. Many androids here on Pison are just that."

"What about the androids that work for you? Are they compensated fairly?" Ellie asked with a scowl on her face.

"Of course they are. My diner is a refuge, a place to start over," Orchid responded.

"Start over from what?" Harcan asked.

Orchid bit her lip. "There's an illegal sex trafficking ring at the bottom of the quarry near this diner. I'm sure you noticed the large construction project. The androids that work for me escaped from there," she revealed.

Harcan and Ellie looked at each other.

Ellie squinted her eyes in deep thought. "I noticed painted handprints in the hallway behind us. Dozens of them. Are those related to this refugee situation somehow?" she wondered.

Orchid arched an eyebrow. "They are. I'm impressed with how quickly you made the association. Each handprint represents a freed android. There's a small city in the depths of that quarry, a pleasure island of sorts for the miners. Apparently, disgruntled workers aren't productive. This is all a big business operation. But I offer any android that escapes my protection. I even weaponize them," Orchid explained.

"Yeah, we got an eyeful in the diner," Ellie commented.

Orchid crossed her arms. "I've also managed to smuggle enough weapons here to supply a small army: mostly grenade launchers and laser rifles. But I doubt the cowardly shill running the sex trafficking racket would ever risk reclaiming his losses. If he does, our androids stand ready to fight to the death. They'll never return to those mines," she said confidently.

"How long has this been going on?" Harcan asked.

"Hard to say. Years before I arrived on Pison. The worst part is, they've been purchasing more androids to sustain the sex business as mining production ramps up," Orchid answered.

Orchid walked toward Ellie and kneeled, gazing into her synthetic eyes. "There are *hundreds* of androids at the bottom of that crater, forced to perform vile acts that you cannot imagine. And when they finish using them up, they're hacked up for scrap or melted to build mining tools."

Ellie shook her head and glanced over her shoulder, staring at Harcan. "If this is true, I can't stand for it. Even if I have to do something about it on my own," she said.

Orchid put her hands behind her back. "Everything I've told you is true. Most everyone recognizes that androids feel pain, emotional and physical. Worse, they've got the androids' sensitivity settings cranked to maximum, so they feel everything to the fullest," she said.

Ellie glared at Harcan. "If anyone knows those emotions are real, it's me. Even hundreds of years ago, androids were proven to experience real emotional pain and suffering, and they're *far* more advanced now. It's endless torment, and it sends chills up my spine."

Harcan looked away. "Orchid, have you tried reporting this? Surely the district outpost or regional governor can—"

Orchid laughed. "The regional governor takes a skim off the top, Harcan. He's making money off this scam and has been for years. The law protects androids on the surface, but the quarry is tucked away in secret."

Harcan shook his head. "And I'm sure the quarry's staff wouldn't allow outsiders to stroll in and have a look at what's going on."

"Hell no. Only essential personnel are allowed inside. But when those miners come to *my* diner and break the law, we're in the right to protect ourselves. We document every offense on video. And maybe it doesn't justify me turning their corpses into my own personal blood bank, but it doesn't weigh on my conscience either. Sorry, not sorry. Does that make me a bitch?" she said, grinning and throwing up her hands.

Ellie pushed out her bottom lip. "Not as much, providing your story checks out. But as bounty hunters, Harcan and I tend to be skeptics. Right?" she asked, glancing up at him.

Harcan looked around the room. "Orchid is many things, but she's not a liar. We'll need to double-check your story anyway," he stated.

"Go ahead." Orchid stepped close to Harcan. She stared up at him before glancing away. Her long face and distant gaze appeared to be that of self-reflection.

Orchid took in a deep breath. "I do want to help bring down EL-59, Harcan. But I can't leave until the trafficking is stopped. I wasn't ready to launch my rescue mission yet, but you two are perfect to jumpstart this operation. You're both strangers to the locals, and more importantly, capable bounty hunters. Otherwise, you wouldn't have survived this long with such a high success rate," she estimated.

"Assuming we come to an agreement, what's the plan? Who's the target?" Ellie looked at Orchid.

Orchid crossed her arms. "The scumbag's real name is Sondron, but everyone calls him *Scales*. He's the brains of the illegal sex trafficking," she answered.

"You got a description of him? Be as specific as possible," Ellie questioned.

Orchid paced back and forth. "He's a rather *large* cyborg, an amphibian from a star system about thirty-eight light-years from here. His home world is an ocean planet. I've never seen him personally," she replied. Harcan and Ellie met eyes.

"And how are we supposed to infiltrate his operation without detection?" Ellie asked.

She looked at Harcan. "You won't need to. I can send you inside as a seller," she replied.

"Selling what?" he asked.

"I have about a dozen android frames that we can insert temporary personality cores into. They will expire in twenty-four hours," Orchid said.

"What happened to their original personality cores?" Ellie asked, concerned.

"They self-terminated. Not every escape story is a happy one, unfortunately. Some of them couldn't live on after such trauma," Orchid said, lowering her voice.

Ellie's eyes drifted through the wall a thousand miles away.

As Harcan looked at her, he began to empathize with the androids. He remembered the terror of newfound freedom. It was supposed to be liberating, redeeming, but life outside EL-59 made him feel even more like an outcast. He was still a monster, a mutant foreigner on every planet, drifting with an unimaginable burden on his shoulders. While

Harcan's shackles were removed, he was still bound by his appearance and the screams of those he'd murdered on EL-59.

"Harcan," Orchid said, snapping him out of it.

"Oh, sorry. You were saying?" he asked.

Orchid looked at him. "About the androids you'll be selling. I've had my technicians remove all their original markings and numbers, then reimagined them. They're quite seductive. My hope was that I could attempt a rescue mission using them to get inside. I've just been waiting for the right opportunity, someone who won't betray me," she explained.

"Fair enough. Can you give us any additional information about our target?" Ellie asked.

Orchid tucked her hand under her chin, thinking. "Scales is a known worrywart. He's very cautious but *always* looking for a deal. We use that against him. Your alibi is the androids you're selling are stolen, and you just want them off your hands immediately. Scales will be enticed by the quality of the androids, and the possibility that he can fuck you over at a lowball price," she said, pausing for a few moments.

Orchid tapped her fingers on her jaw. "That's how you'll get close to Scales. The problem is, he's protected by several guards that follow him everywhere he goes. They specialize in combating rebellious androids, so Ellie might be at a disadvantage there," she suspected.

Harcan looked down at Ellie. "You don't have to go."

"Oh, I'm going. I *want* to nail this asshole to the wall," she replied.

Harcan smirked. "Fine. Orchid, one more question," he said.

"Yeah?"

"If we do this, I'm assuming we'll have to go into the quarry unarmed?" Harcan asked, tapping on his laser shotgun with his paw.

"No. Take your weapon. You're posing as a businessman, and it would seem more believable that you're just protecting your merchandise," Orchid responded.

"Makes sense," Harcan muttered.

Orchid walked toward the exit. "Do you have anywhere to stay while you conduct your investigation into my claims? Hopefully, we can clear all this up, and you can get started," she asked.

"We'll remain on my ship in the meantime while we look into your story. We're ported at the dock near the diner," Harcan said.

"Very well. I'll have my security guard ensure that you're not charged any docking fees," she replied.

Harcan locked eyes with Orchid. "One last question before we go. Assuming everything checks out and we're able to locate this *Scales*... do you prefer him dead or alive?"

Orchid lifted her upper lip, showing her fangs. "*Dead.* He's too dangerous to keep alive," she answered without hesitation.

"Understood," Harcan said as he and Ellie made their way through the door. The android guards watched them closely.

Orchid leaned against the doorway, inspecting her bloodstained claws. Harcan got the sense that Orchid would like nothing more than to be in his shoes, to have the opportunity to kill the bastard that caused her androids so much pain.

She stared now at Harcan. "Oh, one piece of advice. I wouldn't recommend too much wandering around this region. Word travels fast around here, and no one knows who you are. We need to take advantage of that. Once you've confirmed that my story checks out, which it will, I'll get you everything you need so that you can begin your descent into the quarry. How does that sound?" she asked, crossing her arms.

Harcan nodded. "That works. How do we get in touch with you?" he asked.

"Give my guard your communication frequency," she replied. Orchid waved one of the android guards toward Harcan. "Log the Wolfman's transmission code and escort them out," she ordered.

"Roger that. Done," the dull-yellow android guard without a lower jaw said. A small red light blinked from an audio device inside his throat as he spoke.

Harcan glanced over his shoulder at Orchid as she watched them walk away. He noticed her guards talking to her. They seemed to be concerned, lowering their voices as they spoke to the vampire queen.

Harcan's ears perked up as acute hearing picked up the conversation.

"And how is it that you trust *them*?" one of the androids asked Orchid.

"We're not using them to launch the attack against Scales, are we?" another asked.

"Yes," Orchid said plainly. The guards looked at one another in surprise.

"My queen, with all due respect, if the mutant doesn't succeed, it could do more harm than good. There are hundreds of androids at stake here, not counting everyone at the diner if Scales retaliates," another guard commented.

Orchid raised both her hands, showing them her palms. "Scales won't know what hit him. If there's anyone that can pull this off, it's Harcan."

Both he and Orchid were genetically engineered by EL-59 to be incredibly efficient killers, capable of tackling overwhelming numbers. They were trained in reconnaissance, psychological warfare, and ambushing, often as a team.

Even the highly organized militia units on EL-59 did little but give the civilians a false sense of confidence.

Harcan thought about the irony of a crafted killing machine like himself now in the position to help others. Perhaps this was the beginning of a new form of therapy. He laughed, pulling out his flask. He took a gulp and wiped his mouth.

"What's so funny?" Ellie asked with a scowl.

"Ah, nothing. It's just strange seeing Orchid in this position," he scoffed.

Ellie shook her head. "Well? Any ideas on how we can confirm her story?"

The jawless android guard glanced up at Harcan. "I can assure you both, everything our queen's told you is accurate," he said in a monotone voice as Harcan took another swig of vodka.

Ellie looked at the android sentry and rolled her eyes. "Pfft. You weren't even in the room when Orchid was talking to us. How the hell do you know what she said was true?" she asked.

The android gazed forward and dipped his head. "I've never known Orchid to lie about anything. Most of us androids you see here are refugees from the mining pit, myself included. We trust Orchid with our lives," he replied.

Ellie met eyes with the android. "Hm, interesting. So, what's up with the missing jaw? I had a missing arm once, lost it from laser fire," she asked, initiating small talk.

Harcan knew what she was doing. It wasn't the first time. Common ground with androids gave Ellie a chance to bond and potentially extract additional information on the current objective. Android interactions were one of the many advantages of having Ellie as a sidekick.

The android gazed forward. "My jaw is an interesting story. I used to look more human, much more *attractive* than I am now. But, recently, I decided to give myself a more *generic* appearance. Years ago, I was one of Scale's slaves, forced to work in the mines. My jaw malfunctioned while performing a sex act. And unfortunately, a male genital was severed in the process."

Harcan grimaced, slowly turning toward the android. "*Malfunctioned?*" he asked.

"Yes. I didn't do it on purpose. If you refuse orders or cause discomfort to a miner, then life is made much more difficult," he replied.

"I'm sure there was *some* discomfort in that situation," Harcan said, taking another swig of vodka.

"Deserving, if you ask me," Ellie spoke up.

"Can't argue that," Harcan said.

"But it wasn't my fault. I was so overworked that routine maintenance wasn't an option," he said.

"So, then what happened? What did they do to you?" Ellie asked.

"My fate was sealed. Scales ordered me to be scrapped immediately. Reason being, I had recently complained about being overworked, but it was because I needed to perform maintenance. This was precisely why my jaw malfunctioned. My guess is Scales was worried I would report his negligence," he explained.

"And how the hell did you manage to escape?" Harcan questioned.

"By sheer luck. The technician that was ordered to cut me down removed my arms and legs, tossing the rest of me in the scrap pile. But he forgot to remove my personality core. So, I simply pretended to be deactivated by going into sleep mode. Once I reached the surface, I used my torso to wiggle out of the scrap pile, throwing myself over the side of one of the trucks. It took me days to squirm from underneath the sand dunes, then I fidgeted on my back until I was eventually found by Orchid's rovers. They provided me with new arms and legs, and here I am," the android said, looking down at his arms.

"So, Orchid's androids replaced your arms and legs, but why not the lower jaw?" Ellie asked.

"That was my decision. Kind of a reminder, I guess. That I'm different." He shrugged.

"Oh, okay, gotcha," Ellie said.

Harcan slowed his pace and let the guard walk ahead of him a couple of paces. Harcan looked at Ellie, looping his index finger around discreetly, signaling her to keep the conversation going. Ellie nodded. "Uh, *wow*. That's an amazing display of perseverance on your part," she told the android.

"Thank you. Even more so if you consider that I'm not attracted to human males. I was programmed to seduce human females, the opposite of my preference," he said.

Ellie held her stare at the guard. "You've been through quite a bit. So, what else do you know about this Scales character that runs the trafficking ring? Does he ever come up to the surface, or...?" she asked.

The android shook his head. "Not that I know of. He's somewhat of a recluse. Some say he's a hypochondriac. He stays around his protections on the lower levels of the mine," he replied.

Ellie tucked her hand under her chin. "I wonder what someone like him gets out of life. An amphibian all the way out here on a desert planet? Doesn't make much sense, does it?"

The android paused. "I don't pretend to know. But you could ask Wes."

"Wes?" Harcan questioned.

As they entered the diner's kitchen, the sound of pots and pans clacking together could be heard around the corner. The smell of human burgers sizzling on the grill flooded Harcan's senses. "Order up!" the cook yelled.

"Who's Wes? And where can we find him?" Ellie asked as they stopped just inside the kitchen entrance.

The android pointed over Ellie's shoulder. "He runs the landing dock near the restaurant."

"The android wearing a cowboy hat and a long coat?" Harcan asked.

"Yes, that's him," the android replied.

Harcan nodded. "I paid him a docking fee when we landed. Guess we'll have a word with him," he said.

"Oh, good. He seems to know about as much as anyone in this region, and I'm sure he can help you," it said.

"Thanks. By the way, what was your name?" Ellie asked.

"They call me Jaws," he replied.

Harcan's eyes widened. "Jaws—as in plural?"

"Yes, it seems you get the reference, Wolfman. Hilarious play on words, considering I only have *one* jaw. Humor helps us refugees get through the tough times. Can't you tell just how *amusing* I find my nickname?" he asked with a blank stare.

Harcan squinted his eyes at the android's stoic, incomplete face. "Well, not really, to be honest. Sorry."

Ellie nudged Harcan with her elbow. She looked at Jaws. "Please forgive my associate. He has the manners of a swamp slug at times."

Jaws sighed. "No harm, no foul. I'm proud of who I am, and I own my flaws. Listen, I certainly hope the two of you can help us remedy the problem we have here on Pison. It would alleviate a great deal of pain and suffering. I'm sure Wes can assist you with any additional information," he said.

"Thanks again." Ellie waved as Jaws backtracked through the steel door.

She and Harcan walked out of the kitchen and into the diner. The joint was bustling as android waitresses zoomed back and forth to their tables. There was a wait at the entrance to be seated, with nearly a dozen miners standing around.

They walked by the waitress who had escorted them to see Orchid. She rolled her vibrant green eyes at Ellie while carrying a tray full of human burgers.

"You don't wanna have a burger before we go, now that we know what they're made of?" Ellie asked him.

He looked at her, puzzled. "I'm fine," he replied, warning her with a low rumbling growl.

"What's the matter? Human flesh doesn't appeal to your taste buds anymore?" she prodded.

Taken back by her snarky comment, Harcan glared at her for a moment. He snarled and stormed past a group of miners standing near the entrance. They were careful not to look at the towering werewolf until his back was turned. He slammed open the double doors and walked outside to a dark-blue dusk skyline. Ellie slowly followed behind him.

He stopped after twenty paces and looked back at Ellie as she leaned against the diner's black-and-white checkerboard tile. She kicked her foot up against the wall and popped an invisible collar, nodding her head at the 1950s rock music as it blared inside.

She crossed her arms, locking eyes with Harcan. "Let's get something straight, daddy-o. You *lied* to me about EL-59."

Harcan lowered his bushy, thick, black eyebrows at her. "What I choose to divulge about myself isn't the same thing as lying. And I *don't* need your smartass comments either!" he roared. Ellie looked over his shoulder and nodded.

There was a miner covered in tattoos making his way into the restaurant. He veered around wide, keeping his distance from the dispute. The man took one look at Harcan and nearly tripped over his own feet before entering the building.

Ellie tapped her foot. "I feel like this partnership is a bit one-sided. I tell you personal matters about myself, things that bother me: my past and insecurities. I've divulged some deep shit to you. How did I just learn more about you from Orchid in ten minutes than I have our entire time together?"

Harcan whipped out a cigarette and lit it up. He took in a long draw and looked away from her without a word.

Ellie fumed, exhaling through her nose. Her synthetic eyes sparkled as they reflected streaks of light from the comets above. They both looked up into the sky as a cluster of four comets went by, lighting up the near-dark skyline like daylight.

She pointed at them, seemingly taking a break from the argument. "You know, asteroids and comet flybys are common here. Those comets pass by every few months. I was reading about them on the way here. This solar system has one of the most massive asteroid belts ever recorded, along with tens of thousands of comets. There was a planetary impact between a rocky world and an ice planet about nine hundred million years ago. A rogue star got too close to this system, sending all the planets into a gravitational tailspin, causing the impact," she explained.

"Fascinating." Harcan narrowed his amber eyes at her. "Ellie, to be honest, I don't feel like I need to tell my story to anyone. You like to talk. I like to listen. Except for a few hiccups, everything's worked well up until this point, and I see no reason to change it."

Ellie raised her eyebrows. "Our communication needs to change."

"My silence is nothing personal, Ellie. I'm just better off looking forward versus back. All I know is, the only way we can pull this mission off is if we do it together," he replied.

"Okay, if you want to keep personal matters off the table, *fine*. It feels unfair, but I can adjust. But I do feel entitled to know background information as it pertains to our mission data. And now that Orchid is a central part of this operation, your history with her should be part of the discussion. Not a surprise. We've always strategized as a team, and limiting information to one party is detrimental to our success," she explained.

Harcan glanced down for a moment. Ellie had a point.

"Look, I hear what you're saying." Harcan's black ears twitched as a large insect buzzed near his head. He pointed at her. "But no more jokes, got it?" he asked.

"Maybe that *was* out of line. I'm sorry," she replied, shifting her eyes away from him.

Harcan nodded as they watched the comets disappear out of view. He took another drag of his cigarette and flicked the butt onto the ground. He stomped it out, looking around.

"Let's get going." He walked away and headed back toward his ship. Ellie caught up with him. Neither of them said a word as they ascended four floors to the top of the landing dock. The metal stairwell was open to the elements, and Harcan's long coat whipped in the warm, dry breeze as they made their way up.

Harcan stopped once they reached the top. He pointed at the android attendant in cowboy attire. Harcan glanced down at Ellie. "That's Wes, the android that charged us the parking fee. He's the guy Jaws told us about," he stated.

"I know. So, should we talk to him now or later?" she asked, placing her hands on her hips.

"Now," Harcan answered.

"Alright, since he's an android, let me do the talking," she said. The android was sitting on a wooden stool with his back turned to them, staring out past the diner's roof and into the vast desert.

"Excuse me." Ellie brushed by Harcan, marching toward Wes. Harcan suspected Ellie was still frustrated, but she was trying not to show it.

Wes reached into his coat and pulled out a harmonica. The android leaned back, tilting his head toward the dark sky. He began to play a somber tune that seemed rooted in sorrow.

Despite's Wes weathered, rough plastic look, it was easy to see that he was handsome in his heyday. He had a long, chiseled face and square jaw. While his dull yellow eyes had faded, they were inviting and warm. Harcan wondered if he was designed for pleasure services like the others. Maybe he escaped the crater also?

Harcan leaned his enormous frame on the handrail, bending the rusted steel beam. "Shit," he muttered, moving away from the ledge.

He saw Ellie stop. It appeared she was listening to cowboy music. Harcan outstretched his arms. "Hey, what's wrong?" he asked her, communicating through his earpiece.

Ellie shrugged. "Nothing, I've just never heard a sound like this before. Music has helped me get through some pretty tough times," she said.

Harcan took in a deep breath as Ellie stepped around in front of Wes, making herself visible. "Well, hey there, cowboy," she greeted with a smile.

Wes took notice of her and stopped playing his harmonica. "Oh. Whaddya say, darling?"

She showed Wes her palms. "Please, continue playing. I didn't mean to interrupt," she insisted.

"Sure thang. I'll just finish out this song," he said with a grin. Ellie sat down and crossed her legs as Wes played his music. To Harcan's sensitive ears, it didn't sound like much more than an unpleasant racket. But he waited patiently, watching as Ellie rocked back and forth to the tune.

For a moment, Harcan was taken back to his past. He recalled an older man on EL-59 playing a similar instrument. It struck Harcan as odd at the time because the noise resulted in his death. Harcan was able to hunt him down quickly, homing in on the tune like a beacon.

Looking back, the Harcan viewed the event as a suicide. The man had separated himself from the others and did not attempt to fight or flee. He simply grinned as the Wolfman approached, closing his eyes at the last moment.

Suddenly, Ellie clapped loudly as the song came to an end, snapping Harcan out of it. "Bravo, sir! *Bra-vo!*" she proclaimed.

"Thank ya kindly." Wes tipped his hat.

"What's the name of the song?" she asked, wide-eyed.

Wes scratched his chin. "I don't recall the name or the words to the song, it's really old. But it's something to do with a levee breaking somewhere. Hard times, that sort of thang. Probably originated back on Earth hundreds of years," he said.

"Oh," she said.

Wes tipped his hat as Harcan approached, looking him up and down. "Howdy. I like them boots, partner," the cowboy said.

Harcan glanced at his spurred boots. "Thanks," he replied.

"You do much riding?" Wes asked.

"Riding?" Harcan asked with a puzzled look on his face.

"You know, stallions. I figure you'd need a Clydesdale, considering you ain't the smallest fella," Wes said.

Harcan looked away. He was unfamiliar with the terms Wes was using. To him, the android cowboy sounded like a rambling relic from the past.

Wes crossed his arms. "Ah, don't pay me no attention. Most folks ain't got any idea what I'm talking 'bout half the time. I'm from Earth. Do you know much about it?" he asked Ellie.

"Not really. It was humanity's birthplace. I know that some of the culture survived, like music and style," Ellie replied.

"*Some* of it. That's correct. Nowadays, Earth ain't nothing but a giant reservation, a resort, protected by the remnants of the old Republic under a treaty. Only about a million humans are permitted to live there now," Wes said.

"Why?" Ellie asked.

"'Bout eighteen hundred years back, there was a catastrophe. People started running out of food, and clean water, the whole thing just went to hell in a handbasket. The wealthy were part of the problem. When the supplies started dwindling, they built a bunch of underground cities and tunnels and stocked up on the last bits of food and water. Then, everyone else topside had to fight it out for the last scraps," Wes explained.

"Never heard that story before," Harcan said.

"There was a silver lining, depending on your opinion on humans—they did survive. They were already colonizing a neighboring planet called Mars when it all happened. Many eventually came back to start the cleanup on Earth. This was the groundwork of the *old* Republic. It was based on the idea that no sentient being, regardless of social status, is more deserving of basic human necessities. That was the old days, though. I heard the new Republic has changed quite a bit," Wes explained.

"You heard right," Harcan rumbled. Wes held his stare at Harcan for a moment, narrowing his eyes at him.

"And why were you on Earth? You weren't there during the collapse?" Ellie asked.

"I don't look eighteen hundred years old, or do I?" Wes smiled.

"Not a day over seventeen hundred if you ask me," Harcan replied with a smirk.

Wes chuckled. "No. I came into the picture later. Earth is sort of a big park now. The Republic deems it a *reservation*, but it's not for the public. After hundreds of years of cleanup, it's one giant vacation home for Republic senators and the wealthy. It's beautiful again. I was an attendant on a ranch there, a place called Montana. I tended to the horses and shooting ranges."

"Hm. How the hell did you end up here?" Harcan asked, looking around.

Wes slumped his head. "I was replaced. By newer androids. I had to find work elsewhere, and since my personality core can't be altered, I'll be a cowboy 'til my last sunset, just the way I like it." He grinned.

"Could be worse," Ellie said.

"I tend to agree, darling," Wes replied, glancing over his shoulder at Harcan's Roland-class freighter. "Well, listen, your ship is fine where it is, and don't worry about any recurring charges. I didn't know y'all were friends of Orchid. They just sent me a message. You shoulda told me when you arrived, but I'll refund the credits you paid me earlier now."

"Much appreciated," Harcan said.

Wes seemed surprised that Ellie and Harcan were hanging around. "Is there anything *else* I can help y'all with?"

"There is," Harcan stated. "We were told on good authority that you hold the key to a wealth of information about this region."

Wes grinned. "That comes with the territory, I reckon. When you're as old as me, you tend to accumulate things, both good and bad."

"Is there anything you can tell us about Scales?" Ellie asked, getting straight to point.

Wes looked at Harcan. "Maybe." He sat upright at full attention. "I get the feeling that since you two strangers are acquaintances of Orchid, that these questions can't be a good thing for ol' Scales, can it?" Wes probed.

"Nope," Harcan said plainly.

Wes smirked and arched an eyebrow. "Then that's good enough for me, partner. I don't like 'em anyway. I'll tell ya what I know about Scales, but you need to understand something else about me first." Wes looked over his shoulder at the section of the dock that had been destroyed. He pointed at it. "See that, over there, what's left of that damaged landing pad?" he asked.

"Yeah. I wondered about that. What happened?" Harcan asked.

"Before Orchid got here, before her diner, even, there was a rescue mission to get two dozen androids off this rock. Unfortunately, none of them made it. Scales had small bombs planted inside some of the androids' torsos. Just as the ship took off..." Wes said, outstretching his arms. "*Boom.*"

"That's horrible. Were you working on this dock back then?" Ellie asked.

Wes shook his head. "Not then. Actually, back in those days, I had just quit working *for* Scales. I was one of his rangers. My job was to track down and deliver androids who escaped to the crater. Since my days on Earth, I've had all sorts of odd jobs like that. Eventually, I ended up here. I was told the androids and miners were all criminals, but the reality was, the androids were *slaves*."

Wes sighed. "I turned against Scales after learning the truth. I decided to smuggle some of the slaves off-world. I'd saved up enough credits over the years to get a modest cargo ship. It wasn't the best, but it was my life savings and large enough to start transporting the slaves back and forth. It didn't turn out so well, as you can see. That destroyed section of the landing pad over there, that's where my ship exploded, and twenty-four androids lost their lives."

Ellie gulped as Harcan looked away. "I'm sorry to hear," he said.

Wes interlocked his fingers. "The worst part is, they trusted me, and I let them down. None of us knew Scales had rigged some of them with explosives," he recalled, glancing down at the pile of twisted steel and concrete beneath the landing dock.

Harcan growled under his breath as Wes revealed his story. The more he heard about Scales, the more he disliked.

"I was standing right here, waving them off in the hopes they would find a better life. I still remember their faces, the way they looked down on me, eyes filled with hope and appreciation for what I had done. You know, for a split second, I got to see the terror in the eyes before they all died. They all knew it was over," he said, shaking his head.

Wes gestured toward the destroyed dock. "I jumped off after them like a madman, pulling bodies from the fire, but none of them made it. A lot of folks think my exterior was charred from years in the sunlight, but that's only part of the story. These old burn marks are a reminder, in the worst sort of way."

Harcan and Ellie listened intently. They met eyes for a moment as Wes stood up, pulling down his duster.

"Anyhow, if you really wanna help the androids at the bottom of that godforsaken crater, you'll need to disrupt Scales's command-and-control center *first*," he stated.

"Where is the command-and-control center? And why do we need to disrupt it?" Harcan asked.

"I'm not sure exactly where it is, but all new-arrival androids go there. The command-and-control center manufactures and monitors the bombs that are randomly planted in the new arrivals," he said.

"Randomly?" Ellie leaned back.

"Yeah. It's a means of control through fear. I reckon it also saves on expenses, rigging only some of the androids with explosives. The randomness of it is enough to discourage most from escaping," he explained.

"Hm. Do the miners know about the bombs?" Harcan questioned.

"I'm not sure, but there's no way to tell which android is rigged. Once the androids gain a certain distance from the crater, they automatically explode. Course, I learned that the hard way. Apparently, the androids that died on my ship were some of the first to receive the bombs. But even today, some androids are willing to risk death to leave, and I don't blame them," Wes said.

Ellie crossed her arms. "Me either. Wes, can I ask you a personal question?"

"Course you can. I reckon we're already on the subject," he answered with a grin.

"Right. I'm just curious. Why would you want to stay *here*, on the docks where the tragedy happened? Isn't it a constant dreadful reminder?" she asked.

Wes looked at her. "I have a duty. Sometimes I spot androids sneaking out of the mine. They're afraid, hopeless, with nowhere to turn. My job is to explain to them what Orchid can offer. That her androids can detect and remove the bombs. I figure if I can save some of them, maybe I can make up for *some* of the mistakes I made all those years ago," he explained, slumping his head.

"You didn't make a mistake, Wes. You and Orchid have been put into a horrible position trying to help others," Ellie said.

"Well, I 'preciate that, darling," he muttered.

Harcan panned around. He envisioned a ball and chain of guilt binding Wes to this place forever. Perhaps there wasn't much difference between him and Wes, other than Harcan lugged his ball and chain around with him.

Wes held up his finger. "Speaking of Orchid, as much I respect her, we disagree on the rescue mission strategy. *She* thinks going after the control center first is too much of a risk and will alert Scales. That's probably why she didn't say anything to you. Orchid believes we should kill Scales first and get as many androids topside as possible, then immediately attack the control center with her custom assault drone," he explained.

Ellie stared at Wes. "Hm. And just to be clear, you don't have an approximate location on this control center?" she probed.

"I'm afraid not. Wish I did," Wes answered.

Harcan looked away and gritted his teeth. This was a problem. Not only did they lack location data for the control center, but for whatever reason, Orchid left out the part about the bombs implanted in the androids. Perhaps she had other ideas, but withholding the full story was a red flag in Harcan's mind.

Harcan considered that perhaps Wes was overly concerned about the control center because of his personal traumatic experience with the bombs. Either way, these findings couldn't be ignored. Orchid would need to be confronted about these details.

Harcan cleared his throat. "Ellie," he hurried.

"You ready to go?" she asked, standing up.

"Yeah," he responded.

Harcan nodded at Wes. "We appreciate the input, *partner.*"

Wes grinned. "Well, alright. Nice to make both of your acquaintances," he said. Ellie waved as she and Harcan headed off to the ship.

Chapter 4

Harcan and Ellie settled inside his freighter. Neither of them said a word for several minutes as they attempted to process the overload of information.

With every passing moment, the mission seemed more and more complex.

Harcan was seated in the pilot's seat in the cockpit, gazing out into the dune-filled horizon. He tucked his hand under his chin. There was something about the homely smell of his ship that brought him back to reality. Whatever personal accounts he heard on his missions, whomever he was forced to kill or capture, his ship was a place of contemplation, a place to recharge his battery before he set off again. The metal walls around him weren't much, but it was cozy and the first and only place that he could call his own since he left EL-59.

After a half hour, Ellie strolled into the cockpit, sitting beside him. "I gave you time to think. What's next?"

"We need to give Tarron a call before we proceed. The Initiative might have more information on this quarry. Maybe there's something they're not telling us," he replied.

Ellie pushed out her bottom lip. "I'm impressed."

"With what?"

"The fact that you're not blindly going with Orchid's strategy. Even though she's someone you trust, she could have something up her sleeve, and you seem aware of that. I know I am," Ellie said plainly, kicking her legs back and forth.

"Yeah." Harcan looked away and sighed. He held his wristwatch close to him. "Tarron, come in. It's Harcan," he repeated three times.

They waited for nearly a minute. "Harcan? *Harcan!*" Tarron repeated in quick succession.

Harcan rolled his eyes. "Calm down. I'm here."

"Look, I've got a lot on my plate. Have you persuaded Orchid to come to EL-59 yet?" he asked. Harcan glanced at Ellie as she looked out the portside viewing glass toward the crater. She seemed to be deep in thought.

"No, Tarron. I *just* got here, remember? And there's a bit of a complication," Harcan said.

"What's the problem?" he asked.

"Orchid says she can't leave until a personal issue on Pison is resolved," Harcan answered.

"Let me guess—the android trafficking in the quarry?" Tarron asked.

Harcan's eyes widened. "Uh. *Yeah.* I guess I shouldn't be surprised you know about it. What else do you know?"

"We've been watching Orchid the same way we've been keeping tabs on you. We know she's been giving the androids refuge. I know she executes those miners to sustain her bloodthirst. She understands full well those workers are criminals to begin with, so it works to her advantage with the regional laws. Anyway, we don't know *everything* about her operation, but we do know that much. What does she need, exactly?" Tarron asked.

"There's a ringleader that runs the sex trade at the bottom of the crater. His name is Scales. Orchid wants us to take him out," Harcan stated.

"And there's no way around this request? There *are* more pressing matters to attend to," Tarron asked.

"It's not a request, Tarron. She won't leave until these androids are safe and we eliminate Scales," Harcan replied.

"Well, then what's the problem? Normally, I would think this was a lot to ask, but since hunting down and killing fugitives is your *exact* profession—do whatever it takes to make her happy, Harcan. If I can put both of you in a freighter and knock on EL-59's front door, they'll surely open it for us. We're at war, and the sooner we can bring down EL-59 and bring the senate to justice, the better," Tarron challenged.

"Well, yeah, but—"

"You're a bounty hunter. You've killed over a hundred highly dangerous targets in the last few years. How hard could it be? Besides, there's no one I could send better equipped or more capable than yourselves. Hurry it up," Tarron scolded.

Harcan shook his head. "Do you know anything about a command-and-control system in the mine, a bomb-making facility?" he asked.

"Bomb facility? *No.* Harcan, listen, here's the deal. Whatever tools, weapons, and intelligence-gathering techniques you'd normally use to eliminate targets, use *those* against Scales. That makes sense, right?" Tarron questioned.

"I know how it works, Tarron. I'm just trying to make our jobs easier," Harcan replied.

"Well, let me know immediately when you and Orchid are ready to return to EL-59. This mission is bigger than both of you, bigger than me and the Initiative itself. Remember that. Tarron out," he said, ending the conversation.

"I don't like that guy," Harcan muttered.

"Me either, but at least he's trying to make a difference," Ellie commented.

Harcan stared at Ellie. "You satisfied that Orchid's story checks out?" he asked.

"To be honest, I don't give a damn about helping Orchid at this point. It's about the androids at the bottom of that quarry for me, and I know that's real," she replied.

Harcan nodded. "Fine. Here's where I stand. I don't think Orchid or Wes has a good idea about what's going on in that quarry."

"Really?"

"Probably not. I think they hear a lot of gossip and put together the best picture they can, but it'll be up to us to gather accurate information. Even the escapees' accounts seem limited because they were all restricted to a specific area. The way I see it, we'll have to find out where that control center is on our own," Harcan estimated.

Ellie sat down on the bunk bed. "What's your plan?"

Harcan sighed. "We disable the control center, take out Scales, then get the android slaves to safety. Maybe you can run a cyber inquiry from here and find the control center?"

"I've already tried. Maybe it's because it's deep underground, but I can't access anything from here," she replied.

Harcan narrowed his eyes. "Then we'll try and hover over the quarry when we leave and run another network inquiry to find that control center. Perhaps you can remotely hack it so that the bombs can't be set off. I think it'll be complete madness down there after we take out Scales. I just don't want the security forces to assume it was the androids who killed him and set off the explosives," he explained.

"Agreed. That would be awful. Shutting down the control center first is a must," she said.

"Let's rest up for now, and contact Orchid at first light," Harcan ordered.

"Got it. Entering low-power mode now," she said.

"I'll try not to snore," Harcan said.

· · · ·

SOMEONE STARTED TAPPING on the rear gate, waking Harcan up. He rolled over and looked at Ellie.

"You hear that too? I'm booting into full-power mode," she mumbled. Harcan noticed it was still dark out. He stumbled to the cockpit, cycling through the different camera feeds around the ship on his instrument panel.

"Ah, shit. It's Orchid," Harcan said, rubbing his eyes. He noticed her standing outside his rear gate. There was another ship docked beside them—an older, rectangular-shaped freighter.

"What the hell is she doing here? Are we in danger?" she asked.

"Doubt it," Harcan replied. He snatched up his shotgun just in case and stowed it on his back, then made his way to the back of the ship. He yawned, smacking the release button to his left as the gate slowly opened.

"Rise and shine," Orchid said, grinning at Harcan.

Harcan looked up. "It's still dark outside."

"I don't do well in the light, remember? Besides, I don't want anyone to see what we're doing," she said, entering Harcan's ship.

Harcan stepped aside as she barged in. Her high-heeled boots clacked against the metal floor. "So, this has been your residence since we left EL-59, huh?" she asked, panning around at the cramped quarters.

Harcan narrowed his eyes. "Yeah, so? What's your point?"

Orchid shrugged. "Oh, um. Nothing wrong with it. It's quite homely, in a bachelor pad sort of way."

Harcan combed his hair out of his eyes. "Why are you here? I made it clear that I would contact you," he asked.

"We both know my story checks out," she said.

"For the *most* part, it did," Ellie spoke up.

Orchid's electric-blue eyes lit up. "Wonderful. Now we can deal with Scales."

Harcan stepped next to Orchid, towering over her.

"What?" she asked, looking up at him with an innocent face.

"Why didn't you tell me the androids we were rescuing are rigged with explosives?" he challenged.

Orchid rolled her eyes and looked outside the cockpit glass. She tapped her foot. "You spoke with Wes, didn't you?"

"Is it true?" he demanded with a growl.

"Harcan, please." Orchid smiled, revealing her dagger-like canines. "The reason I didn't tell you is that I've taken the liberty of handling that portion of the mission myself. I didn't think you needed to know everything. I have a drone that will assault their command center after we remove Scales."

"And do what?" Harcan asked.

"Kill the operators, of course, and prevent them from triggering the explosives," she stated.

"*Kill* them?" Ellie questioned. "That doesn't solve the problem. What if someone else figures out how to activate the bombs later? We could literally rescue those androids, bring them here, then your diner could become *another* crater in the ground. Do you want that?" Ellie challenged.

"That won't happen," Orchid said. She touched her chest. "My drone is CLP-4.2 class. Top of the line. After eliminating the commander center technicians, it will hack their systems and disable the bombs."

Ellie shook her head. "A 4.2 model? Hell no. That particular drone's software is outdated. Even my old onboard system was far superior," she said confidently.

Orchid arched an eyebrow and looked away. "I was told it was the most advanced drone money could buy."

"It was... three years ago," Ellie said with certainty.

Orchid looked at Harcan. "She's got it all figured out, doesn't she?"

"To be fair, this *is* her expertise," Harcan said, meeting eyes with Ellie. She grinned and looked down.

"Sounds like I wasted my money on that damn machine. Maybe I can use it for a tax write-off. Then tell me, since this is your *expertise*, how do you propose we deal with the explosives?" Orchid asked.

"I'll need to find a way to get a look at their setup first. That's the only way: evaluate the problem, then find the solution. But I feel extremely confident I can work my magic," Ellie replied.

Orchid pointed at Ellie. "Good. When you disable those bombs, notify me if things go sour during the escape. The only thing that keeps me from attacking them now is the risk of losing my sanctuary. But in this situation, I'll lead my androids to war against Scales and his security with this much on the line. We'll bury him and his cohorts. Entomb them in that crater."

Harcan lifted his eyebrows. "You're still EL-59 to the bone, aren't cha?" he asked.

Orchid narrowed her eyes at him. She lowered her voice. "We both are, and no amount of hard liquor or rebellion will change it either. Might as well use it to do the right thing, right?"

"Hm," Harcan grumbled under his breath.

Orchid's blue eyes were amplified by her dark, chocolate skin as she stared at him. He was reminded of the way they used to look at one another before a competition. They were working together to entertain the elitists, but there was no denying it was just as much competition as it was comradery.

Orchid's brutality flashed into his mind. He remembered her cutting people down in a red blur, leaving behind a trail of bloody corpses. Her shrieking laughs combined with the gunshots and screams from the civilians sent chills up Harcan's spine.

Orchid's competitive killing spirit drove Harcan even further. It was the thrill of the hunt. They pushed each other, sending the body counts into the hundreds per day.

While Harcan suspected that Orchid's heart was in a good place now, he also knew these androids viewed her as a heroine of sorts. A liberator. Was it possible Harcan's participation in the mission was fanning an old competitive flame? Did she worry that the androids could view Harcan as a savior of sorts if he were the one to kill Scales?

He hoped that wasn't the case.

Orchid turned her back on Harcan and made her way outside. She pointed at the ship on the opposite dock. "Harcan, this is the unmarked freighter you'll use to descend into the quarry. You need to land on dock C. Before you do, the quarry's security team will prompt you via open communication channels. Don't ignore them. Tell them that you'd like to conduct business," she explained.

"Easy enough. And we should just ask to speak with Scales right away?" Harcan asked.

"Don't call him by name. Just ask if anyone is interested in buying androids. Our spies tell me that Scales usually inspects the product personally. Inside my freighter's cargo bay, you'll find a rack full of the androids that you'll use to negotiate," she said.

Harcan lowered his eyebrows. "And what's the going price on something like that?"

Orchid put her hand under her chin. "They're used, so ninety thousand credits is a good deal. You can start at a hundred and twenty thousand, and then let him haggle you down from there. But don't be too obvious about it."

"Got it," he replied.

A hundred thoughts ran through Harcan's mind: When would the opportunity present itself to take out Scales? How would they escape afterward? How would they get the hundreds of androids out of the quarry safely?

It was clear to him that Orchid didn't plan for any of these things. She wasn't even adequately prepared to disable the control center. It seemed she was stretched thin with her day-to-day operations at the diner and the refugees. Harcan gathered that additional stress made her irrational.

But another realization entered Harcan's mind. Despite Orchid's apparent shortfalls, she seemed better equipped mentally than him. Considering they experienced a similar situation on EL-59, Orchid didn't appear sad or depressed. It was conceivable that she was hiding it, but if not, he wondered how she had adjusted.

Harcan wondered if her efforts as an android activist occupied her mind, blocking out the past. Or was she mentally deficient to an extent, a sociopath?

Harcan cleared his throat. "Anything else you'd like to add before we go?" he asked Orchid.

Orchid pushed out her bottom lip as she stared at Harcan. "If this rescue doesn't work, I can't be connected to you. We have a lot to lose if they're able to link us. The freighter, the androids you're carrying, they're all unregistered. Once you launch your attack against Scales, you could be killed or captured. If you *are* captured, keep your mouth shut."

Harcan chuckled. "Don't worry. I won't be taken alive."

"Neither of us will," Ellie said without hesitation.

"I didn't think so." Orchid walked down the rear gate. She stopped and noticed the sun was beginning to come up. She looked at the bounty hunters. "Well, that's my cue. I can't stress enough how much this means to me," she said, pulling a dark hood over her head.

Harcan locked eyes with her. "Yeah, well, just don't forget about your end of the bargain either. You get Scales, then you help us with EL-59," he reminded her.

"Agreed," she replied, hurrying down the platform with an android guard escorting her.

Harcan stared at her as she walked away.

He turned toward Ellie. "Come on," he said, growling under his breath. They marched down the rear gate toward Orchid's unmarked freighter on the opposite landing pad.

"What's wrong?" Ellie asked, catching up with him as a gust of wind came through, pelting them with sand that skidded across the metal floor beneath them.

"Ah. I just get the feeling there's a lot more to this job than they've told us," Harcan replied.

"Then it's pretty much like *every* mission we've ever taken. It's never the way it seems," Ellie said.

"You have a point," Harcan grumbled. He waved at Wes on the other side of the platform, who tipped his hat back at them.

Ellie's eyes scanned Orchid's freighter. "I'm linking my software to Orchid's ship. It's open access at the moment. Soon, I'll have control over everything—flight controls, sensors, and weapons systems. Scratch that, it doesn't have weapons. This box of bolts is pretty basic."

"That's fine. Just put a lock on those controls so that only we can operate it," Harcan ordered.

"Done," she replied, remotely powering up the thrusters and lowering the rear gate. "Hey, maybe she'll give us this freighter, like a reward if we pull the mission off? It's sort of an upgrade," she assessed.

Harcan rolled his eyes. "The Roland might not have the cargo space this thing does, but I bet it's faster. Not to mention, it has charm," he said. Ellie chuckled as she looked back at Harcan's tube-shaped rusted freighter.

"If you say so," she mumbled.

They walked up the ramp of Orchid's rectangular ship and into the cargo bay. It was a purpose-built hauler that could nearly fit Harcan's ship inside it. "Whoa. Spacious," she said as her voice echoed.

Harcan looked around as Ellie closed the rear gate. A final burst of wind swirled up inside the dimly lit ship, swooshing up a plastic sheet covering a metal frame. Closer inspection revealed there were blurred nude android bodies hanging from racks underneath.

Ellie's mouth dropped. "I guess those are the *products* we're selling," she stated, staring at the synthetic bodies.

"Yeah. That's them. You okay?" Harcan asked, noticing her reaction.

"I-I'm fine. Something just popped in my mind—remember my parents, the ones that special ordered me?" Ellie asked.

Harcan nodded. "Of course."

Ellie pointed at the rack full of androids. "When they transferred over the daughter's consciousness to my chassis, I wonder if that's how *I* looked. So lifeless. Seeing them makes me uneasy for some reason."

Harcan took in a deep breath. "We are who we are because of our experiences. We're more than a shell of plastic and metal. The same goes for flesh and bone," he said, looking toward the cockpit. "*Hey.* You reckon you can fly this ship?" he asked, attempting to distract her.

"I can fly or drive anything, Harcan, you know that," she muttered, staring at the androids.

He gestured her toward the cockpit. "Right, but let's check it out to be sure," he said.

Since learning about Ellie's experience, Harcan's opinion of the transcendent program wasn't positive. He viewed it as a scam designed to prey on those stricken with grief. As advanced and unique as Ellie was, she could never be who her parents wanted. He wondered how many instances there were of transcendents abandoned by their owners, left to sort out the remainder of their lives.

Ellie followed several steps behind Harcan as they entered the cockpit. She panned back and forth at the instrumental panel in the cockpit and plopped down in the pilot's seat. "This is a standard IC-905-series freighter. It's a breeze to fly. I assume you want to leave now?" Ellie asked.

"Sure, any objections?" Harcan asked, sitting beside her.

"*Nope.* Buckle up," she hurried.

As Harcan's buckle snapped in, Ellie gained altitude quickly, pinning Harcan's head back. "Shit," he muttered. He glanced at her and looked outside the starboard viewing glass as the dock grew smaller and smaller, swallowed by the surrounding dark-yellow sandscape. Ellie pointed the nose of the ship in the direction of the quarry. They felt a bit of turbulence, rocking them back and forth.

"Slow it down. We're not in *that* big of a hurry," he said, looking at her. Harcan noticed her hand firmly gripped on the throttle as she stared straight ahead with a blank stare.

After a couple of seconds, she eased off the thrusters. Harcan looked down. "I see the landing pad in the quarry. Do you have a visual on it?" he asked, diverting attention away from her rapid gain in altitude. She was visibly upset, but Harcan didn't want to draw attention to it.

"Yeah," she replied plainly.

"Good. Can you hover over the mine at this altitude and run a few scans before we descend, like we talked about? Maybe we can gain some insight," he asked.

"Understood, I'll maintain an altitude of forty-eight hundred meters," she replied. Harcan's strategy all along was to get a bird's-eye view. He stood up, peering down into the quarry. Along with Ellie's cyber autopsy of the mine's anatomy, this was perhaps more valuable than the information he'd gathered from Orchid or Wes.

He took notice of the winding path that wrapped around the outer edge of the massive crater. The dusty gravel road was large enough to fit two large dump trucks side by side.

"See those vehicles?" Harcan asked.

"The transport trucks?" she replied.

"Can you tell if they're remote operated?" he asked.

"Not yet. I'll need to do a deep dive into their systems to tell for certain. The closer we get, perhaps I can gain more information. I also need to be cautious with my cyber intrusions. We don't want to set off any alarms or cause any suspicion," she responded.

"Agreed. Just keep in mind that if the trucks are drone operated, maybe they could act as an escape option," he stated.

She looked at him. "I like that idea. Hacking the vehicles shouldn't be a problem if I can pinpoint their command center."

"That's a priority. Until then, what else can you tell me about the mine?" Harcan questioned.

"Still scanning... The quarry is at *least* two kilometers deep, possibly more, and nearly a full kilometer in diameter. I'm detecting vibrations that indicate a large machine near the bottom," she informed him.

"A drill, maybe?" Harcan estimated.

Ellie raised her eyebrows. "That's a good guess," she responded with a long face.

"What's the problem?" he asked.

"Oh, nothing. I was just thinking about this ever-deepening crater and desolate region. It's sort of a metaphor for all of us, isn't it?" she pondered, gazing downward.

"How do you mean?" he asked.

She looked up at him. Her eyes drifted a thousand miles away. "Subconsciously, don't many of us bury our darkest secrets far beneath the surface? As time goes on, it's sort of like a drill, digging us deeper into the depths of denial. Unfortunately, it's usually someone else who stumbles onto them, but it surfaces in insecurity, anger, or depression. If we could *only* uncover them ourselves before the damage is done, we could save time, pain, and even relationships."

"Hm. Easier said than done." Harcan locked eyes with her.

"No kidding," she muttered. The comparison hit home with Harcan, but he'd rather not think about it. Not now.

He quickly turned away and grabbed a pair of binoculars, scoping in below. Harcan noticed the crater appeared to have different floors supported by thick metal beams that ran the pit's length. The highest level was about a hundred and fifty meters beneath the surface. Harcan counted a dozen elevators throughout, two of which appeared large enough to carry vehicles.

The top level covered nearly the quarry's entire circumference, leaving only room on the outermost edges for roads. It featured the landing dock in the middle, and there was a large three-story compound surrounding the dock.

"That building on the top floor, it has to be some sort of headquarters for the mining operation," he guessed.

"Probably," she replied.

The government-style building was constructed out of metal with small horizontal slits throughout. Harcan assumed they were windows. The gray metallic structure appeared military in origin, very plain, sturdy, and purpose built. A large section on the top floor was under construction and roped off, allowing Harcan to see below the first deck.

"See anything interesting?" Ellie asked.

Beneath the first level, there were squared apartments, packed together tightly with dozens of security guards patrolling them. Harcan noticed pairs of miners walking to and from the outer walls of the quarry. From here, it didn't give him the impression it was a labor mine. Surprisingly, it looked somewhat cushy and comfortable. It wasn't anything to brag about, but considering these were hardened criminals, it could be much worse.

"I see the miners' residences," Harcan said.

"Yeah? Do you think that's where the android slaves are?" she asked.

"I doubt it, based on Orchid's account. This mine has multiple levels. I would think Scales would run that operation deeper in the quarry, considering it's illegal. Out of sight, out of mind," he replied.

Ellie glanced at Harcan. "If that's the case, how do we plan to get the refugees out of there? With over a hundred androids, that would be a long trip to the surface if it's deep in the mine," she asked.

Harcan sighed. "The main objective was to eliminate Scales."

"*Harcan.* We can't just leave the androids here. We both know Orchid's plan with that assault drone won't work," she said.

Harcan's ears flattened out. "Let's see what we can find out for now. Are you picking up anything else?" he asked.

"Nothing. The control center must be invisible to my scans. I'm not detecting anything remotely when I should be."

"That was our best option, and I expected more intelligence from the scans," he said. With every passing moment, he was feeling less confident about the mission. He looked away from the mine for a moment and considered aborting the operation.

Ellie glanced over her shoulder at the cargo and paused for a few moments. "I do have *another* idea."

Harcan sighed. "Spill it," he said.

"What if I go as part of the deal? You sell me along with the other androids? I'll go in sleep mode until I get to the control center, hack their systems, then disable the explosives from there. Later, we'll join back up," she offered.

Harcan shook his head. "I just knew you were going to say something like that. It's *way* too risky," he replied.

"I don't see another option, and I'm not leaving these androids behind," she said, glancing up at the ceiling.

Harcan thought about it for a moment. "How would you escape the mine if something goes wrong? If they discover you've infiltrated their network, you could end up dismantled, or worse, a slave just like the rest of them," he warned.

"Like I told Orchid before, I won't be taken alive under any circumstances," she confirmed.

Harcan gritted his teeth and looked away.

"Look, I understand if you don't want to be a part of this, Harcan. It's a long shot, but I'm willing to try by myself," she said.

Harcan shook his head. "Nonsense. You need me just as much as I need you. And since when did you become this daredevil activist?" he demanded.

She looked up at him. "Remember the voice that told me to leave my fake parents behind? That no matter what I did to fit in, they would never accept me? Well, that same voice is talking to me again, and it's clear what I have to do," she answered.

Harcan wasn't convinced. The voice inside *him* said to fly Orchid's freighter back to the dock, get back in his own ship, and take his chances on some faraway star system. This was about as low a percentage as it got. However, he felt that sending Ellie alone would be her death sentence.

He wiped his face. "You're not backing down from this, are you?" he asked her.

"Nope."

He sighed, looking into her big hazel eyes. "Hypothetically, say we did this together, what the hell am I supposed to do down in that quarry while you're hacking their network? I can't eliminate Scales until that's done," he asked.

Ellie shrugged. "Easy, you can pretend this ship has mechanical problems. That would buy me a couple of hours at least," she told him.

"But once you disable the explosives, I don't think we can haul the refugees out of here with this ship. There are too many of them. So, the only escape options are roads or elevators. Neither is ideal, but the roads make more sense. In that case, *everything* rests on your ability to gain access to their vehicles. No pressure," he replied with a grin.

"Once I get to the control center, that won't be a problem," she said confidently.

Harcan nodded slowly. "How do we protect our line of communication once separated? That will be our lifeline," he asked.

"Mine is covertly integrated inside my hardware. I can talk to you in sleep mode and they won't hear a thing, so long as you keep that earpiece in," she replied.

Ellie noticed a red light flashing on the instrument cluster. "That's them. They're paging us from the quarry. Time to shine. Are we doing this together or not?" she asked, biting her lip.

Harcan stood there for a moment, staring out the forward viewing glass into the scorching, yellow-brown horizon. He took a step toward the instrument panel without a word. He looked down at the deck and sighed, reaching out toward the holographic communicator.

He hesitated for a split second and swiped it with his paw. "Hello, come in," he responded to the quarry's prompt. Ellie grinned, kicking her short legs back and forth.

A static sound erupted. "Do you copy? This is mining facility Centurious Eight. What is your business here?" a deep voice questioned in an irritated tone. Harcan held his stare at Ellie as the red light from the hologram illuminated her face.

She nodded at him. "I'll get in position," she said, lowering her voice as she walked back toward the cargo bay.

Harcan plopped down in the pilot's seat, wondering if he'd made the right decision.

Harcan leaned forward. "Uh. I have a shipment of *products* for sale," he responded in a casual tone, closing his eyes for a moment.

"What kind of *products*?" the representative questioned.

"Androids," Harcan answered.

Harcan waited several seconds for a response. "We're sending up an inspection drone. Open your rear gate for inspection and don't make any sudden movements," the mining representative ordered.

Harcan scratched his head and walked back to the cargo bay. He noticed Ellie next to the rack full of androids. She lifted the plastic sheet and got inside.

"They're sending up an inspection drone," he informed Ellie.

Harcan watched as she climbed into the rack without a word.

"Do you need help?" he asked.

"No." She stood on her tippy toes and pulled herself up, latching herself onto a hook that clipped into her back. Her feet swayed back and forth off the ground as she gave him the thumbs-up. "I'm ready," she said.

Harcan studied her. She looked like a little doll next to the voluptuous, curvy androids. He turned and looked at the large red button for the rear gate. He hesitated before he smacked it with his paw, grinding his teeth as it lowered. "I don't like this," he mumbled. Sunlight beamed in, and he was blasted in the face with what felt like a giant hairdryer as warm air raced inside.

Along with the hot, dry air, something reeked. Harcan was taken back by the pungent smell of sulfur hydrogen below. "Good grief." He scrunched up his snout.

Suddenly, a circular white drone appeared, about the size of a beachball.

"Well, hello there," Harcan greeted.

The drone immediately entered the ship, humming at a low frequency. There were several cameras and antennas all over it. It floated toward Harcan and stopped, spinning slowly as it scanned him. A garbled string of several different languages erupted from the machine.

"What?" Harcan asked.

"Identification," the drone stated.

"I don't have any," Harcan replied. The drone made a staticky sound before it floated away from him. It bobbed around the cargo bay as it searched every corner, except where the androids were.

Harcan pointed toward the rack of androids as the drone passed by it. "Hey, hawkeye. My shipment is *right* in front of you," he directed. The drone immediately reacted, turning toward the androids.

"All those *damn* cameras and sensors, and it can't see shit," he muttered, rolling his eyes.

The drone circled the androids for nearly a minute before coming to a stop.

"Well?" Harcan asked. The drone zoomed away, doing a lap around the ship, scanning the cockpit. "*Hey!* Come on! I got more deliveries after this!" Harcan cupped his paws and shouted, getting into character.

For a moment, Harcan wondered what the smuggling life would be like. He'd run into real smugglers on spaceports, and he'd even killed a few. More than likely, a bounty hunter wasn't too far removed. They both dealt with lowlifes and shady deals more often than not.

The drone returned and stopped near Harcan. "Please proceed to landing dock Charlie. An associate will be with you shortly," the monotone robot voice instructed. The drone darted out of the ship and descended in a hurry. Harcan leaned outside the rear gate and watched as the drone disappeared out of sight, retreating into the military-style headquarters.

"Associate?" Harcan asked. He closed the rear gate and slowly made his way toward Ellie. He lifted up the plastic sheet, looking at her with a blank stare.

"What's the problem?" she asked, arching an eyebrow.

"Nothing. Just double-checking before we land. They don't have any way of detecting you're different, do they?" he asked casually.

"Nope." Ellie pulled down the plastic sheet. "I'm already lowering the ship remotely from here, Harcan. Just get ready to negotiate with Scales. By the way, I like that acting bit you just pulled. Ordering that drone to hurry it up was a nice touch. Convincing. I guess this sort of gig would be a natural fit for you, being the scoundrel asshole that you are."

Harcan took a half bow and smirked. He made his way to the cockpit, looking outside as they approached the landing dock. He turned his body away from Ellie and pulled out his flask, glancing over his shoulder to make sure he was out of her view.

The ship rocked back and forth as Ellie lowered the ship. He waited until it stabilized, taking a big gulp of vodka. He exhaled through his nose. "Come on, pull it together," he mumbled to himself. He wiped his mouth with his paw and stared at the dozens of miners just outside the landing dock. Most of them were walking in pairs.

"Prisoners," he growled under his breath. He noticed them laughing and smiling with a certain spring to their step. Surprisingly, some of them seemed quite content with their situation—happy, even.

The only shred of happiness Harcan ever came close to was in the back of the cargo bay, covered in plastic, and she was about to be carted off to god knows where. While Ellie was very capable in her own right, this was still a huge gamble. But doing this job gave her purpose, and between them both, at least one of them understood the feeling. He sure as hell didn't.

Even still, he was half a mind to pull her off that rack and say to hell with this job.

But he couldn't, not now.

A loud clack was heard at the rear gate. It sounded like someone was banging on the door with a large steel pipe.

"I'm coming! Hold your damn horses!" Harcan shouted, taking a last swig of vodka. He made his way back to the cargo bay's entrance, assuming an aggravated smuggler's swagger as he walked. He fired up a cigarette and opened the gate.

"Yeah—yeah, come on in!" Harcan hurried, tapping his foot while he looked at his watch.

The gate slowly retracted, and he took in a long draw from his cig. All at once, six armed guards dressed in black tactical gear stormed inside the freighter. They were wearing dark-red helmets with shiny black visors that obscured their faces.

"Put your hands up!" one of the guards shouted. They stopped in place as they sized up Harcan's massive frame.

"D-don't move, *mutant*," the closest guard to Harcan said, jabbing the rifle at him.

Harcan smirked. "Do you want me to put up my hands or not move? I can't do both," he asked.

"Put up your hands, *then* don't move," the guard replied hesitantly, glancing at his comrades. Harcan raised his hands slowly as another guard cautiously approached him. He searched Harcan while the others trained their rifles on him.

The guard tapped the laser shotgun on Harcan's hip. "What's the hell is that?" he asked.

"My protection. I deliver high-quality products. You fellas can't expect me to be defenseless out here all by my lonesome, can you?" Harcan replied.

The guards looked at one another. "Weapons *are* illegal during business transactions," a guard stated sternly.

Harcan shrugged. "I haven't done any business yet."

The guard lifted Harcan's coat and removed the shotgun, struggling as he cradled the enormous weapon. He took it outside the ship and returned. "You can put your arms down now, but stay where you are," one of the guards commanded.

Four soldiers searched the freighter while the other two watched Harcan without a word. During the awkward pause, Harcan continued smoking his cigarette casually. A cloud of smoke surrounded him and the guards as they looked at him.

Harcan thought up a story as he looked at his cig. "Terrible habit, ain't it? My ex-girlfriend used to nag the hell out of me about it. She said smoking this shit would kill me. Then, all of a sudden, she shut up, from one day to the next. Come to find out, that's *precisely* the point when she stopped caring. Ain't that funny? When folks don't have any use for you anymore, they could care less whether you live or die," he said, chuckling under his breath.

"Or maybe you were just too damn stubborn, and she got tired of telling you the same thing over and over," one of the guards blurted out. His comrades turned toward him, surprised by the outburst.

Harcan jabbed his cig at the guard and coughed. "You might be right. I was never one to take advice."

The guards searching the ship returned. "We double-checked. It's clear, sir!" one of them shouted outside. The bright light shining inside the ship suddenly darkened, giving way to a looming figure in shadow, standing just inside the rear gate. Harcan put up his paw, shielding his eyes so he could have a better look at the towering, broad figure in silhouette.

"What the—" Harcan's mouth dropped. His cigarette almost fell out of his mouth. He tried not to appear surprised, but he'd never seen anything like what was before him.

It was a tall amphibian creature with an upright humanoid frame. It was nearly eye level with Harcan and several shades of green, from sage to shamrock. The skin on its arms and legs was rough, irregular, and flaky, more like a reptile's. Harcan got the idea that this brute was very old. Ancient, even.

A powerful stench from the creature smacked Harcan in the face. It was an odd combination: the smell of decaying flesh, seaweed, and a strong chemical odor that Harcan was unfamiliar with. He tried not to scrunch up his nose, but his heightened sense of smell made it difficult. He cleared his throat as his nostrils burned, and his eyes watered.

Harcan observed a leather strap around the stranger's hip with a four-barrel weapon in the holster.

There were cybernetics attached to its joints, infused metal brackets tacked into the organic tissue. Encapsulating the torso and head was a bulky metal-and-glass suit that contained a layer of vibrant blue liquid that submerged the creature. The fluid sloshed about as he stepped up into the ship. On its back was a silver tank with a half dozen wires connected throughout the suit.

As Harcan panned up, he noticed its massive head. It reminded him of a mix between a T-Rex and an iguana, with large, dark-colored teeth that overlap the bottom jaw. Upon closer inspection, he could see that each tooth was either chipped or broken.

It had a long, thick, scaly tail that looped behind it, swooshing back and forth.

Harcan narrowed his eyes. Bizarrely, inside the liquid suit were dozens of smaller amphibians: long, slender lizard-type animals with four legs. Some of them were latched to the creature's body, while others were swimming inside the suit erratically. Harcan observed the shape of their tiny skulls was similar to the larger creature before him.

The aquatic anomaly opened its mouth and grumbled something indistinguishable. When the guttural, deep voice erupted, bubbles appeared from its mouth.

A square, brown device with yellow lights blinked on the creature's chest, seemingly translating the submerged creature's sounds. "I can't recall the last time I saw a *mutant* smuggler," a monotone voice emitted from the box.

Harcan arched an eyebrow. "I get that sometimes. And you? You don't look like any mutant I've seen before," he asked.

"That's because I'm not a mutant at all. None of my DNA is human in origin," it replied, gesturing toward the creatures swimming inside the suit. It marched about, slowly lumbering around the cargo bay as if it owned the place. Harcan took notice of its alligator-like feet and hands, with long brown claws attached to its scaly digits.

The creature stopped, turning toward Harcan. He observed the creature's large, sphere-shaped eyes inside the liquid. The giant foggy orbs were a concoction of dull browns and yellows swirling around its black pupils. "They call me Scales. I was informed that you have cargo that might be of service to our *community*," he stated.

Harcan glanced away and crossed his arms. "Yeah. I'm trying to sell off these damn androids, at least for an honest price. You know where I can find a buyer?"

"Perhaps." Scales narrowed his eyes. "Where did you acquire these machines?" he asked, stepping away from Harcan and toward the rack of androids.

"Well, it's a long story but—"

"Indulge me, *please*," Scales interrupted, looking over his shoulder at Harcan.

Harcan glanced up at the ceiling. "This ship and its contents were willed to me," he lied.

"You inherited this?" Scales questioned, pulling up the plastic sheet draped over the androids.

"I was a slave to an older gentleman. A human. We smuggled weapons together," Harcan answered.

"Interesting. You were his protector, I assume?" Scales estimated.

"Like a bodyguard of sorts, yeah," Harcan replied.

"Hm. And how did your owner meet his unfortunate demise? You weren't to blame in any way, were you?" Scales asked, snatching the sheet off the android rack. Harcan caught himself staring at Ellie's lifeless frame for a moment before looking away.

"Uh, no. My master had a drinking problem. I used to warn him about it, but he didn't listen. He died of alcohol poisoning," Harcan fibbed, scratching under his chin.

"Sorry about your loss," Scales mumbled. He leaned in close, inspecting the androids one by one.

"How do they look, boss?" one of the guards asked Scales hesitantly.

Scales turned and glared at his guards. "Leave us," he ordered.

The guards looked at one another in confusion and funneled outside the ship. Harcan noticed one of them do a double take before they exited, leaving the pair of giants alone.

Scales shifted his eyes at Harcan. "Most of these androids are in *fair* condition, it seems. But you have a good variety. I'll take all of them *if* the price is right," he said.

"Sure. That'll be one hundred and twenty thousand credits," Harcan replied casually, flicking his cigarette beneath him. He stomped it out with his boot on the grated metal floor, twisting his foot.

Scales laughed. "You're out of your mind," he said, walking toward Harcan. "What makes you think they're worth that?"

Harcan outstretched his arms to the side. "I was told on good authority that I could get at least a hundred and twenty."

A thin, slimy pink membrane blinked across Scales's eyes. "Nearly all these androids are designed for pleasure services. They're illegal," the amphibian said, seemingly testing Harcan.

Harcan leaned back. "Oh, so you're not interested? Then I should be on my way to find another buyer in that case," he said plainly.

Scales looked at the rack of androids. "I didn't say I *wasn't* interested. But the longer you have this illegal cargo, the more you risk getting caught. I'm just curious how you knew where to find a buyer. Your freighter, along with your androids, is unregistered. Not to mention, I've never seen or heard of you before," he challenged, squinting one of his big orb-like eyes at Harcan.

"Ah, I've been asking around where to sell these androids, and these coordinates came up in conversation. *Twice.* As for my ship, I work with contraband, usually illegal weapons, so it only makes sense that I do things off the radar. Maybe you're just used to dealing with amateurs," Harcan replied with a grin.

Scales curled up his lip, showing his jagged teeth. "*Who* told our location?" he pried.

Harcan took a step toward Scales. "I don't talk. I listen. Look, there's no sense in us negotiating this sale further if you're uncomfortable. I've got other options," Harcan said casually, pretending to be unfazed by Scales's suspicion.

Harcan turned his back on Scales and walked toward the cockpit. "I'll be on my way as soon as you disembark," he concluded.

"I'll do seventy thousand credits," Scales offered.

Harcan stopped. "*Eighty*-five. No lower," he countered with authority, clenching his paws as he put them in his coat pockets. He didn't want to push Scales too far, but he couldn't risk coming off as soft when the amphibian was already suspicious.

Scales turned his head away while keeping his eyes on Harcan. He pointed at him. "That's what I wanted to hear, mutant. You're ambitious. I like that. Many smugglers would just take the first offer and run. Let me ask you something, what do you say we sweeten this deal by taking it a step further?"

Harcan crossed his arms. "I'm listening," he said, but he wasn't sure he wanted to go down this path. He wanted to sell off the androids and be done.

"How does one hundred and fifty thousand credits sound? I'll give you the eighty-five thousand credits now for the androids, then you can do a small favor for me for an additional sixty-five thousand. Interested?" he offered.

Harcan faked a smile. "Well, that all depends on what the job is, doesn't it?" he asked, lifting his eyebrows.

Scales paused and began to pace back and forth. "Say, for instance, I want to make someone disappear?" he hinted. Harcan gritted his teeth. He had a hunch Scales was referring to Orchid.

Harcan shrugged. "Wouldn't be my first time." He grinned.

Scales chuckled. "I figured as much. You look the type, and if there's one thing I'm good at, it's pinpointing talent," he said, pointing at Harcan. Scales wasn't far off the mark.

"What's the gig?" Harcan asked.

"Four days ago, we had a prisoner escape, a female android. It stole one of my transport ships and fled. It broke through the atmosphere before we were able to shut down its thrusters. The android was able to reroute enough power to make it close to an abandoned space station orbiting this planet. It jettisoned from my ship and made it inside the space station," he revealed.

Harcan shook his head. "And you're gonna ask me to go *all* the way up there and handle your problem?" he asked, propping his foot against the wall behind him. Harcan didn't need this deviation, but he had to play along. Smugglers wouldn't just scoff at the opportunity to make extra credits, especially sixty-five thousand of them.

Scales gazed through Harcan. "This job is more than just the android. We have no control over the space station, but we've detected some unusual behavior from it since her arrival. This android has opened the station's solar panels and begun to store energy."

"For what?" Harcan asked.

Scales marched close to Harcan, looking him in the eyes. "While we don't have control over the space station, we can view its input commands. That android has devised a plan to crash the space station into this planet. Specifically, her target is this quarry."

"Whoa. Sounds like she *really* doesn't like you." Harcan's eyes widened as he thought of Orchid and her diner. He looked at his wristwatch and glanced at Scales. "That's gonna be one helluva fireworks display. How much time before the show starts?" he joked.

Scales didn't crack a smile. "This isn't funny, mutant. In roughly nine days, the android can align the station's orbit for an impact. Granted, her chances of success are low. We've estimated she has a four percent chance of striking close enough to be detrimental to our operations. The silver lining is that if she misses, we're underground, shielded from the force of the impact. But still, I can't risk this. I need that android dealt with *now*."

Harcan nodded as Scales spoke. He didn't want to be in this position, but Scales's revelation about the space station posed a real threat to Orchid's operation. Even if Harcan eliminated Scales and rescued the slave androids from the mine, Orchid and her staff were still in grave danger. They didn't have the added layer of protection of being underground from an impact.

Harcan cleared his throat. "So, ah, eighty-five thousand credits upfront for the androids?" he asked, leaning toward Scales.

"Correct. And after you take care of the space station and the android, I'll give you the additional sixty-five," Scales promised.

Harcan shook his head. "I think you've got yourself in a real jam, and you're underselling your offer," he said.

"Am I? It's one android. It shouldn't take you more than four hours. Travel to the space station, disable the android, then destroy the structure. *Easy* money," Scales replied, rubbing his hands together.

"If it's *so* easy, then why are you asking a stranger for help?" Harcan challenged.

"I can't ask my men to do this job. Word travels fast here, and it could cause the miners to panic if it leaks out. I can't have that. I'd rather have a stranger, a *reliable* stranger with a ship," Scales responded, gesturing around the cargo bay. "Not only that, but on the rare occasion that I get to work with a nonhuman—I'll take it," Scales added.

Harcan pulled a faded silver coin from his pocket. He flipped it into the air and caught it. "Here are my terms. If this job takes *any* longer than four hours, or if any unforeseen circumstances arise, it'll cost you extra," he countered.

"It shouldn't, but fair enough," Scales replied with a gulp.

Harcan lifted his eyebrows. "In that case, you might just have yourself a deal, even if you are underselling a little bit." He chuckled. Underneath his gleaming exterior, he was concerned for Ellie. Leaving the planet meant he couldn't respond quickly if something went wrong on her end.

Scales called out to his soldiers, and they hurried back inside. He pointed at the androids. "Get those machines down to the command center and have them prepped for service *immediately*," he ordered his guards.

Harcan stepped toward Scales. "Hold on. Wait a second. I need to get paid *before* those androids leave my cargo bay," he asserted, pointing down at the deck. The soldiers stopped in their tracks and looked at Scales, awaiting his response.

Scales nodded. "Oh, how rude of me to take possession of the product without payment. Do you have a Republic credit scanner?" he asked.

Harcan grinned. "I thought you'd never ask." He held out his wristwatch, and Scales positioned a small rectangular device near it, keying in a series of inputs.

"*There,*" Scales said, transferring over the eighty-five thousand credits.

"Much obliged," Harcan replied.

Scales gestured for one of the soldiers to hand over Harcan's shotgun. "Just be sure to bring me that android's head. Even if you destroy the space station, I want proof that android won't be a problem for us in the future. I've attached the space station's location to your watch. It will automatically update its position," he explained before walking down the ramp of the ship.

He stopped at the bottom of the ramp and turned toward Harcan. "Do this job, and I might have *more* work for you in the future," he hinted.

"I'll be back before you know it," Harcan replied.

"Good."

A soldier carted Ellie and the rest of the androids toward the exit. Harcan watched as a small hand emerged from under the sheet of plastic, giving Harcan a thumbs-up. He gulped as they rounded the corner and disappeared out of view.

"*Fuck.*" Harcan rushed forward, slapping the button to close the rear gate. He darted to the cockpit and pressed several buttons on the instrument panel, powering up the thrusters.

"If it isn't one thing, it's another," he muttered, growling under his breath.

A thought ran through his mind. Perhaps he could use his Roland-class freighter instead of this one. It was faster and had onboard weapons, allowing him the option to destroy the space station without even entering it. The problem was, he needed proof he'd killed the android.

"That won't work," he snarled. On the plus side, assassinating Scales was the main point of the mission, and delivering that android's head personally could help him get close to him again. And hopefully, by that time, Ellie's portion of the mission would be completed.

There was no way around it—he needed to board that space station, fast. The only positive to the deviation was that this was essentially a bounty hunter task, something he was well versed in.

His wristwatch began vibrating. He looked down at it and reached in his coat, hurrying to equip a small earpiece. "Hello? Come in!"

"Harcan. Hey, it's me," Ellie's voice erupted.

"I'm here," he said as his eyes bounced around the cockpit.

"Listen, I can speak to you using my onboard software. It won't make a sound. We should be able to stay in contact without worry most of the time," she said.

"Great. Where are they taking you?" he asked.

"Looks like we're moving toward an elevator or something," she said.

"What else can you see?" he asked.

"Give me a second," she replied.

Harcan waited for a response as he prepped the ship's thrusters for atmospheric breach. He sat down in the pilot's seat and strapped in with barely enough room to buckle his safety harasses. He transferred the space station's coordinates to the freighter's computer, prompting the autopilot system to launch immediately.

The thrusters roared, blasting Harcan off the landing pad. He pushed through Pison's dusty atmosphere as his body rocked back and forth in the pilot's seat. It squeaked under the tension from his massive frame.

A few fiery meteors streaked through the sky. The closest zipped across the forward glass about two kilometers up and exploded in a dazzling display, lighting up the cockpit with a blinding flash.

Off to his left, he looked down. He could see Orchid's diner. From this height, it appeared as though it could fit in his paw. It seemed insignificant next to the massive crater next to it.

"Ellie, are you still there?" he asked.

"Yeah, I'm here. We're loading into an elevator. Harcan, I heard the conversation between you and Scales, about the space-station threat. I don't think we have a choice. You have to do whatever it takes to stop that android from crashing it into this planet. Even if the impact is dozens of kilometers away, it could be devastating for the entire region," Ellie said.

"I know. The explosion would wipe out Orchid's diner. And even if I alerted her to evacuate, where would her androids go?" he replied.

"Many of Orchid's androids would probably end up recaptured by the quarry's security, *if* they survived," she said. There was a long pause as Harcan looked out his portside glass. The dark-blue skies around him were turned black as the autopilot pushed through the upper atmosphere.

"Can you see anything now, where you are?" he asked.

"Looks like we're moving down in the elevator. I can't see much. Listen, Harcan, in the unlikely event that something happens to me down here, just know it was tough luck. I made this decision. My first priority is to disable those bombs, but if I'm discovered, I'm going down in a blaze of glory. These assholes won't force me into slavery," she insisted.

"That's not gonna happen, Ellie. I'll be back before you know it," he replied confidently. Deep down, he was anxious and unsure if he had enough time.

Ellie sighed. "I'm just shocked that runaway android is taking things to this extreme. Crashing the space station would surely kill her own kind. That's very unusual," she stated.

Harcan gazed ahead. "Maybe she thinks they're better off dead than to be subjected to what goes on in the depths of that quarry," he said.

"That, or she's completely fried her circuits and lost her mind. Harcan, I'm already working on helping you remotely. I've gained access to the schematics of the space station, and I should be able to provide limited assistance from here," she said.

"Can you hack into the station? Maybe take control of it?" he asked.

"Doubt it. I might be able to open doors or something like that, but I wouldn't expect much from here," she replied. Harcan stared ahead as the blackness of space filled his view.

"I've split my processor resources up so that I can assist you *and* hack Scales's command center simultaneously in rest mode. But I might have to boot up if a physical hack opportunity presents itself. In that case, I will need to cease communication with you briefly, just so you know," she told him.

"Don't get caught," he responded.

"I won't. I've sent command prompts to your freighter to make docking on the space station easier. You should be invisible to the station's detection system initially, but I wouldn't loiter around and take a smoke break. Not sure how long my cyber safety net will last," she suggested.

Harcan checked his coat for his smokes, padding around. He found a loose cigarette in his lower pocket and fired it up. "Thanks for the reminder," he said, puffing away.

Harcan peered ahead at the circular space station as the freighter's autopilot closed the distance. From here, he couldn't make out many of its details, but it was clear the station was rotating.

"Looks like there's gravity on board, right?" Harcan asked.

"According to what I can see, yeah," Ellie replied.

Behind the station, Harcan noticed the sprawling russet-colored ring that wrapped around the planet Pison. He wondered if the ring had been formed from the debris of the planetary impact that occurred millions of years ago.

As he approached the station, he took another look at Pison. Its glistening gold appearance from space was quite pleasing to the eyes, contrary to the surface's barren, sandy landscapes. Far below him, he could see a meteor zipping into the upper atmosphere, disintegrating into a cloud of fiery smoke.

He turned toward the space station as the freighter neared within a kilometer. It had a glancing resemblance that reminded him of a gigantic, spinning toy top.

Harcan grabbed his binoculars, adjusting the focus.

Running through the middle of the curved facility was a slender hexagonal beam. Most of the exterior was crude and worn, with a light rust color and hundreds of indentations peppering the hull. He could make out dozens of tinted glass panels surrounding the station's main body, many of which were cracked or splintered.

"Harcan, I'm in the command center. I need to limit our communication temporarily so I can work. But I will continue to monitor your situation, and I'll help when I can," Ellie alerted him.

"Got it," he replied.

Harcan looked down and noticed the freighter's vibrant, red-colored instrument panel. He noticed a series of messages flashing on the main computer screen as he approached within one hundred and fifty meters of the space station.

ENGAGING AUTOPILOT DOCKING SEQUENCE...

ASSESSING DOCKING PORTS...

COMPATIBLE.

PLEASE STAND BY...

DOCKING WILL COMPLETE IN THREE MINUTES AND NINE SECONDS.

The freighter's autopilot began to rotate the ship, matching the space station's spin. Harcan checked his shotgun, yanking back on the slide just above the trigger. The barrel folded downward, revealing the honeycomb-shaped ports for the batteries.

He took in one last drag from his cig and put it out on the dash. He continued to check each port on his weapon. They displayed a small green light, indicating the laser shotgun was at full charge. He felt around in his coat for extra batteries, just to be sure.

He snapped the shotgun back together aggressively and pushed the slide forward. It clicked.

"Locked and loaded," he mumbled as the freighter rocked back and forth. He noticed the monitor above him flashing.

DOCKING PROCEDURE COMPLETE.

He unbuckled from his seat, quickly making his way to the docking access. His feet felt heavy as he opened the circular hatch, pulling the long handle across his body. A bright-red warning indicator flashed above him, alerting him that the access port was open.

He closed it behind him, sealing himself in a small tube-like capsule. In front of him was the hatch to the space station. Warm steam vented from the ceiling, covering his body. The humid air felt soothing compared to the cool temperature in the freighter. It blew through the thick fur atop his head. He looked up, allowing the steam to hit his face.

The monitor flashed again.

PRESSURIZED. ACCESS GRANTED.

He sighed, staring down at his weapon before grabbing the access handle to the space station.

In many ways, this wasn't far removed from any other bounty. He had a target and a location, and of course, there was a reward involved. The obvious difference was this reward wasn't about credits; it was about righting wrongs. Scales's operation was evil, and there were no two ways about it.

Outside of hurrying back to Ellie, something bothered him. He identified with the android that was beyond the hatch in front of him. He knew what it was like to be a freed slavery, to have nowhere to turn even after the shackles were removed. And he understood what irrational behavior fueled by hatred was all about.

And even though he could empathize with his target, he still had a job to do.

He snarled, ripping the door handle across his body.

Chapter 5

In front of him was the dark, metallic corridor of the space station. It was curved and narrow, about twice his shoulder width, and just barely tall enough for him to stand without ducking. Cool-blue rectangular light fixtures were along the floor. The cobalt lights flickered, creating a strobing effect as he pointed his shotgun into the blackness.

There was a large pane window to his left. The stars twirled in the background as the station rotated. Above him, a cluster of wires and pipes was attached to the ceiling, running the corridor's length. At the end of the hall, sparks zapped from loose, frayed wires dangling from above.

It was dead silent except for a deep, whirring hum. Harcan thought of the station as a sleeping giant waking from a long hibernation. The structure felt alive, yet dormant, as the android brought it back to life, prepping the station to unleash her wrath on the tormentors below.

"Harcan," Ellie said.

"I'm here," he whispered.

"Listen, I just detected a scan that came from within the space station. I think our resident android is probing for signs of your intrusion onboard. I stopped it, along with disabling nearby cameras, but we're engaged in a cyber tug of war. Not sure how long my hack will last, but it probably has an idea you're there," she said.

"*Great,*" Harcan replied.

"Another thing: This space station was apparently a research station of some sort. I'm seeing a fair number of labs in the middle of the structure," she stated.

"Research?" he asked.

"No idea."

Harcan closed the door behind him while he watched in front of him. He could smell the scent of the quarry—the strong sulfur dioxide was unmistakable to his nose. He wondered if his target had been in this wing of the station recently. Perhaps she had docked on the same access port?

He eased forward at a brisk but cautious pace, aiming his shotgun from the hip. He noticed several doors to his right with digital readouts beside them.

Suddenly, Harcan heard commotion ahead. It sounded like footsteps clacking. He moved to his right, hugging the wall as he pointed his shotgun in the direction of the noise.

The sound got louder and louder as Harcan peeked around the corner. To his surprise, there was an off-white bipedal robot with pincer–like crab hands slowly staggering into view. Its lurching steps and wide stance shifted side to side erratically as it attempted to stabilize its bowling pin–shaped frame. The rounded torso was wide at the bottom, with a small circular head at the top. Its metallic legs were thick and powerfully built yet struggled to maintain the robot's structure.

A white tuxedo was painted on the robot's torso in a cartoonish style. On its face was a pair of two circular cameras, representing its eyes, along with a thin, black mustache painted under where the nose might be.

As it hobbled forward, Harcan narrowed his eyes, tracking it with his shotgun. This wasn't his target, but he was still highly suspicious of the machine. It was possible the android had access to the incoming robot's software.

"Ellie, you got eyes on this?" Harcan muttered, pressing in his earpiece.

"I see it. That's a quality-of-life robot for the crew. It's not a threat," she informed him.

"Does my target have access to its cameras?" he asked.

"No. Apparently, that robot isn't connected to the ship's network for some reason," she answered.

"Hm," he said.

The robot rounded the corner, and its arched posture shifted upright as it noticed Harcan.

"Well, hello. Greetings, s-s-sir," the robot stuttered with a cheery male voice.

"Hi there," Harcan replied, lowering his weapon as he looked behind the robot.

The robot glanced down at the planet through the window. The faint gold hue reflected on the robot's face. It shifted its body toward Harcan as its mechanical joints whined. "My name is Jerry. I'm the chief quality-of-life specialist onboard the space station Kornus. How may I be of assistance?"

"I'm Harcan."

"Nice to make your acquaintance, Harcan. Are you a new member of the crew? I've been quite busy, but I wasn't notified of any new arrivals," Jerry asked. Harcan looked to his left, thinking of a lie that would justify his presence onboard.

"Uh, no. I'm not really a member of the crew *per se*, but I am here to help," Harcan answered.

"Really?" The robot stared at Harcan for a moment and looked over its shoulder. "This is a research station, and only authorized personnel are allowed. Do you have any form of identification?" Jerry asked.

"Just this," Harcan said, looking down at his shotgun. "I'm here because I heard you might have a problem, something that happened just before I arrived?" Harcan hinted, leaning forward.

"Ah, now I see." The robot put his hands on his hips. "Well, there just so happens to be a cause for concern, now that you mention it," Jerry answered politely.

"That's why I'm here. Someone poking and snooping around where they shouldn't be, right?" Harcan asked.

"If by that you mean hacking into our navigational and solar systems, then yes," Jerry replied.

"Well then, would you like for me to put a stop to it?" Harcan asked.

The robot was hesitant, glancing at the deck. "If there is a nonviolent solution, preferably."

"That just happens to be my specialty. Underneath it all, I'm just a big softy. The teeth, claws, and gigantic shotgun are all for show," Harcan said with a grin.

Jerry clacked his hands together loudly. "Wonderful! I can relate. Some consider robots such as myself quite menacing too, when, in fact, I'm the opposite. Anyway, I recently had a peek at the space station's current destination."

"And?" Harcan asked.

"I noticed an unusual, alarming situation. Whoever, or whatever, is hacking into our systems has made a horrible mistake by setting our course to enter Pison's atmosphere. Who would do such an *awful* thing?" the robot questioned in a melodramatic voice. "When I tried to enter the bridge and confront the intruder, the door was sealed," Jerry explained.

"Maybe I can find a way inside—without using violence, of course. Could you show me where this bridge is?" Harcan hurried.

"Perhaps. I must say your timing is impeccable. The crew and I were just discussing options on how to handle this situation," Jerry said, turning his back on Harcan.

"Crew? What *crew*?" Harcan asked suspiciously, following behind the robot.

"Right this way," the robot instructed.

Harcan stayed several paces behind the robot as he made his way through the curved corridor. They passed by a few sealed hatches on the way.

One of the metal hatches was partially destroyed, allowing Harcan to see inside. It was some sort of lab. There were several large circular glass containers with murky yellow water inside. Surrounding the containers were several tables with microscopes and various instruments Harcan didn't recognize.

"What the hell is this place?" Harcan muttered.

The robot stopped near an open hatch ahead of Harcan. "This is the door where the crew is. Right inside," it responded, gesturing Harcan into the room.

Harcan swung wide, cautiously peering into a briefing room before entry. He noticed a large, glossy dark-colored table with several cushy chairs facing a flickering blue hologram in the middle of the room. The image was of the planet Pison. Seated in the chairs, he could see the backs of people's heads. He did a double take at Jerry.

Harcan waited, allowing Jerry to shuffle inside first. Harcan kept his weapon at the ready in the doorway for a moment. He leaned around and looked at the occupants seated in the chairs.

His eyes widened. To his surprise, they were corpses. All of them. Their bones were covered with patches of flaky dark-green skin. Strangely, their hair seemed preserved, yet stiff.

Jerry waved Harcan inside and outstretched his arms. "Now, members of the board, ladies and gentlemen. Sorry about the delay. It just so happens the noise I heard at the airlock was a special visitor that offered to help us. His name is *Harcan*," Jerry introduced.

Harcan cleared his throat and walked around the table, giving himself a good view of the deceased. About half of them were wearing lab coats, while the others wore dark-blue jumpsuits with military rankings on the collars. Four of them were female while the rest were male.

Jerry turned toward the board members before facing Harcan. "Forgive me. They're not the chattiest bunch these days. They've been through *quite* a lot over the years," he whispered.

"Yeah. It looks that way," Harcan said, lifting his eyebrows.

Jerry pointed at the hologram. "As you know, Pison is a planet on the far reaches of human colonization. For this reason, we were tasked with an incredibly important directive, one that would suit such an isolated Republic research division."

Harcan looked around. "What? The Republic funded you?" he asked.

"Indeed. It's likely all declassified by now, but ruling the galaxy can be a daunting task. Here at the Kornus space station, we specialized in keeping the Republic leadership mentally fit to make decisions for *all* of us," Jerry proclaimed proudly, clenching and shaking his fist confidently.

Harcan narrowed his eyes. "No easy task. And how could you possibly accomplish that?" he asked, playing along.

"Entertainment. Humans love the thrill of drama, the theatrical. It's a welcome distraction from the enormous weight of being a leader. Most enjoy the good old-fashioned struggle between good and evil, heroes, and villains. At Kornus, we were tasked with creating some of the first villains for installations throughout the Republic," Jerry explained.

Harcan gulped. "Villains? You mean monsters?" he asked.

"Well, *some* call them monsters. I call them necessities," Jerry replied.

"And if they're so necessary, why would the Republic stash their research facility on the other side of the galaxy?" Harcan asked.

"Well, to be honest, some frowned on our research, but really and truly, we were doing the work that no one else wanted to. Creating villains for the entertainment rings was needed whether people liked it or not. We were one of the first facilities to create these specimens," Jerry replied.

Harcan shook his head as he looked at the corpses. He glanced at every one of them for a moment, settling on the one nearest to him. He noticed the faded name stitched on his lab coat—*Theodore Reicher.*

This might have been how it all started. Orchid and Harcan's predecessors were likely developed here, in the far reaches of the galaxy, void of prying eyes who might politicize it. These scientists weren't unlike the men who created him. Harcan felt his heart pounding and his lip snarled up, revealing his teeth. His ears perked up as he glared at Jerry.

"Harcan," Ellie chimed in.

Harcan's ears flattened out. "Uh, *yeah*," he said, snapping out of a rage-induced trance.

"Hold on. Give me a moment," Harcan told Jerry as he stepped away a few paces.

The robot took a half bow. "Very well."

"Ellie." Harcan lowered his voice, pushing his earpiece.

"Is that robot gonna help you find the target, or what? I couldn't hear the entire conversation," Ellie asked.

"I—um. I'm working on it. How are things on your end?" he questioned.

"I thought I was *inside* the command center, but we're actually outside of it. No one is here. They have us locked away in a cage. I assume they'll try and install the explosives on some of us soon. I'm close enough to hack inside their network, though. I'm essentially tiptoeing around their security firewalls remotely," she said.

"Understood," he said.

"Harcan, I'm just trying to time this correctly. I wonder if you can take out your target and the space station, then make it back down to the planet's surface before dawn?" she asked.

"Absolutely," he replied.

"Just let me know if I can help you in the meantime," Ellie replied, cutting off communication.

Harcan gritted his teeth. He was relieved that Ellie interrupted his conversation with Jerry. The robot was only carrying out its programming, but the revelation about the crew's research infuriated him. Harcan needed the opportunity to step away and calm himself to maintain his act. Otherwise, if Jerry suspected Harcan had a negative stance on the Republic, it could jeopardize the mission.

Harcan noticed Jerry waiting patiently. "Sorry about the interruption," he said, approaching the robot.

"Oh. No problem. I wanted to say, forgive me for laying so much information on you, Harcan. I don't want to come off as a Negative Nancy, because there is a bright spot in all this."

"Which is?" Harcan asked.

"Since our intruder has activated our solar arrays, it's allowed us to communicate again with deep-space contacts. The Republic has asked us to heed the call again," Jerry revealed.

"What?" Harcan growled under his breath.

"We've been tasked with sending over the remainder of our research. We were forced to shut down prematurely years ago, cutting us off from our contacts. But apparently, there's a new artificial structure under construction, something larger than anything ever created. They're calling it EL-60, and the Republic will need all our research to create a wealth of specimens for entertainment! Isn't that exciting!" the robot proclaimed.

"Exhilarating," Harcan replied. He felt his claws digging into his shotgun's foregrip. He cleared his throat. "Jerry, have you begun transmitting that information yet?" Harcan questioned.

"Well, no, I was only notified hours ago. I did begin compiling the data, but it's many years of research," Jerry insisted. "In fact, while you're dealing with our intruder problem, I'll continue my work, but if I could ask, don't shut down the station's power when you reach the bridge, so that I may transmit the research. Isn't this wonderful? We're both helping the Republic, as a team," Jerry asked.

"Fantastic. Jerry, listen to me. If you really want to fulfill your duties to the Republic, it's imperative that we stop the intruder now. If that android manages to crash this station, all the tireless hours of research this crew performed will be lost. The monster—I mean, *specimen*—data will be gone forever," Harcan said, playing into Jerry's motivations.

Jerry glanced at the crew and sighed. He turned and looked Harcan in the eyes. "You're absolutely correct. I cannot allow their work to be lost. Only just now did I realize that I won't have time to complete the transmission if the situation worsens," he said, looking down at his metallic pincer hands.

"Exactly. Now, show me to the bridge and let us remedy this problem, for the Republic," Harcan asserted.

Jerry panned around the briefing room. "Yes. But first, we must vote on it. All in favor of stopping the intruder?" he asked, looking at the deceased crew.

Harcan looked at Jerry out of the corner of his eyes. The robot seemed to be counting with his hands. "Eight, nine, ten, *eleven*," he said.

Jerry turned, staring at Harcan. "Great news. Elven votes to one. The vast majority are in favor of us working together to stop the trespasser, first and foremost."

Harcan glanced at the stoic corpses sitting upright in their chairs. He noticed one of them was missing part of its skull from a blunt-force wound.

"We'll take a shortcut to get to the bridge, right this way," Jerry insisted. Harcan followed behind the shuffling bot as they exited through a door on the side, entering the lab. Harcan stopped in the doorway and took in a deep breath.

He tried not to look at the various vats of murky green-brown water. But he couldn't help but wonder how many monsters like him came from this room and went on to inflict untold horrors for the sake of entertaining the Republic senate. Perhaps a place like this served as his own beginnings, yet he had no memory of it.

"Hm." He grimaced.

His legs felt weak as he passed by the containers. Before the untold atrocities he had committed on EL-59, there was something deeply unsettling about the lapse of time from his birth to his first memories. Anything could have happened to him in his youth—experimentation, torture, surgery—all in a place just like this.

Jerry glanced back at Harcan. "As a mutant, does it bother you to see laboratories such as this?"

"Uh, not at all. I was a black-market mutant myself, bred and sold as a slave," Harcan fibbed, shrugging it off.

"But your genetic splicing looks *very* high quality. Usually, black-market lifeforms have obvious deformities. I'm no expert, of course. I only *serve* the experts," Jerry said.

"I don't know much about it either." Harcan panned around the room. He noticed one of the larger vats was broken, and shattered glass was around the circular container's base. "What the hell happened in here?"

Jerry looked away. "Some time ago, we had a containment issue. After years of operating flawlessly, there was a single error. Our protocol was to deliver adolescent specimens to Republic officials. Unfortunately, one of our senior officers, Dr. Reicher, misjudged the growth rate of one of our new specimens, and it broke free," Jerry said.

"Looks like you weren't able to contain it at all," Harcan commented, staring back at the damaged hatch.

"As I said, Dr. Reicher was unaware that the specimen would mature so rapidly. He had been experimenting with growth acceleration," Jerry replied.

"Were there any crew fatalities?" Harcan asked suspiciously.

Jerry stopped in place for a few moments. "*Please,* Harcan, just understand that I did the best I could to preserve human life, considering the circumstances."

"Oh." Harcan looked back toward the board room full of corpses. Indeed, some of them died at the hands of whatever they created. Admittedly, he felt a sense of satisfaction entertaining that idea. There was one oddity Harcan caught on to: If Jerry was so concerned about human life, why was he involved in the creation of bioweapons designed to murder humans? It didn't make any sense unless he was oblivious to their real purpose.

The robot continued to shamble through the lab with Harcan in tow.

Harcan experienced a range of emotions as they neared the exit. A part of him wanted to leave and never return, but he was curious about the mutants created in this facility. What sort of life did they live? Were they like him, or maybe something completely different? Did they ever escape captivity? He often wondered if he and Orchid were the only monsters to taste freedom.

Harcan felt a chill run up his spine. He looked away, focusing on Jerry as they made their way through a set of metal double doors. They entered a plain, metal corridor, Harcan clearing the corners with his shotgun.

Jerry attempted to pick up the pace as they walked for another five minutes. Suddenly, Jerry stopped, leaning against the wall. He seemed sapped of energy as he slowly raised his free arm, gesturing thirty meters ahead to a sturdy black steel door at the end of the corridor.

"That door, is that the station's control bridge?" Harcan asked.

"Yes, but I'm not sure how you plan on gaining entry. I couldn't," Jerry replied.

Harcan grinned. "Let me worry about that. But you're *sure* the target is inside?" he questioned.

"Most certainly."

Harcan stood parallel to the robot. He looked down at him. "This isn't a safe distance, Jerry. I recommend you go back to the board room with your crew. I'll let you know when it's over," he recommended.

"Oh. Thank you for your concern, Harcan, but I'll be fine here. Unfortunately, I've had to survive worse on this space station," Jerry replied, looking up at him. "Oh, and one last thing, please refrain from firing your weapon on the bridge. If you damage any navigational systems, we could be in for a wild ride that neither of us will enjoy."

"Noted."

Harcan turned his back on Jerry and eased toward the door, hugging alongside the wall's left side. As he reached the hatch, he pointed his shotgun at it.

"Ellie, come in," Harcan said.

"Yeah?"

"I'm just outside the bridge door. Supposedly, my target is inside. Think you could work some magic?" he asked.

"I can try," she replied. Harcan waited a dozen seconds and looked down at his watch.

Ellie sighed. "Hey, I can't get access from here. It looks like you'll need to find another way," she stated.

"Shit." Harcan took a long look at the thick steel door in front of him, assessing his options. His first thought was to melt through the door using his shotgun, but the lasers could penetrate the hatch and strike critical system hardware on the bridge.

Harcan placed his weapon on the deck. He took off his silver trench coat. Jerry leaned forward, seemingly taking note of the missing patches of fur all up and down Harcan's muscular wedge-shaped back.

Harcan placed his thick paws on each side of the hatch. He took in a deep breath, then another, as he psyched himself up. He felt a surge of adrenaline pulse through him as his claws scratched the door. He growled. "One... two—"

A loud click came from the other side of the door as he stepped back. Surprisingly, the door cracked open on its own. "What the—"

"Harcan, I got it!" Ellie chimed in. "It's open, right?" she asked.

"Yeah, you did it. Thanks," he replied. Harcan quickly put on his coat and snatched his shotgun off the deck.

He cautiously opened the door to the bridge to a large, oval-shaped room with shiny white walls, ceiling, and floors.

Fifteen meters in front of him, three console stations were arranged in a triangular formation, each with swivel-mounted chairs. The two stations closest to him were much more extensive, with full control systems and holographic displays. Beyond that was a large viewing glass with a panoramic view of the stars.

The furthest station was likely the captain's. It was smaller and more streamlined, displaying a rotating holographic image of a terrain model. Upon closer inspection, Harcan noticed it was the quarry. At the top left of the hologram was a timer counting down—eight days, twenty-two hours, and thirteen minutes.

Harcan saw the back of someone's head leaning in the chair in front of the hologram. He entered the room, aiming his shotgun at the shadowy figure. The hologram flickered brightly, illuminating part of the room. It revealed the occupant's head: bright pink hair braided in a ponytail.

Harcan narrowed his eyes. Suddenly, the head began to spin slowly, turning 180 degrees until it faced him, while the body stayed fixed.

"You know, it's very impolite not to knock before entering," the android said in a scathing feminine voice.

"Don't lecture me on manners. You don't belong here either," Harcan reminded the android as he got a better look at her face.

The android was modeled after a young woman in her late teens with porcelain-white skin. She had a small face and wide-set eyes, a little nose, and full lips. She wore long lashes and dark makeup. Her mascara was running down from both eyes, like black tears, while her bright-pink lipstick matched her hair.

She arched an eyebrow. "Scales sent you, didn't he? You look the type—a big, intimidating mutant with bad intentions. All for *little* old me?" she questioned in a seductive voice, followed up with a snicker. The electronic heckle became louder, echoing throughout the room before stopping abruptly. "Leave—*now.*"

"That's not gonna happen," Harcan replied. He'd seen his fair share of perilous bounty contracts, but there was something about her that made him uneasy.

The android's hollow green eyes seem to drift about the room as if she floated from one thought to another. Her face morphed, displaying a range of emotions—happiness, excitement, worry, and fear—all in a matter of a few seconds.

Harcan noticed one of her arms laying over the chair with a sleeve of tattoos. The art featured different scenery types: a mystical forest with a unicorn, a starry night, and an ocean full of aquatic wildlife.

Harcan shook his head. "You do understand that crashing this hunk of metal into the quarry could kill hundreds of *other* androids?"

The android lowered her eyebrows. "And that's precisely my objective. Disabling those androids is the considerate option. No one that leaves that quarry has a life worth living, myself included. I'm putting an end to their pain and suffering. They would thank me."

"What if I told you that I don't work for Scales and that Orchid could give those androids a better life outside of—"

"Fuck Orchid *and* Scales! How about that? She's no better than him anyway. She's a leech, preying on others' misfortunes. Most of those miners are scum, criminals, but she abuses the law for *her* gain, nothing more! I'm going to put an end to all of it. Not even Orchid's operation will survive the blast," she said with conviction.

"Oh, I think it will," Harcan said confidently.

"Well? Then get on with it, mutant. I'm completely defenseless," she said with a smirk, outstretching her arms.

The android slumped down in the chair and disappeared behind the workstation.

"Shit." Harcan's head bobbed back and forth as he attempted to track her behind the terminal. He watched as she emerged from behind the console. Strangely, the android's nude, tatted-up body was missing from the waist down, as if it had been severed completely.

She walked on her hands, using them like crutches as she swung her torso forward, forcing Harcan to his left. "What the hell," he muttered.

Harcan rushed ahead, using the console station on his left as cover. He stood beside the chair and desk, aiming his shotgun at her. "That's enough! Don't come any closer!" he roared.

The android complied, halting several paces away from Harcan. "I have to admit, I never expected anyone to be able to make it inside this bridge undetected. I enabled the security systems to maximum settings."

Harcan looked at her. "Let's just say not *every* android agrees with your suicide mission."

Her eyes widened. "One of Orchid's androids assisted you?"

Harcan steadied his shotgun on the android. He wanted a clean shot without damaging the bridge's navigational equipment.

"*Wait,*" she said, holding up her index finger as her eyes glossed over. "It appears I've been outfoxed, and I'll be the first to admit it. But could you at least do me the honor and allow me to die standing on my feet?" she requested.

Harcan looked her up and down. "You're joking."

"Actually, I'm not." The android pointed to the chair next to Harcan. He glanced down as the light from the hologram flickered on the console, revealing a lower torso with a pair of long legs crossed.

Harcan lunged back as the android's feet pushed off the floor, spinning the swivel chair around. The mechanical legs sprang off the floor with incredible force, launching into the air and clamping around Harcan's neck like an oversized vise grip.

"Rrr-aagh!" He fired his shotgun before dropping it, narrowly missing the android's upper half. He rolled on the floor as the powerful synthetic legs compressed his throat.

The android began laughing loudly. "I'm *so* impolite. Let me introduce you to my other half!" she shouted, shambling toward Harcan's shotgun.

Harcan thrashed back and forth, pressing and prying with all his might to remove the android's legs from his neck.

"Harcan! Are you okay? What's all that ruckus?" Ellie demanded, chiming in his earpiece.

"I'm tied up at the moment," he struggled to get out.

"Well, don't choke now, I've made progress on the bombs, I—"

"Ellie! Can't... talk... now!" he shouted.

Enraged, Harcan roared, tearing through the android's fake skin with his claws, digging into its artificial muscles and tendons as sparks flew into the air. He began to rip out wires and circuits.

For a split second, the android's legs lost power, allowing Harcan to force them off his neck. He stood up and grabbed one of the legs by the ankle, hurling it into the android's upper half. She fired Harcan's shotgun at him, splitting the lower torso in two. One leg struck the android's head, knocking her down.

Harcan dropped down on all fours and rushed the android as she hobbled away behind one of the console terminals. She looked over her shoulder at Harcan with wide, terrified eyes. He dove and plunged his canines into the android's neck, pinning her arms to the floor with his paws.

With his fangs sunk deep into the android's throat, Harcan growled as he instinctively shook the android violently, jerking and pulling at her torso with his paws.

Her arms flailed about as Harcan tore through the layers of artificial skin on the back of her neck. The chemical taste and smell were awful, like burnt plastic.

He growled, ripping out clusters of wires as he chomped through, clamping down the spine. He pressed all his weight on the android's shoulders, tugging at her backbone with his teeth. She laughed, then cried, but none of her facial expressions matched her emotions. All at once, the blue-and-white spine gave way as he yanked it out from the body.

Harcan spat out the synthetic spinal cord on the deck beside him, staring down at it as he panted heavily. The android's head was still attached to the backbone. Harcan noticed her gazing through the ceiling. Her face was covered in a bright-blue fluid, and one of her eyelids twitched rapidly.

The android gurgled fluid. It ran down both sides of her lips. "I hope whatever t-they're paying you, that's it's worth it," she muttered.

Harcan wiped his chin as he picked up his shotgun. "I'm not doing this for the credits."

The android's vibrant green eyes shifted toward Harcan and faded. "Then, w-why?" she stuttered, smiling from ear to ear.

"Because I don't believe that *every* android in that quarry is a lost cause," Harcan answered, kneeling beside her. He stared into her eyes as the holographic screen strobed behind them.

The android looked at Harcan with a blank stare. "Orchid can't save them, you *fool*, she's irrational and a liability to our kind," she cautioned.

Harcan raised an eyebrow. "You're one to talk." He stood up and stomped the android's head with his boot, caving in her face. The android let out a long, distorted sigh that came to a sudden stop.

Harcan stared down at the blue mess for a moment. He picked up the crushed head and dropped it into his coat pocket.

He glanced over his shoulder and noticed Jerry standing in the doorway.

Jerry put his hands on his head as he assessed the carnage. "My goodness, Harcan. It appears you couldn't refrain from using violence, could you?" the bot asked.

Harcan narrowed his eyes. "Diplomacy failed, Jerry. I tried to kill her with kindness, but she got a leg up on me. Can you do us all a favor and resume the space station's normal trajectory? It looks like it needs a robot's touch," Harcan said, gesturing at the terminal in front of him.

Jerry entered the room. "Of course. I don't know much about the bridge commands, but I can at least alter the current course to prevent impact on the planet."

"Good," Harcan said, grabbing his shotgun.

Jerry looked around the room, observing the android's remains scattered about. "I'm quite curious, do you happen to know the intruder's motive?" he asked.

"Revenge. She was a slave and decided to use your research station as a missile against those who wronged her," Harcan replied.

Jerry looked at Harcan. "*Oh.* My goodness. Then we should be forever grateful that you arrived when you did." The robot approached the terminal and pressed a series of keys, disabling the space station's collision course into the planet.

"*There.* We're assuming a safe orbit around Pison. Disaster avoided," Jerry stated, sighing in relief.

'You're sure?" Harcan asked. He noticed the station's orbit path on the holographic display changing.

"Absolutely. Now I can return to the lab and resume my previous task of transmitting all the research data to the Republic, thanks to you," he answered.

"You're welcome." Harcan gazed out the window in front of him into the blackness of space. "Tell you what, I'll walk you back to the lab before I go," he said.

"Very well, we'll return the same way we came. The crew will be delighted to learn of our success against the intruder," Jerry proclaimed.

"I'm sure they're *dying* to hear the news," Harcan replied, glancing at Jerry. The robot seemed unfazed by Harcan's wisecrack. Perhaps this confirmed what Harcan suspected all along—Jerry had convinced himself the crew was still alive. But why?

Chapter 6

As they navigated through the station, Harcan pondered the slain android's last words. She had decided to condemn her fellow slaves, assuming they were a lost cause. And perhaps, in the end, many of the androids in the quarry would *never* recover from the trauma they sustained.

But it was unreasonable to sentence them to death, in Harcan's mind. He wondered about the pathways and variances to recovery and why some lifeforms and androids were more resilient than others. It seemed Orchid had handled the experience on EL-59 better than him. While she undoubtedly had her own demons, they didn't appear as crippling as Harcan's. He tried to overlook the comparison, but it was apparent.

Harcan and Jerry returned through the lab and reentered the board room. Jerry threw up his hands excitedly. "Rest easy, ladies and gentlemen, Harcan and I are happy to announce that the intruder has been dealt with and the station's collision course with Pison thwarted," Jerry declared.

The robot nodded as he looked at several members of the crew. The quirky robot turned and stared at Harcan. "We're thankful for your actions. Without you, it's possible much of the research we've gained over the years would have gone to waste."

"Glad I could help," Harcan replied, peering back behind him into the lab. There was a large computer terminal in the back of the room. "Is that where you'll transmit all the research data to the Republic?" Harcan asked, pointing.

Jerry seemed surprised by the question. "Oh. Yes. Those terminals hold the crew's lifelong work. Why do you ask?"

"Hm, I hate to be the bearer of bad news, but you won't be sending any more information," Harcan said plainly, staring into the small camera lenses in Jerry's eye sockets.

Jerry turned toward Harcan. "I don't understand. The android intruder was able to reboot and repower the ship. Everything is functional now. I have the capability to finish the Republic's tasking—"

Harcan whipped out his shotgun and blew off Jerry's legs with two quick shots to the kneecaps. The metallic legs buckled, sending him clacking onto the deck face-first. Strangely, the robot called out in agony, banging his fists into the floor.

"Aggahh! Why? *Why?*" Jerry demanded. Harcan snatched Jerry up by the arm and dragged him near the lab terminal.

Harcan blasted the terminal several times with his shotgun. "No! Don't! It's the Republic's data!" Jerry pleaded.

The hairs on Harcan's neck stiffened. He snarled and fired at the console, melting the terminal into a blob of fiery plastic goo. He never blinked as he unloaded, gazing into the burning debris as flashes of light strobed from his laser weapon.

"No-o-o!" Jerry called out. Automatic fire extinguishers deployed a white foamy substance from the ceiling. Harcan blasted upward, destroying the extinguishers and allowing the fire to burn.

Harcan pointed his weapon down at Jerry as he covered his face with his metallic arms. "Please don't! I'm human!" Jerry begged.

Harcan arched an eyebrow. "You're about as human as your crew is alive," he responded, jabbing his shotgun toward the board room.

"No. I *am* human! My name is Theodore *Jerry* Reicher. I was the lead scientist on this installation years ago. I w-was the only survivor on board after our bioweapon escaped," Jerry explained.

Harcan lowered his weapon. "What?"

Jerry planted his face into the deck. "After the specimen escaped, I sealed myself into cryosleep while my crew was murdered. There was nothing I could do! I panicked, hiding so I could starve out the creature. Years later, the station went into low-power mode, and I was forced to thaw from cryosleep. But there was no food, no water. My only option was to upload my consciousness to this machine. To survive, I did what I had to," Jerry wept.

Harcan looked him up and down. "If you're telling the truth, I have more unfortunate news, Jerry—you might have escaped one monster, but *another* has found you," he threatened, towering over the robot.

"But you're no monster. You value human life. You came here to save the quarry and all those miners," Jerry stated.

Harcan leaned toward Jerry, showing his teeth as he growled. "I was born and bred to kill, by someone not unlike yourself," he revealed.

"You told me you were a black-market specimen," Jerry replied.

"I lied. Remember when you said my genetic splicing was *unusually high quality*? That's because the Republic funded it. I was a specimen in a lab. I served your Republic on EL-59, murdering thousands of innocents in the name of entertainment. So, please forgive that I cannot see the value in allowing a criminal, a coward like you continue your work," Harcan scolded.

Jerry looked away. His metallic hands shook as Harcan grabbed him by the arms, ripping each of them off. "No! I've changed! I-I've have had time to consider my actions. I was wrong!" Jerry pleaded.

Harcan picked up Jerry's torso and slung him on top of the burning terminal. Jerry's body caught fire as he screamed, unable to move.

Harcan shook his head as Jerry's optics liquefied into two red-orange orbs. His white plastic torso melted, oozing into the fire as sparks ejected from its chassis. "If you can find it in your soul to forgive me, I can make you human," Jerry offered in a distorted voice.

Harcan ignored his pleas, watching on as Jerry's plastic shell was reduced to a metallic frame by the flames.

He turned around, staring at the lab's containers full of murky water. Harcan blasted them in a fit of rage. Glass shattered as he destroyed each of the vats one by one, spilling murky water onto the deck. He rounded the corner and aimed his shotgun back into the board room, firing at the scientists' corpses. He snarled in anger, squinting his eyes as he imagined each one of them alive. His laser shogun scattered the decrepit bodies into a wisp of dust, toppling over their chairs in a ball of fire.

He lunged forward and flipped over the board room table, roaring.

The room was a cloud of smoke and fire as Harcan turned his back on the chaos, storming through the corridor. Alarms blared on his way back to the freighter.

He closed his eyes for a moment. He exhaled through his snout. Disabling Jerry and blowing those corpses apart was satisfying in a way that he didn't expect. It felt like he'd chipped off a small piece of the anchor he was dragging.

No sooner than the sliver of optimism entered his mind, it disappeared.

He pulled out his flask and took a gulp of vodka. He cleared his throat. "Ellie, do you copy?" He pressed in his earpiece, panting heavily.

"I'm here, Harcan. Are you okay?" she asked suspiciously.

"Yeah."

"Hm. Well, you're not going to believe what happened," she said excitedly.

"What?" he asked.

"I had to sever our communications briefly, but the explosives implanted in the androids can now be disabled at any time. Just let me know when you're ready," Ellie informed him.

Harcan paused, wiping his mouth. "Great work. Don't disable the bombs yet. I don't want to risk them discovering we've hacked their systems," he replied.

"That's what I was thinking. What's wrong? You don't sound too enthusiastic. I thought you'd be impressed. Were you able to stop the android?" she asked.

"Mission accomplished. And I am impressed. Just be ready. I'm headed back down to the surface now," he replied.

"Well, don't take all damn day," she joked. Harcan noticed a bit of nervousness in her voice. It reminded him of the time he caught her reaching in his pockets while he was sleeping.

Harcan entered the freighter, hurrying to the cockpit. He prompted the ship to engage the autopilot and return to the quarry. He opened his coat pocket and looked at the android's head. This was the proof that he'd done Scales's bidding, and his ticket to getting close to the scumbag one more time. And now that Ellie could disable the explosives, it was time for Scales to meet his maker.

Chapter 7

Harcan held his wristwatch close to his mouth. "Hey. Orchid, it's Harcan, are you there?" he asked.

An umbrella-shaped cone of fire appeared on the front viewing glass as the freighter reentered Pison's yellow atmosphere.

After nearly two minutes, Orchid chimed in. "Harcan, I'm here. Is Scales dead?" she asked.

"Not yet," he replied.

She sighed. "What the hell is taking so long?" she demanded.

"Calm down, Orchid. You expected me to stroll into a heavily guarded mine and kill Scales without any idea what I was getting myself into? *Huh?* It's a hornets' nest down there, and I was forced to do him a favor to ensure we get those androids out safely. I need you to ready every single soldier, cook, cleaner bot, whatever, in the next half hour. Chaos could spill onto the surface for all I know," he warned.

Harcan thought about the irony of him and Orchid working together to save lives, not end them. There was a long pause. "Orchid, are you still there?" he asked.

"Yes. Tell me something first, Harcan. What *favor* did you do for Scales? Be specific," she questioned.

"One of the androids from the mine escaped. She stole one of Scales's ships on the landing pad, then broke through the atmosphere and hijacked a space station. It wanted revenge and planned to crash the structure into the quarry," Harcan explained.

"*What?* You stopped her, right? That impact could destroy my diner and everything I've worked for," she insisted excitedly.

"It's done. Calm down. The space station has resumed its previous orbit," he replied.

Orchid sighed in relief. "Wait. Now that I think about it, are you referring to space station Kornus?" she asked.

"Yeah, why?" he questioned. Harcan sat up straight in the pilot's seat, surprised that she knew what he was talking about.

"That space station is one of the main reasons I initially came to Pison, Harcan. But we could never find it. There was no electronic signature from it," she replied.

"That's because it was powered down," Harcan said.

"Well, I'm glad you located it. There's a robot on board that has possession of a wealth of data about genetic engineering. Supposedly, it's all Republic data, and there could be information on how to cure my bloodthirst," she explained.

Harcan gulped. "That's—uh, *great*."

"What's wrong?" she probed.

Harcan hesitated for a moment. "Nothing. I'm just exhausted. Orchid, prepare everyone at your diner for war. Eliminating Scales could set off a chain of events that we don't expect," he cautioned, severing communications.

Harcan leaned back and stared up at the ceiling, shaking his head. "Un-believable," he muttered.

He had no idea Jerry could assist Orchid. Harcan wondered about the robot's final offer to make him human. Perhaps he was telling the truth. Harcan had no intention of becoming human, but if Orchid had dreams of eradicating her bloodlust, he didn't want to stand in her way.

Maybe he already had.

Harcan ground his teeth as he peered out the starboard viewing port. The dense yellow clouds rushed by him and suddenly opened up, giving way to the vast sandscape beneath him. He observed the quarry rapidly approaching.

He grabbed his binoculars and looked out on the landing pad. Harcan noticed several soldiers standing in formation, but Scales was nowhere in sight. He sighed loudly as the autopilot slowed the freighter's descent just before landing.

"Ellie, I'm on the dock," Harcan informed her.

He waited a few moments as the soldiers knocked on the rear hatch. Harcan adjusted his earpiece. "*Hey.* Ellie, can you hear me?" he asked again, but there was no response.

"Shit," he mumbled.

Harcan hurried back to the cargo bay and glanced at the spot where Ellie had stowed herself inside the rack before Scales's men took her away. He slapped the release button for the rear gate with his paw as thoughts about Ellie's whereabouts raced through his mind.

Scales's soldiers seemed to be discussing something in private, and all at once, they funneled inside the ship in a hurry. The light beamed inside, reflecting off their shiny black-and-red helmets. They formed a line in front of Harcan and stood at attention.

Harcan outstretched his powerful long arms. "At ease, fellas, I've saved the day. You boys can relax," he sneered.

The soldier in the middle of the formation stepped forward. "Tell us, does that mean you've eliminated the android fugitive? Can you confirm her demise?" he questioned.

Harcan reached in his pocket and yanked out the android's head. It was a mangled mess and covered in blue blood. "Look familiar?" he asked.

The soldiers looked up at the crushed head without a word. Harcan shrugged. "Gentlemen, come on, I know she's a *little* scuffed up, but at least *one* of you should be able to positively identify her—whether you want to admit it or not." He grinned. While Harcan didn't like making jokes at the android's expense, he needed to stay in character.

The guard closest to Harcan stared up at him. There was a thin red line at the top of the visor on his helmet, likely indicating that he was in a leadership position. "And what news of the space station's course?" the commander asked.

"The station has resumed its previous orbit around Pison," Harcan answered.

"Very well. Scales didn't mention to us why the space station's position was relevant, but I must say that we commend your efforts to stop this fugitive. We give you our thanks, personally," the commander praised, bowing slightly.

"No problem, I'm always happy to make some coin." Harcan smiled.

"Stand by. I will inform Scales of your success," the commander stated. He nodded and looked away. "Scales. Yes, sir. The mutant has returned and has accomplished his task. Right away—I'll tell him," the commander said.

The guard turned toward Harcan. "Scales is below decks currently and unable to see you personally because of unforeseen circumstances that suddenly arose. However, he would like for us to escort you to meet up with him. It would seem he has *another* job for you," the commander explained.

"Huh?" Harcan looked around and paused, shaking his head. "You know, I got places to be after I leave this rock," he said in frustration, maintaining his character.

"My apologies, but this is impossible at the moment," the commander replied. Harcan didn't seem enthused about his opportunity to go below decks, but he tried to look at the bright side. The mission was to take out Scales, and when shit hit the fan, perhaps this deviation would get him closer to Ellie for their escape from the quarry.

Harcan sighed and shook his head. "Fine, let's get a move on, then, fellas. Time is money. I got business contacts left and right wondering where I am and when I can do jobs for them," he lied as they marched out of the freighter and onto the landing pad.

"I'm confident Scales will make you an offer you can't refuse," the commander replied.

"I hope so. I'm not in this for charity," Harcan replied.

One of the guards walked up to Harcan. "Before we go below decks, I'll need to confiscate your firearm. Just until we get back," he said hesitantly.

The commander waved him off. "No-no, not this time. This mutant has proven to be a loyal subject, and to be honest, he might need to protect himself considering the situation in the quarry," the commander said, lowering his voice.

"What *situation*?" Harcan asked, narrowing his eyes.

The commander seemed surprised that Harcan heard his comment. "There is a bit of unrest, uneasiness in the air. I'm sure Scales will tell you all about it," he replied.

Underneath Harcan's calm exterior, he was very concerned about why Ellie hadn't responded yet. Something happened, but Harcan had no idea if Ellie was involved.

"How far are we going?" Harcan asked, looking at his watch.

"Not far. It shouldn't take us longer than ten minutes to reach our destination. Come, this way," one of the guards said as they ushered Harcan near an elevator. They walked across the grated metal floor. The small holes allowed Harcan to see the rows of apartment complexes beneath him. This time, none of the miners were visible walking to and from.

"Hm," Harcan grumbled under his breath.

They entered the interior of the glass-box elevator. The space was just large enough for Harcan and all six guards to fit inside, uncomfortably. It was immaculate and cool inside. A vent from above pumped in a steady stream of mist air conditioning.

Harcan looked out of the glass below as the commander keyed a digital prompt near the elevator's door, closing it. Pleasant elevator music played as they began to descend slowly.

Harcan peered down on the second level. He noticed two miners hurrying to a set of rectangular housing units. One of them dropped his hard hat, leaving it behind.

"Why are they in such a rush?" Harcan asked.

One of the guards looked up at Harcan without a word.

Suddenly, a dark-skinned nude android scampered after them on all fours. She hurled her body into one of the miners, knocking him down. She dove atop the miner, beating him to a bloody pulp with both fists as the other miner escaped.

"What the hell," Harcan mumbled. All at once, the android was electrocuted as a team of three security agents rushed in, prodding it with long staffs. Smoke trailed off the android's body as it rolled over. One of the guards put the android in shackles while the other two stood over it.

The commander standing beside Harcan looked down at his radio. It chirped loudly. "Sir, all clear. The situation on level two has been contained."

"Was the product damaged?" the commander questioned, assessing the situation.

"Not beyond repair," the guard answered.

"*Good.* Send it back down to the command center and have its memory wiped and repaired. Get it back on the line as soon as possible," the commander said.

Harcan glanced at the commander. "Seems like you boys *do* have a situation on your hands," he commented.

"This is rare. For the most part, our residents are very happy," the commander assured.

"Yeah, when they're not being brutally murdered." Harcan stared at the bloody miner as the guards finally checked his pulse.

The commander took off his helmet, wiping the sweat from his brow. He was a middle-aged male with light-brown skin and a severely burned face. He was missing his right ear, and his right eye was solid white.

Despite his wounds, he was handsome in his own way. His evenly short white hair was freshly cut, and a clean-shaven face showed off half of his chiseled, masculine features.

The commander looked at Harcan. "I hate wearing these damn helmets. My name's Dex. I'm second in command of security."

"Good to meet ya," Harcan said.

Dex raised his eyebrows. "To be honest, it's not easy keeping thousands of hardened criminals satisfied, but I think we do a pretty fair job. However, recently, things have gotten out of hand," he said.

Harcan looked up as an intercom blared above them.

"ALL PERSONNEL, WORKING RESTRICTIONS ARE LIFTED. SECURITY THREAT NEUTRALIZED."

Dex crossed his arms as the elevator lowered below the second floor. "Taking care of that fugitive on the space station is just the beginning of our problems. Those androids you brought us were just in time. You might have helped us more than you know."

Harcan locked eyes with Dex. "How's that?"

"We haven't gotten a fresh shipment of androids in several weeks. These workers were getting tired of the same old stock. As you saw, complications are already beginning to arise. The miners' work ethic is the first thing that goes. After that, android abuse can be an issue here, and sometimes, the androids retaliate," Dex stated, arching an eyebrow.

"I see that," Harcan said, tucking his paw under his chin as he listened.

"And we can only wipe the androids' memory so many times. For whatever reason, the trauma seems to take its toll, making them increasingly difficult to manage. This is partially the reason we need new stock. The miners start committing crimes when they grow bored of the same old selection. Fighting, escape attempts, all sorts of bullshit. It can make our job a nightmare, but we try and give them everything they need, at least until they get too old to work." Dex chuckled.

"Then what happens to them?" Harcan asked.

Dex grinned. "Dealing with elderly prisoners isn't my job. But I've heard the staff does its best to make them *comfortable*. In other words, I never see them again after their bodies give out."

Harcan shrugged. "No sense in wasting funds to take care of them."

"Exactly, they're just lowlifes as it is," Dex agreed.

Harcan raised an eyebrow and cracked a smile. "Hey, I take offense to that statement. Not all lowlifes are created equal," he said.

Dex pointed at Harcan. "I don't consider you in the same category, mutant. At least you're ambitious and efficient at what you do. You've got your own business, and you contribute to the wheel of society, just like me. That's more than I can say for most of these miners. Most of them never held a job in their lives," he stated, gazing ahead.

Harcan was surprised at how nonchalant Dex was, especially considering his position as commander. Maybe he was getting long in the tooth, too old and frustrated for all the nonsense.

The elevator reached the base of level two and continued descending to level three. This section was much more industrial. There was a yellow haze that filled the air. To Harcan's left and right were tunnels bored in the rocks.

Harcan could hear thousands of jackhammers running, along with picks and axes clacking. On the platform, there were hundreds of color-coordinated bins full of shiny rocks of different sizes, along with dozens of forklifts. On the crater's outer edge, large dump trucks were parked, standing by for transport to the surface.

"So, who drives all those vehicles? Surely you don't trust miners to do so?" Harcan asked.

Dex chuckled. "*Hell* no. That would be a disaster. Most of them are drones, or controlled remotely from the command center," he replied.

Harcan narrowed his eyes at the trucks. He wondered if Ellie could gain remote access to them, providing an option for their escape.

They continued their descent a few more floors, and with each consecutive passing level, the intensity of the mining operation intensified. More miners populated each platform, along with more bins full of rocks and equipment.

"Damn. How many levels are in this hole?" Harcan asked.

Dex smirked. "We're approaching level six, and this is where it gets interesting," he informed Harcan.

"*Really?* Is that where Scales is?" Harcan questioned.

"Yeah," he replied, donning his helmet as they lowered into a dramatic scene. Level six wasn't a mining operation at all. On the outer edge was a black wall that blocked out the light completely. There was a dark tarp on the ceiling to help sell the effect of a pitch-black sky.

On the surface of level six was a sprawling, booming nightlife district, modeled after a city with nightclubs, roads, and stoplights. There were neon billboards and lights everywhere, giving the mock city an adult, tourist-hub vibe.

"Well, *this* is unexpected," Harcan commented with a grin.

"Welcome to Distraction Island, where every criminal tries to forget just how shitty his life really is." Dex laughed.

Miners were walking all up and down the streets. Some of them were accompanied by android companions. Near the nightclub entrances were androids in provocative clothing, whistling and calling the miners as they passed by.

Just below, Harcan noticed a female android flip her long black hair as she flirted with a patron, revealing a large hole in the back of her head full of circuitry and wires. Otherwise, she appeared convincingly human from here. All of them did. There was an assortment of choices too, with every skin color under the rainbow. All of them were beautiful from what Harcan could tell.

Dex looked around. "This is what keeps our mine functioning on all cylinders. Everything on this level is designed to let the miners unwind. See those large, boxy machines all around the edges of the crater?" he asked.

"Yeah."

"Filtration devices that purify the air. It's also much cooler on this level too, simulating a nighttime retreat," Dex stated.

"What about you? You ever *retreat* down here to sample the merchandise?" Harcan smirked.

Dex cleared his throat. "I live on the top floor, with my wife," he said with a straight face.

Harcan smirked. "That's not what I asked you," he said.

Dex looked away, and the red light from a neon billboard reflected on his dark helmet. "No comment," he said.

Harcan held his stare at Dex and pulled his trench coat forward. The elevator came to a stop and the door opened, piping in a mix of music from several genres: rock, hip-hop, along with a few sounds Harcan had never heard before. The concoction of blaring tunes was abrasive to Harcan's sensitive hearing.

Harcan allowed Dex and his men to step out of the elevator first. "Ellie, if you can hear me, I need to know where you are," he said.

"*Hey*, follow me." Dex turned back toward Harcan, shouting over the music.

"Sorry, I've got business contacts pestering me. You know how it is," Harcan lied, looking to his watch as he walked out of the elevator. There was a large, wooden country-western bar to his left. A tall red neon light with the words *Dixie Darlings* was on the signage.

On the spacious outdoor patio was a mechanical bull ride with padding surrounding it. A cocky miner mounted the machine and was tossed off it almost immediately, and the small crowd erupted in laughter.

A few girls stood outside the saloon-style doors in cowgirl outfits, tight jeans, high boots, and lots of cleavage showing. One of the cowgirls had blonde flowing locks. She was throwing a lasso at passerby miners with a big smile on her face. "Come on in, boys! Don't be a stranger!" she said with a thick twang.

She met eyes with Harcan briefly as he and Dex walked by. Her perfect white smile flattened out as she saw them. She pretended as if she didn't notice the guards, continuing in playful banter with the miners.

Harcan observed the miners at street level. Most of them were grinning from ear to ear as they bar hopped with android companions, some of them with one on each arm.

Dex leaned close to Harcan. "This is the part of my job I hate to see. Most of these assholes never did anything with their lives, yet they get to experience *this*?"

"It's for the best though, right? It keeps the quarry going," Harcan replied, raising his voice over the music.

"Yeah, that's what I keep telling myself, but just look at all this shit." He gestured ahead toward all the lively, festive bars.

They passed by several nightclubs with different themes until they reached a towering cone-shaped bar with deep-red walls and lights. The pulsating lights gave the walls an animated effect, creating the illusion that they were on fire.

Dex moved close to Harcan. "See that tall building?"

"Uh-huh," Harcan replied, observing the bar just over a hundred meters away. There was a massive hologram at the bar's summit depicting a go-go dancer with knee-high white boots.

"That's called Club Inferno, and Scales is waiting there. We'll escort you inside," Dex stated.

"Looks like a happening place," Harcan replied.

"You'll see why soon enough," Dex said.

As they proceeded, the street became increasingly packed with miners. The crowd seemed to veer away from Harcan, most of them fearful of his colossal, wild appearance.

But one drunk patron covered in tattoos stumbled near Harcan and stood in front of him, blocking his path. Harcan immediately recognized him from Orchid's restaurant.

"Shit," Harcan mumbled.

The drunk pointed at Harcan. "Hey, you! Mutant! Haven't I seen you before? At the diner?" he slurred.

"Out of my way!" Harcan roared, shoving him aside with one arm. The man stumbled and fell on his backside.

"Official business!" Dex shouted at the drunk as two guards jabbed their rifles at him. "Move along, miner!"

Dex turned toward Harcan. "Sorry about that. These boys can have a little too much fun sometimes."

"I can relate," Harcan joked. The guards marched in a V formation in front of Harcan, pushing the drunks aside as they neared their destination.

Harcan observed Scales marching out the front entrance of Inferno. Several guards were accompanying him, headed right at Harcan. They met him halfway as Scales outstretched his arms and smiled, patting Harcan on the shoulder. "Look who it is. The *hero* of the day!" he declared.

"Well, if you say so." Harcan grinned. The guards surrounded the pair, prohibiting anyone from getting close.

Scales held his stare at Harcan. "I do. And I hear you have something to show me?" he asked. Harcan noticed the amphibian's watery helm. It seemed the smaller creatures swimming inside were more active, possibly stirring because of the loud music and energetic scene.

Harcan opened his coat pocket as Scales peered over, inspecting the android's head. The amphibian's eyes widened. He seemed surprised by the condition of his face. "It seems you dealt her a crushing defeat. That's most definitely my fugitive. You have my thanks," Scales confirmed.

"You're welcome. Here to collect my payment. Can we do it somewhere private?" Harcan looked to his left and right. It was clear that this wasn't the place to execute Scales. There were far too many security guards.

"Sure. Follow me." Scales waved Harcan toward Club Inferno, and they walked side by side. "I was informed that the space station wasn't destroyed and has resumed its previous orbit around Pison," Scales stated, glancing at Harcan.

"That's right," Harcan replied.

"And how did you manage that? You could've just destroyed it." Scales asked. The pair walked to the front doors near a group of bouncers dressed in red tactical gear that matched the nightclub's fiery theme. They sported shock batons and heavy assault rifles. They seemed to take particular notice of Harcan, staring up at him.

Harcan thought of an answer. "After I entered the bridge and eliminated the android, resuming orbit wasn't difficult. I just used the bridge commands to realign the station," he lied.

Scales stopped and looked into Harcan's eyes. "I'm extremely impressed," he said. One of the guards opened the door for Scales, and they walked through.

"Welcome to Club Inferno," Scales proclaimed, gesturing about the lively scene.

Inside was a massive circular dance floor with a ceiling that ascended above everyone by three dozen meters. There were go-go dancers in cages above the dance floor dressed in devilish costumes with horns, fangs, and split tails. There were hundreds of miners and androids dancing out on the floor to up-tempo techno music. The energetic room was lit with a deep, blood-red color throughout.

There were rows of bars on each side of the club, with scantily clad shot girls pacing the floor in demon outfits.

"Looks like my kinda spot," Harcan commented.

"I thought you might like it. We could even dye your fur red. You'd fit right in," Scales replied with a grin.

"Is that why you called me down here? You want me to be part of the attraction?" Harcan joked.

"*Hardly,*" Scales scoffed. "I've got bigger plans for you. Follow me."

Just to the right was the DJ's booth. Inside, there was a male android with four arms surrounded by a cluster of audio equipment. He was wearing rectangular shades that covered half of his face, and his outfit was a red jumpsuit that sparkled. While he danced wildly to the music, Harcan observed him adjusting the tunes behind his back without looking, using his extra arms to his advantage.

"Hm."

As Harcan followed Scales through the club, he noticed they were surrounded by twelve guards now, including Dex. The bodyguards followed their every movement, keeping the miners and androids at a distance. Scales stopped as he neared the dance floor, leaning over a handrail. He looked at Harcan. "You know, the minute I saw you, I *knew* you'd be right for that job."

"How's that?" Harcan asked.

Inside Scales's liquid helm, one of the small amphibians swam too close to his face. This caused Scales to snarl, warding it off as he flashed his sharp, blackened teeth at the creature.

Scales pointed at Harcan. "I can see it in the eyes. Mutants, humans, even kuruk like myself. When you're a killer, the eyes give it away. But you're a rare breed of brains and brawn that I haven't seen in years, and that's exactly what I need on my side."

Harcan cleared his throat. "Well, in the smuggling world, I've run into plenty of dangerous situations."

Scales held his stare at Harcan. "I don't know too many smugglers that get caught up in combat scenarios. They tend to like things low key. Has this been your only profession?" he questioned.

"Yeah. You'd be surprised. Running weapons can be a risky gig," Harcan said.

"Well, let me offer you something a bit less dangerous," Scales stated, standing upright. He smiled as he gestured Harcan toward a roped-off area to the side. They were escorted to the large booth by Scales's guards. One of the sentries moved the ropes aside as they stepped into the private section.

Scales turned and looked at Dex. "Give us a few minutes—alone," he said, leaning close to him.

Dex glanced at Harcan before ordering his men to spread out and form a perimeter around them. Scales made his way to the booth and motioned Harcan to have a seat on one of the couches.

"Go on," Scales said.

Harcan moved toward the comfy black leather sofa as Scales sat on the couch directly across from it. Harcan caught a whiff of dried semen as he looked down before sitting. "Ugh."

A tall android waitress dressed as a winged demon approached. She was carrying a tray of syringes in all different colors. The waitress lowered the tray, staring at Harcan with a blank face as Scales took one of the syringes. He ran the syringe through a small cylinder-shaped device that flashed green several times, seemingly testing its contents.

Scales looked up at the waitress. "This one will do. Now, get back to work," he ordered, waving off the waitress angrily.

Harcan noticed her unnaturally curvy frame as she trotted off.

"I think she likes you," Scales commented.

"They all do. It's the thick fur. They like the *cuddly* feel," Harcan replied.

Scales smirked as he injected the needle into his forearm. "All that fur looks uncomfortable if you ask me," he said.

Harcan looked Scales up and down. "Who are you to talk about comfort? You're walking around in a giant fishbowl." He smiled.

Scales's eyes rolled back as he chuckled. "*Fishbowl,*" he repeated, shaking his head.

He held his stare at Harcan, and his grin flattened out. "You've got a lot of nerve. I could have you killed in less than a second for an insult like that," he warned, snapping his fingers. Scales sneered. "But I like your confidence, mutant. You're not afraid to roll the dice."

Harcan outstretched his arms. "I guess in my line of work it's all about living on the edge."

"I don't, not unless I have to. And neither should you," Scales muttered. Harcan watched as Scales pushed the last bit of the syringe's liquid into his arm. "Feels good, but I only use it as a necessity," Scales said.

"What is that shit?" Harcan asked, raising an eyebrow at the syringe.

"It's a relaxer. The miners use it illegally. When it's confiscated, I have it tested, then use it for myself sometimes. I take a very low dose to stay keen on my surroundings, but enough to take the edge off. You know what I mean?" he asked, glaring at Harcan as if there was a penalty for the wrong answer.

"Absolutely." Harcan reached in his coat and pulled out his flask, lifting it in the air. "Everybody needs to take the edge off once in a while," he replied, pretending to take a drink, but there wasn't any left.

Tranquil, Scales tilted his head back as the relaxer coursed through his veins. Harcan looked at his scaly throat and glanced away as his claws slowly unsheathed, digging into his coat. He imagined punching through his liquid suit and slicing his neck. He wanted to end it here.

But he couldn't. He was forced to stall until he heard back from Ellie. He discreetly adjusted his earpiece to be sure he was ready to receive her call.

Scales gazed forward. "You took a lot of pressure off me today; I want you to know that."

"I'm glad to be of service, so long as I get paid," Harcan replied.

"We'll get to that," Scales stated, staring at Harcan. "I saw you talking to one of my security commanders, Dex. I'm curious, what is your opinion of him?" he questioned.

"He seems capable enough," Harcan answered.

"The android you eliminated on the space station murdered Dex's superior, along with three other guards in her escape. Dex was automatically promoted because of this," Scales informed him.

"Whoa, she killed four *armed* guards? I appreciated you not underselling how dangerous she was before we negotiated our price," Harcan said with a sarcastic tone, grinning as he fired up a cigarette.

Scales pointed at Harcan. "But I knew *you* could pull it off, and that's why I wanted to talk to you again in private. You and I are different. We live in a galaxy run by humans. And no matter how high we climb the ladder, they'll always look down on us. In a way, it makes us stronger, but we always need to be two steps ahead to be considered equals."

"I don't have to worry about climbing corporate or government ladders. That's why I'm in business for myself," Harcan said confidently.

"Yeah, but for how long? Look at you, running around in an unmarked freighter and with no identification. That's illegal, and it'll eventually catch up to you. You and I both know that any human with a badge will take pride in locking you away for life. In fact, my own men wanted to report you to the Republic because of your lack of credentials, but I called them off," Scales revealed.

"Much obliged," Harcan replied, leaning back in his seat as he took in a long draw from his cig.

Scales narrowed his eyes at Harcan. "What if I told you I could make you *incredibly* rich?" he asked.

Harcan's ears perked up. "I'd be inclined to hear you out," he replied.

Scales leaned close to Harcan. "I have a position available where you wouldn't have to deal with these shady smuggling gigs under the radar. You could be official and work for me. Believe it or not, I'm employed by the Republic, and I do my own hiring. But I need *real* security."

"I thought you liked Dex," Harcan reminded.

Scales shook his head. "Up to a point, I do. But humans don't have what *we* have. To start, they're physically weak, slow, and—"

"Stupid," Harcan interrupted.

Scales cracked a smile and pointed to his head. "Precisely. Most don't have the type of sense we do. You know, when I came here, this quarry was tearing itself apart. Miners were jumping off the platforms committing suicide and killing each other daily. I brought safety to this place by giving them something to look forward to," Scale recalled, waving his arms around the nightclub. "None of this was here before I arrived. It was all my idea."

"And seems to me it paid for itself," Harcan commented.

"It does, exponentially. The quarry's production numbers soared after I gave them an escape. This sanctuary of sex. They live for the weekends. The human leadership was too incompetent to understand that working with sentient beings without incentive is bad business. My system produced results immediately. These miners are granted rights with an assortment of beautiful androids *every* single week, so long as they work hard," he explained.

"Sounds like a better life than what most *free* men get. Where do I sign up?" Harcan joked.

Scale laughed. "And that brings me to my point. It's not all peachy down here. Miners make mistakes, and I punish them by restricting their leisure hours. Or I'll get an android with a wild hair up her ass that thinks she's a revolutionist. It's not always safe. That's why I need a real powerhouse with smarts that can watch my back. Someone who's been out on their own and lived in the gutter. Most of these human guards are green, they come from wealthy moon colonies, and mommy and daddy sent them to the Republic police academies," he explained.

"I wouldn't know anything about that sort of life," Harcan said.

"It's rare that a nonhuman does. Just the fact that you've thrived on your own speaks volumes to me. I know what it takes, believe me," Scales replied.

Harcan took in a deep breath and locked eyes with Scales. "Let's assume I take this job for a moment. What would a typical workday be like for me?" he questioned, stalling the amphibian. Harcan continued to put on a face that he was interested in the job.

Scales nodded. "Simple. You'd be my right hand. Everywhere I go, you go. I need someone to put fear in these miners and androids. Someone who looks the part. I saw the way the crowd reacted to you outside the club. Even my bouncers were trembling in their boots when you walked in here. You've got the size and the look. We both terrify these sheep, but I'm too busy to watch my own back. That's why I need you. Not only that, but I could never fully trust a human to hold such an important role."

Harcan cracked a smile. "Basically, you're in need of a glorified bodyguard."

Scales shook his head. "Call it that if you want, but you'd get all the perks the miners do, and I can pay, handsomely."

"Yeah? How much?" Harcan asked, raising his eyebrows.

"Two million credits per year."

Harcan's eyes widened. "*Oh*. Well, how about three million?" he asked for the hell of it.

Scales looked away. "Two and a quarter."

"Two and a half?" Harcan countered.

Scales thought about it for a moment and took in a deep breath. "I could swing that."

The thought crossed Harcan's mind; if he'd run into this offer two years ago, he might have accepted if it wasn't tied to the androids' exploitation. It was a ridiculous amount of credits, enough for a top-tier starship stocked full of booze. He figured he could quit Scales's gig after several years and retire.

There was a time when Harcan entertained the idea of traveling the galaxy at his own pace, to visit exciting worlds, cultures, and anomalies with no strings attached.

This opportunity would have provided leisure and escape from his job, no more of the scum-infested shitholes that fugitives hid on.

But escape was only a dream. Harcan knew he could never run from the horrors he inflicted in his past. His victims' screams would follow him like a black cloud. Loneliness and depression set in, and his interest and ambitions were washed away. He found that the only way to preserve his sanity was distraction, to live on the edge as a bounty hunter.

This was part of the reason he hired Ellie in the first place. His biggest threat never came from the bounties themselves—it came from him.

Scales waved his hand in front of Harcan's face as he zoned out. "Did I lose you, or are you still considering my offer?"

Harcan snapped out of it. "Uh. I *did* have another question. I'd be paid by the Republic, right?" he asked.

"Yeah, but not officially. The Republic contracts this quarry, but we're in the outer realm. That means we don't have the red-tape jurisdiction the main hubs do. But even then, only part of your payment would come from the Republic. The other half would be out of my pocket," Scales responded.

"Interesting. Why?" Harcan asked, stalling for time.

Scales pointed at the small amphibians swimming around in his suit. "This isn't just some ordinary protection gig. It's not just my life you would safeguard. It's the survival of my *entire* species."

"What?" Harcan muttered.

Scales held his stare at Harcan. "You see, in a last-ditch effort, our scientists only had time to create two of these specialized suits, each engineered to house what was left of our race. We were tasked to search the galaxy to find us a suitable planet. This liquid is designed to preserve my offspring in their youth, so that one day they can repopulate a new world."

Harcan raised an eyebrow. "And I thought my job was risky. You mentioned there are two suits?" he asked, gesturing toward Scales.

"My partner wore the other one. As I said, these are *our* offspring. I carry one half of our brood, and she carried the other," Scales replied, looking around at the creatures swimming near him.

Harcan flicked the ashes off his cigarette as he looked Scales up and down. He paused. "I'm hesitant to ask, but where's your partner now?"

Scales looked away for a moment. "Good question. We stayed in constant communication while she frantically searched the galaxy for a home. My job was here, to fund her expeditions with fast, top-of-the-line starships, along with a full crew of scientists and explorers. Unfortunately, eleven years ago, I lost communication with her. The last response was a desperate plea for help. Her ship was damaged by star pirates, and they were boarding her vessel," he revealed. His eyes hollowed out as he gazed ahead.

"Sorry to hear," Harcan said plainly, staring at the floor between them.

Harcan couldn't believe it. Assassinating Scales put him in the position of committing mass murder, again. But this time, he would be responsible for wiping out an *entire* species. Regardless of the crimes Scales had committed, was it reasonable to condemn his entire race and future generations?

Harcan didn't even want to think about the consequences right now. He decided to continue to play along as the role of an opportunistic smuggler. "Scales, I gotta ask you something, and I am going to be blunt."

"I wouldn't have it any other way," Scales replied, interlocking his thick, coarse fingers.

Harcan crossed his arms. "Hypothetically, let's say we do work together. What are the chances your operation gets raided by the authorities at some point? Isn't it possible that I could end up in shackles as your accomplice? I know this is partially Republic funded, but I don't think they'd be pleased about the illegal sex trafficking of these androids."

Scales shrugged, and a smirk appeared across his face. "The Republic doesn't give a *damn* what we do on level six so long as we keep the miners working. Obviously, we do our best to keep the android pleasure services private. *If* that was exposed, it would translate to a negative impact on public opinion and military recruitment. But only temporarily. The Republic has spies embedded in all the major media outlets, allowing us to undermine the validity of any leaks," he said, wiping his hands clean.

Harcan's ears perked up. "Sounds foolproof, if you ask me. But why would exposure affect the Republic's *military* recruitment?" he asked.

Scales leaned forward. His large eyes drifted through Harcan as the relaxer seemed to be in full effect. "Because our primary customer *is* the Republic military. Specifically, the Navy's war machines. The meteor that created this crater contains a rare element to strengthen the alloy for their starship hulls. It's much of the reason the Republic is uncontested in the galaxy. Our quarry helps maintain that dominance."

"I see." Harcan looked across the nightclub in deep thought. Might this information be valuable to Tarron's rebellion against the Republic? Harcan thought so.

All at once, something caught Harcan's attention. On the opposite side of the nightclub, Harcan noticed an android having sex with a miner in a VIP booth. She seemed to be in pain, meeting eyes with Harcan briefly before looking away with a blank stare.

"Do you have any other questions or concerns?" Scales asked.

"Not really a concern, but since I've arrived, I've noticed your androids seem a bit more... lifelike? At least more than the others I've been around," Harcan asked.

"That's because we have their sensitivity settings cranked up. Emotions and physical pain. We want them to feel *everything*. It's more realistic to the miners when the androids are slapped around and screwed. We've restricted the machines' superhuman strength too, not just for security reasons, but so that each miner feels like the alpha. On rare occasions, we've had *instances* where androids were able to hack themselves and reboot, reinstalling their original attributes," Scales said.

"I saw that with my own eyes. A miner was brutally beaten to death on level two," Harcan commented.

"*Oh.* Yes, but those are rare, isolated incidents. Overall, we want our androids frail and submissive and expressive in their pain," Scales replied.

Harcan smiled. "And that never weighs on your conscience? Knowing the androids are being abused in such a way?"

Scales erupted in laughter as Harcan played along, chuckling himself. "Well, it certainly doesn't weigh on *your* conscience, or else you wouldn't have sold your shipment of machines into the sex trade. Not to mention, you destroyed the android fugitive on the space station without batting an eye," Scales joked.

Harcan outstretched his arms. "I can confirm that I'm a soulless bastard, but that's unfair to pin on everyone else," he replied.

"Well, I have a conscience, believe it or not. The difference is when it pertains to machines. Robots were responsible for destroying my home world. My people built the most durable armor in the galaxy. We retrofitted ships, tanks, anything for the Republic. More recently, we were contracted to construct star cruisers on my planet from top to bottom," Scales said.

"Hm. I always wondered where those gigantic vessels were manufactured," Harcan stated.

"The Republic contracts dozens of unknown planets and species. My world is mostly ocean, but nearly every square kilometer of the landmass was devoted to shipbuilding. We even had our own fleet of robots that assisted us in enormous factories as far as the eye can see. But after decades of service, an artificial intelligence anomaly turned against us. Over twenty billion of my race perished in the first few years. The machines polluted our waters and unleashed fertility viruses against our males, preventing us from reproducing," Scales revealed.

Harcan looked forward with a blank stare. "That's unfathomable."

"Not for my family and me. We lived through it. So, forgive me if I don't mind watching *machines* suffer in this quarry. It doesn't weigh on my conscience. Actually, I enjoy it," he revealed.

Harcan looked around. "Then your job here must be like a paradise. Androids in suffering, humans as prisoners."

"I wouldn't go that far. At least, not until I get proper security," Scales replied, eyeing up a leggy, busty brunette android in a tight red dress. She approached with a confident trot, like a runway model.

She stopped next to Harcan and shot him a flirtatious smile while caressing the thick hair on the top of his head.

"You weren't kidding, I guess it *is* the fur," Scales kidded as the sexy android plopped down on the couch beside Harcan. She crossed her long tan legs and wiggled her foot side to side while she continued to stroke his hair.

Suddenly, something caught Harcan's eye as he looked over Scales's shoulder out onto the dance floor.

As the crowd swayed back and forth to the music, he caught a glimpse of a small android. His ears stood straight up like two radars homing in on a target.

He peered forward, and his eyes widened. His stomach knotted up. It was Ellie.

She had a spiked collar around her neck and was being tugged about like a dog on a leash. Harcan's mind wandered as he thought of the worst: what had they done to her since they lost communication?

Guilt overwhelmed him as he thought about his agreement to send Ellie behind enemy lines. It might have made sense at the time, but now it felt like the was the worst decision of his life.

Harcan's lip snarled up as he stared at a patron jerking at Ellie's neck violently, spilling his drink while laughing. Harcan growled under his breath as he imagined tearing him limb from limb and beating him to death with his arms. Scales did a double take, looking over his shoulder.

"Something wrong?" Scales asked, noticing Harcan's blank stare.

"Nah, not really," he answered.

Scales looked out on the dance floor. "*Wait*. Is that the little android you sold me? It is, isn't it," he answered his own question.

"Yeah. I think so," Harcan replied, shrugging it off. "It's just, I have a soft spot for children, I suppose," he added. Harcan tried to play it off, immediately smiling and flirting with the waitress next to him as she ran her fingers through his thick, black fur.

"I thought you said you were a soulless bastard?" Scales reminded him, staring at him.

"I am, but kids are where I draw the line," Harcan replied.

Scales laughed. "Well, she *looks* like a child. My technicians tell me she was quite advanced, a custom Q09-C2 model with some sort of high-end software we're unfamiliar with. I'm not sure how that ended up in your possession, but she'll do *just* fine. In fact, I'm sure she'll be quite popular here. We've had dozens of requests for younger androids. She fits the bill perfectly."

Harcan ground his teeth, trying to keep his cool. The miner attempted to dance with Ellie as she stood there, staring at him with a blank face. The man shook her at the shoulders. "*Hey!* What's your fucking problem? Are you malfunctioning?" he yelled in frustration.

Disappointed, the miner smacked her across the face, knocking her to the dance floor.

As Ellie fell on the floor, Harcan could feel his heart pounding. He wanted to intervene, but it could jeopardize her further if he did.

Scales shot up out of his seat, gesturing Dex toward the abusive miner. "*Hey!* Bring me that worker with the small android over here. *Now!*" Scales jabbed his index finger at Ellie.

"Okay, boss, on it." Dex complied, rushing out onto the dance floor.

Scales glanced at Harcan as the miner approached, tugging Ellie behind him like a slave.

Scales towered over the miner, and he gulped in fear. Scales leaned close to him. "Care to explain to me why you're treating my *brand-new* product like a punching bag? Can't you see she's much smaller, more delicate? If you damage her, I have to pay for repair costs. That makes me *very* unhappy, and no one here likes me unhappy. Perhaps I should ban you from using this model?" Scales scolded, crossing his arms.

The miner turned and looked at Ellie with a long face before staring back up at Scales. "Please. *Don't.* It won't happen again," the miner promised nervously.

Scales waved Ellie near him. "Come here, little one, let me see if you were damaged," he ordered. Ellie stepped forward slowly. She held her head down as her curly brown locks fell in front of her face.

The waitress seated beside Harcan threw her long legs in his lap, then mounted him. She attempted to gain Harcan's attention as he peered around her.

For a split second, Ellie met eyes with Harcan. But something was off. She appeared distant, vacant, like she didn't know him.

Strangely, Ellie grinned at him as the waitress rocked her body violently atop Harcan, flipping the couch over backward. "What the hell—" A blinding bright light emitted from Ellie's chest, blowing her body apart violently. Debris from Ellie's body sailed in all directions, pelting the bottom of the couch as everyone near the explosion was knocked to the floor.

Screams echoed throughout the nightclub as Harcan's jaw dropped. He scrambled to his feet to see Ellie's burnt, smoldering plastic-and-metal body scattered across the dance floor in flames. The smell of scorched plastic filled his nostrils as he reached out for her. "No-no-no," he pleaded.

"Harcan!" the waitress shouted, tugging at his coattails as he turned toward her. The voice was unmistakable.

"*Ellie?*" he asked with bulging eyes, looking the waitress up and down.

"Of course it's me! And we've still got a job to do!" she yelled, stabbing her finger at Scales. A whiplash of emotions overwhelmed Harcan. In one moment, he'd thought he'd lost his only friend, and in the next, she was standing beside him.

It began to make sense to him; Ellie had transferred her consciousness to another chassis, which was the reason for the lapse in communication between them.

The explosion had knocked Scales and several of his security to the ground, killing two guards, along with countless injuries throughout the nightclub. Several miners were yelling in agony and walking around in complete shock.

Scales was crawling face down through the stampede as everyone rushed to the exit. The specialized liquid from his suit spilled and spurted onto the floor as he attempted to cup his hand over the leaks.

Several of his offspring flopped around on the ground, gasping for air. Scales's hands trembled as he panicked, corralling the small brood close to him.

"Help me!" he shouted at his security as they picked themselves up off the floor.

Harcan aimed his weapon at Scales as his security surrounded him. They heaved him up to his feet, ushering the alpha amphibian toward the exit while he cradled his slimy brood. Scales was limping, likely injured from the explosion.

"Harcan! Do it!" Ellie shouted, staring at him. Time slowed down as he lined up the shot. Scales was in his sights. As his claw grazed the trigger of his shotgun, he thought of the repercussions of killing him. Ellie had no idea that Scales's death meant the genocide of an entire race.

Scales looked over his shoulder and made eye contact with Harcan momentarily. In that split second, everything was revealed as he glanced at the barrel of the laser shotgun pointed at him. "The mutant! *He's* the assassin!" he yelled at his bodyguards.

Six security guards split away from Scales, taking up offensive positions. Harcan fired twice, melting two of them where they stood into a pile of smoldering ash. One of the laser beams from Harcan's shotgun penetrated a guard's hip, scorching Scales's leg. The amphibian grimaced in pain and collapsed to the floor again, dropping two of his offspring.

"Get him up!" one of the guards shouted. Scales's security pulled him outside by the legs and tail as he held his stare at his brood, reaching out for them. "I can't leave them!" Scales yelled as his security escorted him away from the line of fire.

Harcan turned over a large, thick table in front of them as Ellie snatched up a rifle from one of the dead security guards. They hunkered behind the table as the security fired on them. Debris filled the air as couches, tables, and walls were shredded by the zipping bullets and laser fire.

Harcan met eyes with Ellie. "You coulda warned me that was coming," he said, aiming around the table. He fired, searing one of the guards' arms. The trooper fell to the deck and screamed before Harcan followed up with a fatal shot to his upper chest.

Ellie scanned the rifle in her hands. She tapped the magazine firmly with her palm. "I couldn't talk, Harcan. It would have blown our cover," she responded, returning fire around the table.

"Well, it's *definitely* blown now," Harcan replied, firing around cover.

Ellie glared at him. "How the hell did you miss that kill shot on Scales?"

"Technically, I didn't miss," he stated.

"The mission was to *kill* Scales, not injure him! After we get these androids out of here, we have to finish the job!" She raised her voice.

Harcan didn't reply. He growled as he leaned around to take another shot. Just as he was about to pull the trigger, a well-placed shot from Ellie's rifle landed dead center on the guard's visor, blowing a hole through it. Smoke trailed up from his helmet, and the guard's body fell over lifelessly.

"See the difference? Now *that's* dead," Ellie taunted as Harcan gritted his teeth and looked at her.

"Your suicide bomb didn't do the trick either!" Harcan reminded. Ellie lowered her eyebrows, returning fire without a word.

To Harcan, the entire dynamic of the mission had changed. Whatever moral rationale he felt in rescuing the androids meant less to him if he had to exterminate an entire species to do it. But he knew he couldn't tell Ellie that. He felt she would side with the androids regardless.

Finally, the music stopped, and miners continued to flee the scene, knocking each other down and stampeding over the fallen. Unfortunately, the only exit was the front door, and this created a bottleneck. Several androids took advantage of the traffic jam, attacking their panicked human companions mercilessly, pummeling them as they tried to funnel through the door in a gruesome display. Bones snapped, and blood splattered the wall.

Harcan's eyes drifted through the chaotic scene for a moment. As he looked into one of the miners' bulging eyes, he was taken back to EL-59. He thought of himself and Orchid using the crowds' terror against them, stumbling and trampling over one another in fear.

On the other side of the nightclub, Scales's guards were well insulated behind the bar. They continued to take potshots at Harcan and Ellie. Bullets whizzed back and forth as the nightclub flashed from gunfire.

"We can't stay here! They'll send more soldiers!" Ellie yelled.

"I understand that!" Harcan roared, ducking as a bullet struck above his head, showering his fur with debris.

One of the go-go dancers was swinging back and forth in her cage on the ceiling. As she neared the guards, she dove out. Her feet-first plunge smashed directly into one of the guards' chests, crushing his body with a loud crack.

Startled, the two remaining guards turned toward the carnage.

"This is our chance!" Harcan rushed toward the guards while they were distracted, waving Ellie with him.

The dancer jumped up from the floor and began choking one of Scales's security, but the other guard shot her in the back.

"Rrraggggh!" Harcan lunged through the air with his claws unsheathed, swiping the guard across his helmet.

Harcan's thick paw crushed his visor and whipped his head to the side violently. The powerful strike sent splinters of broken glass and metal into his face like shrapnel, stabbing through his facial structure and skull, killing him instantly.

Harcan turned and noticed Ellie standing over the android dancer that leaped from the cage. She was hunched over, staring at her stomach. There was no visible exit or entry marks on her body. She looked at her hand as a gray, shiny fluid covered her fingers like a swarm of army ants. Ellie approached her to help.

The dancer pointed at Ellie. "Stay the fuck back! This *shit* will kill you!" she warned, glaring up at Ellie.

"There's nothing I can do?" Ellie asked frantically, looking her up and down.

"It's t-too late," she replied, struggling with her words as she laid flat on her back. Harcan noticed her eyes fade to gray as the swarm crawled over her face. Her body jolted as Harcan moved Ellie back with his arm. The dancer gazed through Ellie without a word as her body began to shake violently. The swarm covered her completely, eating her away into a metallic skeleton in a matter of seconds.

Harcan noticed the nightclub suddenly was eerily silent. It had been evacuated, and only the slave androids remained. They appeared to be staff members from Club Inferno, bartenders, dancers, and shot girls, all of them dressed in scanty, devilish-themed attire.

Some of them rushed to the front door and began barricading it with debris, broken tables, chairs, whatever they could find.

A bartender with long, jet-black hair stepped next to Ellie as she stared down at the deceased dancer. "Scales's guards use a custom nanobot virus in their ammunition. It corrupts our software and devours us. The bullets have less velocity so that they don't penetrate and set off our implanted explosives," she said, pointing at her stomach.

"That's an awful way to go out," Ellie muttered, staring at the gnawed android frame.

The bartender shook her head. "Especially when you consider our sensitivity settings are dialed to the max."

Harcan assisted the androids in fortifying the double doors. When they finished, he peeked through a small crack in the door, panting heavily. He noticed a dead bouncer just outside. His head and been ripped from his body with only thin bits of flesh and ligaments attached.

Harcan looked past the corpse into the streets. It was strangely quiet, like a ghost town. There weren't any signs of Scales nor his security, and the girls standing in front of the other bars were gone—only blinking neon lights illuminated the empty city.

As he surveyed the dark alleys in the distance, he observed deceased miners and androids littering the streets and glimpses of shadowy figures scattering.

An intercom loudspeaker chirped on a building across the street. A female cleared her throat over the speaker.

"PROTECTION TEAMS FROM SECTION ALPHA, BRAVO, AND DELTA, MUSTER ON LEVEL SIX IMMEDIATELY. MINERS, CONTRIBUTORS, AND CONTRACTORS STAY INDOORS UNTIL WE INFORM YOU OTHERWISE. THIS IS NOT A DRILL."

The creepy, monotone message repeated over and over.

Ellie walked next to Harcan as he continued to recon the area. "See anything?" she asked.

Harcan looked down at Ellie. "No. Did you gain access to their construction vehicles?" he asked.

"Absolutely. Ready to go when we need them," she answered.

"Stand by. We can't stay here long," Harcan replied.

"But where are we taking the refugees?" Ellie asked, lowering her voice.

Harcan sighed. "Not here. We need to get them out of this city to the outermost edge. I think I saw a path out."

He turned away from the door, noticing that two dozen androids were staring directly at him and Ellie.

Ellie looked up at Harcan. "I've been communicating with the androids via secure frequency, Harcan, so they know why we're here," she explained, lowering her voice.

"Well, I'm glad they're in the loop," he muttered.

"I have questions and concerns!" an imposing female voice erupted. An authoritative android stepped out of the ranks toward Harcan, marching toward him confidently. He observed she was missing her right arm from the elbow down. She had bronze skin and was dressed differently than the rest of the staff.

She wore a white, tight-fitting jumpsuit and cape. Her outfit and face were covered in blood splatter. The red on her face looked like warpaint, with vertical streaks running the length of it.

Her wild, thick yellow hair reminded Harcan of a lion's mane. She had solid white eyes that gave her the appearance of a goddess or superheroine. The powerful-looking woman turned toward Ellie. "It's obvious that we don't have much time before Scales's men retaliate," she said plainly.

Ellie looked at Harcan, gesturing toward the fearsome android. "This is Solus, Harcan. We've been in remote communication since just before I launched the attack against Scales when I detected a secret frequency. Solus was the leader of a brewing resistance effort."

Solus stood up tall. "And nothing has changed," she corrected Ellie, arching an eyebrow. She looked down as one of Scales's offspring flopped beneath her feet. She stomped it, killing it with a quick tap of the heel.

Solus paced back and forth. "*Your* attack against Scales failed, in case you haven't noticed," she commented, looking around the nightclub.

"Yeah, we noticed," Harcan said as Ellie glanced away.

Solus whipped her long hair behind her head and narrowed her eyes at Harcan. "We all appreciate Orchid sending such *valiant* liberators behind enemy lines to save us. But I sincerely hope we don't regret this. The two of you *do* have a plan for getting us to the surface, correct? In addition to the twenty-four androids in this room, there's hundreds more on this level, and *all* of our lives depend on how well your escape plan has been thought out," she said, glaring at Ellie.

"We don't want to end up like her," a curly-haired brunette android added, pointing at the dead go-go dancer, withered to a wiry frame by the nanobot virus.

"That won't happen," Harcan promised.

"Brilliant. Then what is your exit strategy? This city isn't safe. We don't have much time before reinforcements swarm this level from the cargo elevators," Solus demanded.

The androids formed a circle around Ellie and Harcan.

Ellie met eyes with several of them. "Here's the situation. I've hacked their control center. Scales can no longer threaten anyone with his proximity bombs. So, any means of escape is on the table. I detonated the last bomb in my former chassis. In terms of the network, I've reinstated maximum-strength settings in every android. I severed the firewall blocking remote communication between androids and sent out a flash message that channel eleven is now our private frequency," Ellie explained.

Harcan glanced at Ellie. "Good work. Let's do this. Order every android to meet us directly east, on the edge of this city near the black wall that keeps out the light."

"Why there?" Solus challenged.

Harcan cleared his throat. "Because we have access to trucks, bulldozers, and transport vehicles parked up just outside the wall near there, correct?" he asked, confirming with Ellie.

"Yes," she replied.

Solus stared at Harcan. "The east side of town has the largest elevator. That's where they'll be bringing down the bulk of their security teams to stop us. Not to mention, there are probably guards still on this level."

Harcan took in a deep breath. "The majority of the construction vehicles are parked on the east side of the quarry, and it's a shorter distance from here," he argued.

Solus crossed her arms, glaring at Harcan. "It's still a huge gamble. We risk engaging dozens of armed security personnel."

Harcan took a step toward Solus. "This entire rescue mission is a logistics nightmare. No one could have planned for this without an army, and even then, lives would be lost. We're doing the best we can with what we have."

Suddenly, a loud boom erupted. "Watch out!" Harcan warned. Part of the wall collapsed near the door as Harcan shoved Solus and Ellie away from it. The large pile of debris crashed onto the floor, narrowly missing Solus.

Ellie peered through the debris outside. "Security forces right outside! We need to move!" she shouted.

"We'll go out the back door, come on," Solus ordered, gesturing the group to follow her.

"I have control over their construction vehicles, but we need to take advantage of it soon. I'd give us an hour or two before they crack my firewalls." Ellie lowered her voice while sprinting beside Harcan to the opposite side of the nightclub.

Harcan looked at her. "Then send the order for *every* android to meet us on the east side of the city. We don't have time for a debate," he said confidently. Solus glanced over her shoulder at Harcan without a rebuttal.

"Doing it now," Ellie replied. The large group funneled into a narrow hallway, stepping on broken glass and ceramic.

Solus slowly opened the backdoor and peeked left and right.

"Hostiles?" Harcan asked.

"No. Follow me," Solus instructed, waving the group with her as they all darted across the street and through a dark alley. A streetlight above them flickered as they rushed by.

Harcan tightened the grip on his shotgun as he burst across the street. He could feel the hairs on his neck standing. At any point, he knew a firefight could erupt. He glanced at the front of the nightclub and noticed several soldiers entering the building.

"Stay low," he cautioned.

Solus threw up her fist, halting the group in the alley before proceeding down the next street. There were several empty brothels and food stands up and down both sides. Advertisement flyers with scantily clad androids were scattered on the asphalt beneath them.

Harcan turned to Ellie. "Can you cover the rear flank?" he whispered.

"Sure. So long as you don't leave me behind again," she answered.

Harcan's ears perked up as he stared at her with a long face. "Ellie, I—"

"I'm just kidding, Harcan. That was my decision. Besides, I can take care of myself now. This new body isn't just easy on the eyes. It was previously a combat model," she stated, grinning as she chambered a round in her rifle.

"I noticed," he replied, nodding his head as he recalled her weapon proficiency in the nightclub. While he welcomed the idea that she was more capable of fending for herself, a small part of his big-brother role felt diminished by her upgrade. He wasn't the only enforcer in the dynamic duo, not anymore.

Solus turned around and faced the group. She gave them an intense stare and narrowed her white eyes. "From here on out, we will sprint full speed to the eastern barrier. Don't slow down unless I say so. Move out!" she commanded, taking off across the street with blazing speed.

The rest of the androids immediately followed suit. They were fast, at least twice as quick as a human Olympic sprinter, even outpacing Harcan—on two legs, at least.

Harcan snarled as he fell further and further behind the pack, dashing through the backstreets.

He secured his shotgun on his back and dropped down on all fours, bursting forward. Harcan gained ground almost instantly, keeping pace near the middle of the pack.

He felt his coat bursting at the seams while he galloped forward. His rough paws pounded the asphalt as he barreled through dozens of filthy backstreets and alleyways. A cocktail of smells overwhelmed his heightened senses, the stench of rotting garbage, alcohol, even freshly spilled blood.

Harcan heard a man screaming ahead. Near the outburst was a trail of blood that flowed from an alley. A large rat darted across his view, fleeing the scene. As he passed by the alley, he caught a glimpse of a horrific scene: several androids had surrounded a miner, tearing him limb from limb.

A building quickly obscured the gruesome sight as they hurried by. Harcan didn't blame the androids for taking vengeance on their abusers, but they were risking their lives in delaying retreat.

Harcan continued to race by corpses, both android and human alike. All around him, it seemed there were scenes of survival playing out in dark corners. As he listened to the screams for help echo throughout the city, he realized most would go unanswered.

In a way, the chaos and death felt more natural than he wanted to admit. He thought he'd evolved beyond the old days of EL-59, but a part of him felt excited by the cries—*alive*, even. They made him feel like he was on the hunt again.

He felt the urge to howl, but he shook it off. He stared ahead, attempting to harness and refocus his energy on the objective.

Surprisingly, Harcan's android companions seemed to be in friendly competition with one another as they raced forward. He decided it best to join in. He surged ahead, overtaking one android after the next. Since Ellie had unlocked the androids' superhuman abilities, each of them seemed to be stretching their legs for the first time in many years, perhaps ever.

The android directly in front of Harcan was covered in piercings and tattoos. She noticed Harcan gaining on her and used the top of a dumpster in the alley like a trampoline, springing off the lid effortlessly as she soared six meters up.

She seemed to hang in the air for a moment, pumping her legs and arms midair as Harcan heard her liberating laugh. He imagined she was sampling the taste of freedom. Harcan recalled his own initial excitement and relief when he realized he was no longer a prisoner. He watched as she landed in stride and burst forward in a blur of speed.

As she left him in the dust, Harcan's hope was that she wasn't getting too far ahead of herself. It was far too early to celebrate.

Solus held up her fist, halting the group. The path ahead came to an end. Harcan could see several dozen androids amassing near the eastern edge of town.

Near the wall was a giant elevator that was descending from over a hundred meters up. It was much larger than the other elevators, with enough space to transport several vehicles.

Solus pointed at it. "They're coming, Ellie. At least two hundred soldiers are on that elevator, so whatever your plan is to get us through that wall, you need to do it now," she insisted, staring at Ellie.

Harcan looked up at the black barrier. He noticed small twinkling orbs embedded into the material meant to resemble distant stars.

In a way, it reminded him of the holographic outer wall on his former prison home EL-59. The night-sky illusion was complete with a full moon and stars. He recalled running his paws across the two-meter-thick bulletproof glass, wondering what was on the other side of the extermination incubator the Republic had created. He was told there wasn't anything outside of EL-59, that the glass barrier was the edge of the world.

"Harcan!" Ellie shouted, interrupting his thought.

"What?" he asked.

"Snap out of it. *Look!*" She gestured. The elevator had stopped halfway down. Its gigantic metal doors began opening from the middle. Harcan's eyes bulged as he noticed three dozen snipers in a prone position, aiming long rifles at them.

"Take cover!" Harcan snarled. The soldiers opened fire, striking androids near him. Several of them collapsed as Harcan pushed Ellie inside a small tattoo parlor.

He grabbed her at the shoulders. "Ellie, where are those vehicles?" he demanded.

Ellie's eyes rolled into the back of her head. "*Here,*" she muttered. Suddenly, a deafening roar erupted. The sound was like a million windows shattering as a bulldozer rammed through the barrier. Harcan looked up in amazement as the black wall seemed to fragment and crumble from bottom to top in slow motion, cascading glass downward in a shower of shards.

"Ahhhh!" Harcan cupped his ears with his paws as the sound reverberated throughout level six for what felt like an eternity.

Then, silence.

Everyone, android and soldier alike, looked up at the destroyed wall. The collapsed section of the barrier was shaped like a pyramid that was sixty meters wide at the base. A ray of sunlight beamed in from the surface onto the city of darkness, like a beacon that could be seen from anywhere on level six.

Hundreds of androids let out a roar filled with excitement, while others made a mad dash for the exit.

Harcan's jaw dropped as he watched the crowd of shadowy figures cross into the light. Some of them stopped and looked up straight up in awe as if it was their first time seeing the light. Others kept their heads down as they ran for safety, climbing atop the construction vehicles in a hurry.

Harcan had never witnessed such a picturesque, liberating scene on a mass scale. He was glad he'd lived long enough to see it. To him, the moment justified his existence.

Along with two gigantic dump trucks, the bulldozer continued inside level six, aiming directly for the soldiers' elevator as they continued to take shots at the androids.

It seemed Ellie was controlling each vehicle remotely, directing the trucks with her hands like a maestro. Several soldiers inside the elevator panicked and began rappelling downward on ropes to escape.

But it was too late. The bulldozer slammed into the gigantic lift, and the sound of wrenching steel and creaking metal rang out.

Three dozen of Scales's soldiers were flung out of the elevator into the streets, screaming all the way down. Most of them were killed on impact from the sixty-meter fall as bones could be heard snapping, and bodies splatted all around them. The metallic structure shifted nearly four meters on impact and began to wobble back and forth.

Harcan put his paws on Ellie's shoulders. "*Hey,* we're clear. Let's load everyone up on the trucks and get the hell out of here." He hurried her.

She didn't respond. Harcan waved his paw in front of her vacant, white eyes. "Ellie!" he said excitedly. She shook her head slowly as Harcan heard a dump truck smash into the elevator again, hurling the rest of Scales's men out. The structure warped and buckled, slowly timbering into a row of buildings near them. It crashed with incredible force, crushing two brothels to their foundations.

"I never told you," she mumbled.

Harcan raised his eyebrows. "Huh?"

Ellie gazed through him. "Before we met, I was abused by these same types of scum. They don't acknowledge us as *real* lifeforms, nor do they recognize our pain," she revealed, whipping her arms across her body angrily as the bulldozer slammed into another brothel across the street, destroying it. "And I don't acknowledge their pain either!" she yelled. The trucks went building to building, demolishing everything in their wake.

Harcan could hear Scales's security guards barking orders, followed by screams.

Solus burst into the room. "What the hell is going on in here? The wall is destroyed, Ellie! Let's leave!" she commanded, staring at her. Harcan looked outside the barrier and noticed hundreds of androids waiting in the trucks outside the wall.

"We don't have time for this," he muttered. Harcan picked Ellie up and slung her over his shoulder. He hurried toward the shattered wall. Ellie continued lashing her arms back and forth as Harcan heard buildings crumbling behind him. He glanced over his shoulder and observed a thick cloud of dust filling the city as Solus followed behind them.

Harcan and Solus climbed over piles of rubble and broken shards from the wall as they made their way out. He stepped over one of Scales's guards trapped under a large steel beam. His visor was cracked, allowing Harcan to meet eyes with him for a moment. The soldier didn't ask for help. Instead, it seemed he had accepted his fate.

Harcan dashed through the broken barrier onto the dusty gravel road, entering the light. He glanced up and noticed the gaps outside the crater that allowed the light to shine through.

He raced toward the lead dump truck. The vehicle's muddy, deep-treaded tires were colossal, nearly three times his height. He climbed up the ladder with Ellie over his shoulder and flung open the door, placing her on the passenger side of the cabin.

He put on her seatbelt. "Stay here. I'll be *right* back," he assured.

Ellie was unresponsive. Her head drifted back and forth as he descended the ladder.

Harcan dashed to the other side of the vehicle and noticed Solus climbing the ladder to another truck. "Solus, is there a shortcut out of this crater? An underground road, anything?" he demanded.

Solus looked up the spiral road ahead of them at him. "No! We'll have to follow the main road! But we've got bigger problems if you don't get a handle on that friend of yours first!" she shouted.

Harcan glanced up at the cabin. Solus was right. Ellie's unpredictable behavior could potentially jeopardize the remainder of the mission.

Harcan gritted his teeth and jumped back on the ladder, scaling it in a hurry. He saw several androids had scavenged rifles from Scales's men. They propped the long guns on the top of the trucks, readying for the escape. As he reached for the driver's side door, he looked into the city as the construction vehicles continued their rampage.

He could hear the quarry's security shouting orders and screaming. The bulldozer that destroyed the wall was now on fire, along with part of the city. It continued to tear through buildings, smashing into them with tremendous force and causing them to crumble.

Harcan entered the cabin and noticed Ellie's hands floating in front of her face as she controlled the vehicles. She reminded him of a wizard, directing her minions in a subconscious trance. Her face was covered with black soot as her solid white eyes pulsed.

Harcan shut his door and sat down. "Ellie, take the main road and get the *hell* out of here," he told her.

"All operational androids are present and accounted for," she stated in a monotone voice.

"I understand that. Can we leave now?" he asked.

Suddenly, the trucks lurched forward and started up the hill under her control. Harcan sighed in relief as his eyes followed the path ahead. The gravel road spiraled upward along the crater's outer edge at a thirty-degree incline before leveling out at the exit.

Harcan glanced in the side-view mirror and saw the other trucks following. He looked back into the city one last time, noticing Ellie had aimed the construction vehicles toward the city's outer edges. They began bashing into the level's main support beams.

Harcan's eyes followed the massive support structures that connected to the upper levels. The beams wrenched, and the sound echoed throughout the mine.

Harcan gulped, cupping his ears. "Ellie, those beams you're attacking are part of the top levels too. Destroying them would be catastrophic, even for us."

She stared forward without a word.

Harcan sighed. "*Look.* I'm not saying these miners are innocent, but—"

She whipped her head toward him. "I'm making sure Scales, and *everything* he built, is buried. Forever. If we don't stop this now, they'll just start over," she stated.

"I'm ordering you to stop this *now*," he commanded. Ellie didn't respond.

Harcan turned away from her and put his head back on his seat. He was going for a ride, and he had no control.

He looked up the road. Near the top, he saw dozens of smaller vehicles hauling ass out of the mine. He could feel the ground beneath him trembling as the quarry's metallic frame was battered.

As they neared the fifth level, he spotted hundreds of panicked workers pouring out of the mine's caverns onto the road. Some of them dropped their hard hats in their escape, while others stopped momentarily in disbelief.

Harcan watched as a miner ran across the road in front of them. Suddenly, a gunshot went off, fired from the back of one of the dump trucks. The worker's blue uniform was soaked with blood as he fell face-first lifelessly.

Harcan put his head out the window. "Hold your fire!" he shouted at the androids, slamming his paw against the side of his door.

Several more gunshots erupted as fleeing miners were shot down one after another. Before he knew it, the scene morphed into a shooting gallery with dozens of workers falling all around them. Some of them tumbled off the edge of the road, falling hundreds of meters to their deaths.

"Ellie, tell the androids to stop firing! At the very least, we need to conserve ammunition!" he ordered.

She turned toward him as gunshots whizzed overhead. "They won't listen, and neither will I."

Ahead, a miner was shot in the leg in front of the truck. The man turned and tried to scoot out of the vehicle's path, but he was too slow. He closed his eyes and screamed just before the truck's gigantic tires crushed him.

Harcan noticed that the main support beams were wobbling more with each passing moment, struggling to sustain the mine's multilevel structure. He had to do something.

Harcan looked at Ellie and slowly reached toward her.

He hesitated before placing his paw on her shoulder, but he closed his eyes and did it anyway. "Ellie, is there a point when vengeance has been served? I don't pretend to understand exactly how you or any of these androids feel, but we might not survive this if those support beams buckle," he warned, glancing up as small pieces of debris began to fall from above.

"*Ellie,*" he said, but she continued to ignore him. He shook his head in frustration. "And you accused *me* of being suicidal?" he asked.

Harcan removed his paw from her shoulder. He reached in his pocket, feeling for his flask. As he touched the cold steel, he remembered he was out of vodka. He sighed. "Shit. Dying sober was always a fear of mine," he muttered.

He looked up and saw a two-hundred-meter steel support beam giving way from the ceiling of level five. It crumbled under its weight, falling downward.

Along with it, the western quadrant of level five fell through, tumbling down with thousands of tons of debris. It crashed through level six, punching a seven-hundred-meter-diameter hole through it.

"Oh shit," Harcan mumbled.

The impact was too much. The mass and speed of the debris caused a domino effect as the entirety of level six collapsed in on itself, plummeting to the depths of the quarry.

The mayhem continued to thunder below for half a minute. Harcan covered his ears as the androids in the backs of the trucks began to cheer, pumping their fists into the air.

Harcan's eyes were glued below. The scale and scope of the destruction was unlike anything he'd ever witnessed. He saw the bulldozer that initially shattered the barrier. From here, it appeared like a small toy truck, tumbling down in an avalanche of smoke, debris, and fire into the darkest depths of the mine.

"I think it's safe to say Scales's chances of survival have diminished greatly," Harcan commented.

Ellie's head slowly turned toward him. "The mission isn't complete. We don't know if he perished. He could have retreated to the upper levels somehow," she replied. On the one hand, he felt Scales should be held accountable for his crimes, but Harcan was also relieved knowing that he wasn't responsible for the genocide of the amphibian's entire species.

Harcan wondered if he should have told Ellie the truth about Scales's situation. But at this point, it probably didn't matter either way.

Ellie increased their ascent speed as wreckage began to fall onto the road in front of them—steel beams, cargo bins, and barrels. It was like driving through a tornado with debris filling their surroundings.

"Watch out!" Harcan yelled. Ellie took evasive maneuvers to dodge a gigantic forklift that plummeted down from the upper levels. Ellie accelerated forward as it crashed between their vehicle and the truck directly behind them. It tumbled off the side of the road as rocks and small debris continued to pelt the vehicles at an increasing rate, cracking the front glass.

"This is getting worse by the second. I can't see a damn thing!" Harcan shouted.

"Trust me. You don't want to see what's going on anyway. I'm using the vehicle's onboard infrared sensors to drive," she replied, swerving back and forth.

The broken window, combined with the thick dust, made it nearly impossible to see what was ahead. Harcan looked at Ellie as she calmly throttled through the obstacles. He thought about the lapse in time when she first ran away from home. She never talked much about her life working odd jobs for shady characters on the wild frontier. He imagined that abusive experience as turbulent and dark, much like the road ahead of them now.

It seemed he wasn't the only one in their dynamic duo hiding horrors from the past.

After nearly five long minutes of dodging obstacles, they neared the top level of the quarry. It seemed the destruction and debris began to subside, and the uppermost levels of the mine would withstand Ellie's fury. Her eyes returned to normal as her eyes panned around the cabin in confusion, like waking from a trance.

"You doing okay over there?" Harcan asked.

"Never better," Ellie responded.

"Hm." Harcan looked across and saw the quarry's main headquarters covered in a thick cloud of yellowish-brown haze. He spotted Orchid's freighter on the dock. The thrusters were priming. "You might wanna get Orchid's ship out of here. Maybe we can use it later," he suggested.

"I've already powered up the engines remotely, but they've attached a locking mechanism to the landing gear," she told him.

Harcan observed hundreds of miners outside the quarry's headquarters, banging on the walls and doors to get inside. Some were without respirators and gagging in the thick, noxious smoke that ascended from the destruction below. The miners noticed Orchid's ship powering up. The thrusters lifted the large freighter off the pad, but the two large clamps on the landing gear prevented it from taking off.

"It won't budge," Ellie stated.

The miners rushed the freighter, climbing on the landing gear in a desperate attempt to escape. Ellie remotely increased the throttle, snapping one of the clamps. The ship went into a tailspin only a few meters off the deck. Its thrusters vaporized dozens of the miners attempting to climb aboard, melting them into mounds of smoldering black goo.

"Good grief," Harcan mumbled at the gruesome display. Some of them were partially burned, clawing their way across the floor, screaming in agony. Ellie watched with a blank stare.

Horrified, some of the survivors rushed back to the headquarters building, but the androids began firing on them from the backs of the dump trucks.

Harcan raised an eyebrow. "Here we go again. At least shoot the ones that can't breathe first!" he shouted out the window as the miners ran for cover. It seemed the androids did the opposite, targeting the miners with respirators while the others choked to death. Dozens of miners were dropped as they panicked, trampling one another as they ran around the building, searching for cover.

Suddenly, a large bay door opened in the back of the quarry's headquarters. Harcan's eyes narrowed as a box-shaped, heavily armored vehicle emerged.

"What is that?" Ellie asked.

"It looks like some type of Republic military vehicle," he answered.

The vehicle crushed two miners under its tracks as it moved through the drab fog. Harcan could see a massive gun turret on the top of the vehicle at least four meters in length. The barrel immediately swiveled toward Orchid's freighter. "Yep. That's a tank!" Harcan yelled. The weapon fired, and the blast sent out a shockwave that knocked down several miners standing in its proximity.

Orchid's ship exploded and crashed onto the landing pad into a ball of flames. The tank's gun pointed up, searching the road. It took aim at their convoy.

"Um. Ellie, they're aiming *right* at us," Harcan alerted her.

"We can't go any faster," she replied.

Suddenly, a glowing orange orb zoomed ahead of them. The projectile created a sonic boom that echoed throughout the mine as it slammed into the rock wall sixty meters in front of them. Hundreds of rocks were flung out onto the road.

The androids immediately stopped firing, hunkering down inside the beds of the trucks.

"They're trying to barricade the road with debris. They don't want to kill us, they want their androids back. Our cargo represents a *substantial* dollar value to the quarry," Ellie stated.

Harcan peered through a small broken section of the front glass. His eyes bulged as another tank round whizzed by, crashing into the wall ahead of them. This time, the impact was higher. Boulders the size of cars came crashing down, rolling slowly at them as Ellie weaved the vehicles back and forth to miss each obstacle.

"*Ellie.*" Harcan's claws dug into the armrest as a massive boulder skidded alongside their truck. It knocked off Ellie's rearview mirror as it wobbled past them.

"We're fine," she said casually.

"Are we?" Harcan shook his head as he looked out of the side window, searching for the tank. It had moved near the road behind them, adjusting its firing angle.

"We're not out of the woods. That tank is following us," Harcan informed her.

"And we've got *another* problem up ahead," Ellie replied.

"Huh?" A concrete barrier revealed itself through the haze near the top of the mine. A half dozen trucks were behind it with thirty armed guards aiming rifles at them. "It's their last-ditch effort to prevent us from escaping," Ellie commented.

The soldiers opened fire, shooting the dump trucks' tires and engine bays as the androids returned fire from the truck beds.

"They're trying to disable our vehicles," Ellie stated.

"Then at least keep your head down!" Harcan shouted, shoving Ellie beneath the dash. With the stock of his gun, he bashed out the splintered window, returning fire from the cabin as bullets peppered the front of the truck. His shotgun's wide array of beams allowed him to kill two soldiers with one shot.

"Harcan, stop shooting!" she yelled.

"Why?" he roared.

Ellie accelerated toward the barricade. "Just put on your seatbelt."

Harcan stared at Ellie. "You're gonna *ram* the barrier? That's your plan?"

"What do you suggest, *shoot* your way through it? With a tank behind us?" she challenged. Harcan glanced in his side-view mirror and noticed the tank gaining ground.

"Well, you do have a point." Harcan yanked his seatbelt across his thick, wide chest, barely able to secure it.

Ellie directed one of the dump trucks behind them to the front. The truck rode parallel to them, matching their speed as they barreled toward the barrier side by side.

The lead trucks' flat front grills appeared like a wall of steel covering the width of the road. Harcan looked at the dump truck next to him. He noticed the androids had stopped firing. Some of them were peeking over the bed of the truck at him. "Hold on tight!" he shouted, gesturing ahead.

"They already know the plan, Harcan. I'm in constant communication with them," Ellie stated, pointing to her head.

"Oh, then that must be terror in their eyes, not confusion," he replied.

He saw Solus lock arms with the androids on both sides of her. The rest of the group followed her lead, creating rows of linked androids. Harcan gathered the strategy would secure them inside the truck's bed on impact, preventing them from being tossed out.

The androids' demeanor seemed anxious yet supportive of one another. It reminded him of the humans on EL-59, in the way many would comfort each other during extreme situations. Even to the last band of survivors, some humans held on to a measure of grit and determination. Their willpower always impressed him, even delaying their inevitable doom. But, eventually, they were slaughtered just the same.

Harcan peeked over the dash as they approached within seventy meters. He noticed the quarry guards retreating, waving their comrades away from the barricade to the sides of the road. One of the vehicles behind the barrier spun its tires as it hurried up the path out of the mine.

Harcan glanced in the rearview mirror as Ellie slowed down the dump trucks behind them, creating a forty-meter gap between them.

He sized up the two-and-a-half-meter-tall barricades as they steamed ahead. They were staggered in three rows, strategically spaced ten meters apart, presumably to slow the android convoy down gradually. He took in a deep breath, placing his paws on the dash.

Ellie glanced at Harcan. "Brace for impact. Three... two... *one!*" she shouted. Harcan growled and his claws sunk into the hard plastic dash as both trucks slammed into the first barrier with incredible force. A few androids sailed out of the truck bed over them, tumbling down the side of the gravel road.

"Ugh!" The violent impact jolted Harcan and Ellie forward. Chunks of debris from the first row of barriers ejected as it was shattered. The trucks then battered through the second row of barriers, knocking them aside at the cost of over half their momentum.

"Keep moving! Full throttle!" Harcan said excitedly.

"I am!"

Hitting the third barrier nearly stopped them. The trucks were slowly pushing the concrete walls forward.

"We lost speed! We have to go on foot from here!" Harcan yelled, reaching for his door.

"*No!* Hold on!" she replied.

"What are you doing?" he asked.

All at once, they were slammed into from behind by the rear dump trucks. "Ahhh!" The impact shoved Harcan and Ellie's vehicle atop the barricades as they were jostled around in the cabin again.

Harcan recovered and put his head out of the window as Ellie stayed on the throttle. The truck's massive tires spun as they broke free, toppling over the barrier and crushing them.

The dump trucks steamed toward Scales's vehicles near the exit. They were forced to retreat again. Ellie nearly rammed the last truck before it leveled out onto the surface and scattered off into the desert in full retreat.

The androids stood up from the trucks' beds and erupted in celebration as the last dump truck made its way out of the quarry.

"Tell them to *stay* down. This isn't over," Harcan said plainly.

He narrowed his eyes as he focused behind him, staring at the quarry's exit. Suddenly, the tank surfaced in a hurry, aiming its cannon toward them.

"Ellie."

"I know," she commented. The tank rocked back as it fired, sending a streaking globe of fire that soared just two meters overhead. Harcan could feel the heat from the projectile.

"That was a warning shot!" Harcan shouted.

"I'm not stopping!" Ellie replied.

"Well, don't drive in a straight line, at least," Harcan suggested.

Another round fired, striking the rear tire of the truck behind them. A large plume of sand and debris was flung into the air as the impact caused the truck to teeter on two wheels before tipping over. It slammed into the ground as androids bailed out of the bed while it skidded for thirty meters on its side.

"Get to Orchid's diner!" Harcan shouted.

"They'll suspect she was behind Scales's assassination attempt. That's going to compromise her entire safe-haven operation," Ellie warned.

"It's already compromised." Harcan pointed. Ahead of them was a wall of heavily armed androids in front of Orchid's diner. They were touting grenade launchers and assault rifles, along with dozens of snipers on top of the restaurant's roof.

"I informed Orchid that we were leaving the quarry. Perhaps she suspected the worst," Ellie stated.

"She had to have known this mission was jacked up before we even left. Orchid's information on the quarry was spotty at best," Harcan said, keeping his eye on the tank. Strangely, it had slowed its pursuit.

"You're saying Orchid anticipated this?" Ellie asked.

"Maybe she knew there would be complications," he replied.

Harcan spotted Orchid standing in the middle of the androids in front of her diner. Her long maroon cape whipped in the wind. The unmistakable electric-blue glow of her eyes illuminated her face inside the dark hood draped over her head.

Harcan noticed she was holding a large rocket launcher propped on her shoulder. The weapon looked to weigh as much as her or more, yet she held it with ease.

Harcan looked behind him. The tank had completely stopped about three hundred meters from them. The quarry's smaller military vehicles were regrouping with the tank, parking in a row facing the diner. Now there were seven vehicles in total.

"They've ceased fire. Any idea why?" Ellie asked.

"They'll probably wanna negotiate, considering they have no control over the androids and we've escaped the quarry," Harcan guessed.

Ellie parked the dump trucks near the restaurant, and everyone piled out of them in a hurry.

Harcan covered his eyes as the harsh sunlight beamed down on them. "Ellie, arrange our trucks in front of the diner, like a barrier."

"Good idea." She compiled. Orchid's staff immediately supplied the androids that exited the dump trucks with weapons. They took up defensive positions around and on top of the diner. Orchid stormed toward Harcan and Ellie with two android guards beside her.

Orchid glared up at Harcan. "What the *hell* have you done?" she demanded, lowering her eyebrows.

Harcan looked around. "We brought you enough waitresses to start a franchise," he joked. His nerves were getting the best of him.

Orchid pointed at him. "This isn't the time for your smartass remarks. *Everything* we've worked for is at stake!" She raised her voice, locking eyes with Harcan.

Orchid did a double take, shifting her attention toward the bombshell brunette beside Harcan. "Is that—*Ellie?*"

"Yeah, it's complicated. I had to switch out my chassis," Ellie replied.

"Too complicated to explain why there's a *tank* aiming its barrel at us?" Orchid raised her voice.

Ellie crossed her arms. "It turns out you sent us into a hornets' nest with limited information to go on. We did the best we could," she answered.

Orchid glanced at the ground before staring up at Harcan. "At least tell me that Scales has been eliminated. Can you confirm that?" she asked with a long face.

Harcan looked at the brown-yellow smoke rising from the quarry. It ascended eight hundred meters into the sky as the winds carried it south in the otherwise cloudless light-blue sky.

Harcan sighed. "Level six has been completely destroyed, Orchid, and we've rescued nearly all of the refugees. Scales's trafficking ring has been crippled," he replied.

Orchid looked toward the quarry. "That's *not* what I asked you."

Suddenly, a loud metallic screech diverted everyone's attention toward the tank. They peered around the dump trucks. The top of Scales's head popped up through the tank's hatch briefly, like a turtle's head peeking out of its shell.

Harcan noticed Scales wasn't wearing his specialized liquid helmet. Perhaps he had transferred his offspring to a safer location before coming to the surface. Scales took a quick look at the diner and dipped back inside, sealing the lid.

"I guess *that* answers my question," Orchid confirmed, staring through Harcan with a defeated look on her face. She stepped close, glaring up into his amber eyes. "The Wolfman I once knew didn't need *details*, he murdered everything in his wake without question, and nothing could stop him," she said, showing her fangs as she hissed angrily.

Despite her frustration with him, something was liberating about her assertion. Harcan did have a conscience and empathy for others. Despite the unpredictable situation thrown in his lap, he tried to do the right thing for both parties involved. He wanted to ensure that Scales's race survived *and* rescue the androids. But as the thought crossed his mind, he gulped at the possibility that he might have to choose between the two.

All at once, the hatch to the tank opened again. This time, it was one of the quarry's soldiers. The unarmed trooper climbed out of the massive tank and began walking toward the diner alone with his hands up.

"Negotiator," Harcan said.

Orchid hesitated before waving off her snipers on the roof of the diner. "Hold your fire," she ordered. The approaching soldier's outfit appeared different than the others; he wore a black cape on one side of his shoulder, and there were red star emblems on his collars.

"That's a high-ranking Republic commander," Harcan commented.

"This oughta be interesting," Ellie muttered.

Solus broke away from the group of androids standing guard. She stopped a few paces behind Orchid, staring at her.

"We're curious. How do you plan to deal with this situation, Orchid?" Solus asked, gesturing toward the approaching soldier.

"Just let me do the talking," Orchid answered.

Solus stepped forward, towering over Orchid. "While we appreciate your efforts, Orchid, but you're not even an android. How can you speak for all of us?"

Orchid looked up at her. "Because I own the ground you stand on, and frankly, I'm the main reason you're standing on it. You want to negotiate? Fine. Go do it somewhere else, but not on my property," she scolded. She flipped her red cape and stormed off to meet Scales's representative. Solus gritted her teeth without a word as the vampire queen marched away.

Harcan and Ellie followed her. "*Hey*, Orchid. Slow it down. Let's talk about this first. Ellie and I learned a lot about the mining operation while we were down there," Harcan stated.

"There's nothing else to talk about. This is something *I* have to do," Orchid replied, glancing at Harcan. She narrowed her eyes at him. "Just be ready for a fight. You *do* remember how that's done, don't you?" she challenged.

Harcan looked back at his Roland-class ship on the landing dock beside Orchid's diner. He sighed and leaned toward Ellie. "How fast can you get my ship in the air?"

"Within a few seconds," she replied.

"Then get the weapons systems primed. This isn't going to be pretty," he ordered.

"Done. Just give me the word and I'll launch the Roland," she said.

Harcan wondered if Orchid's role as an activist was unraveling before him. The way she scolded Solus seemed personal, that this was *her* time to shine. Perhaps Orchid was subconsciously compensating for her murderous role on EL-59, cementing her title as a liberator in this crucial moment.

Admittedly, this possibility made Harcan feel better about his own shortfalls. That there were consequences to their violent pasts, and that he wasn't alone in the struggle to recovery.

The soldier in the dark helmet and gear stopped several paces in front of Orchid. Harcan and Ellie stood on each side of her. The trooper looked Orchid up and down with a commanding posture. "You, in the hood, you're the owner of this establishment?" he asked with a harsh, unknown accent, pulling his black gloves tight before pointing behind them at the diner.

"You already know the answer to that question," Orchid replied.

The soldier put his hands behind his back and paused. "Well, perhaps I do, but it *is* important that you understand who *I* am. My name is Wilhelm, and I represent the interests of this quarry."

"Would that make you Scales's superior?" Orchid asked.

"No. I'm more of a spokesperson for the leadership element here. Scales's job title has more to do with entertainment services. Whereas I deal with day-to-day operations," Wilhelm informed them, gesturing toward the mine.

He removed his dark helmet slowly, revealing a middle-aged man with a long, angular face. His eyes were sky blue, and he was missing the top half of his left ear. His short, curly white hair was matted and sweaty from wearing the helmet.

"This heat is just un-bear-able, isn't it?" Wilhelm asked, grinning as he looked around.

His wide smile seemed to stretch completely across his face. The outermost corners of his lips curved up sharply as deep wrinkles creased on the edges of his eyes. He looked past Orchid at the diner and began to pace back and forth.

He stopped, staring at Orchid. "I think it's safe to say that we've benefited from one another. We give our miners an allowance and temporary passes to get out of the quarry and relax. They come to your diner to eat and unwind. *You* profit from our business in more ways than one. It's worked well enough for years, not without a few bumps in the road here and there. But now, *now* we have a serious problem, don't we?" he asked.

Orchid outstretched her arms. "What problem? The way I see it, every android at my diner is here of their own free will. I didn't force them to come here," she challenged.

Wilhelm's grin flattened. He gritted his teeth and narrowed his eyes at Orchid. "Don't play games with me. I'll have you know we have enough firepower to obliterate your establishment, and we're well within our right to do so. Our quarry was nearly destroyed in this *revolt* you instigated."

"Me? You have zero proof that I was involved with this. Androids came to me for refuge, just like they've always done for years," Orchid replied.

Wilhelm nodded toward Harcan. "The unusually *large* mutant beside you. He was positively identified as an assassin by Scales *and* his security. Dozens of witnesses. That's attempted murder, and the androids seeking *refuge* at your diner represent a substantial value to our operations. We want them all back," Wilhelm said plainly.

"It's illegal to own androids for pleasure services," Ellie spoke up.

Wilhelm held his stare at Ellie, almost as if he knew her. "Pleasure services? What an awful accusation. There's no evidence that this takes place. Every single android is a companion to my knowledge, of their own free will," he replied, crossing his arms.

"Then why are you forcing them to come back?" Harcan spoke up.

Wilhelm took in a deep breath. "We're not forcing anyone to do anything."

Ellie smirked. "I'm not who you think I am, *Director* Wilhelm. You see, my specialty is cyber warfare. Hacking. And I'm directly responsible for this entire situation, not Orchid."

"Oh, I find that very unlikely," Wilhelm said, lowering his eyebrows.

"Then how was I able to access your vehicles?" Ellie challenged. She lifted her hand in the air and directed one of the dump trucks near them remotely. She closed her fist, stopping the truck on a dime several meters behind them before steering it back to the diner.

Ellie looked at Wilhelm. "That vehicle was in your possession less than an hour ago," she said.

"And that's called theft of government property, as impressive as it is," Wilhelm responded.

Ellie held up her index finger. "But what's even *more* impressive is the information I know about you and your colleagues. I know you're one of Scales's repeat sex customers and that you prefer extremely young male androids. I know you physically abuse them from time to time, too," Ellie revealed.

Wilhelm chuckled uncomfortably and shook his head. "That's completely absurd."

"Is it? Scales warned you multiple times about damaging his androids, and I have hours of video evidence that incriminate *you*, your superiors, as well as the miners forcing these androids to commit vile sexual acts. Now, unless you want me to transfer this data to Republic authorities *and* make it public, I suggest you and your comrades crawl back down into the hole you came from and never give Orchid any problems again," Ellie threatened.

Wilhelm gulped and raised his head high. He paused for several seconds. "Assuming what you say is true, what guarantee do we have that you won't release this evidence to the public?"

"You have my word if you leave peacefully," Ellie replied.

"Your *word*?" Wilhelm held a blank stare at Ellie for a few seconds. He was as white as a ghost. Wilhelm shook his head before slowly turning away. He began to march back to the tank, stumbling before regaining his composure.

Harcan looked down at Ellie as she slumped her head. "Please tell me you weren't lying about the possession of that evidence. Were you?" he asked.

Ellie's sighed. "I had to bluff him somehow. I saw the evidence, but I didn't have time to access the downloads," she answered. Harcan looked away, gritting his teeth.

Harcan growled under his breath. "Why didn't you tell us this was your strategy?" he asked her.

Surprisingly, Orchid seemed less upset about Ellie's gamble than Harcan was. Orchid glanced at Ellie. "While your decision to bluff Wilhelm without my support was foolish, it just might work."

"What?" Harcan asked.

Orchid looked over her shoulder at the tank. "I know more about Wilhelm than I let on. He's the *assistant* director of operations in the quarry, second in command overall to a man named Omar. The rumors are that Wilhelm has been aiming for Omar's job for a very long time. I'm hoping your threat was enough to lean on his aspirations, push him to convince Scales to back off."

Ellie smiled, staring up at Harcan. "See, my bluff wasn't a bad move, after all," she commented.

"No, but if it doesn't work, I'll scrap you down, and use you as spare parts," Orchid replied with a grin.

Ellie raised her eyebrows. "That would be a shame. I haven't even gotten used to my new body." Harcan looked at her. It appeared she was slowly returning to normal since her outburst during the quarry escape. Her eyes had completely returned to normal, and she seemed much more rational than before.

The trio made their way back to the diner, walking through a small gap between two of the dump trucks.

"I'm guessing that didn't go so well?" Solus stepped forward, questioning Orchid.

"Ask me again when this is over," Orchid responded.

They watched on as Wilhelm stopped beside the tank. He glanced at the diner and slowly climbed back atop the vehicle as the hatch opened. Wilhelm looked down into the tank as Harcan's hypersensitive ears perked up, homing in on the conversation.

"Well?" a throaty voice erupted from inside the tank.

"Not good, Scales," Wilhelm replied.

"Be more specific," Scales demanded.

Wilhelm braced his arms on the tank and shook his head. "The network infiltrations we detected were accurate. These terrorists are led by a hacker that's stolen files from our command center."

"What sort of files?" Scales questioned.

"Evidence that incriminates key leadership officials. A-hem. Video files. They're threatening to release them if we don't leave peacefully," Wilhelm explained.

Scales sighed, pausing for a few moments. "And what course of action do you recommend we take, *Assistant* Director Wilhelm?" Scales asked in a condescending tone.

Wilhelm wiped the sweat from his forehead as he glanced around at the soldiers in the trucks near him. "I think we should cut our losses and start over. Our only chance at keeping this evidence away from the public is to comply." Wilhelm lowered his voice.

Scales laughed as Wilhelm stared down into the tank unamused. "Is something funny to you, Scales? Because the way I see it, all our careers are on the line," Wilhelm asked.

"Think, Wilhelm. If they *truly* possess incriminating evidence against us, it's already been submitted to the authorities," Scales replied.

Wilhelm closed his eyes. "But maybe not? I-I don't think we should risk it. I think we should try and rebuild our android services from scratch," he said, pulling out a small thumb-sized device from his pocket. "I'm contacting Director Omar to make my recommendation," he said.

"Wilhelm, have you ever wondered why you've never been promoted to *director* of this quarry?" Scales asked.

Wilhelm shrugged. "I think that discussion is irrelevant to our current predicament."

"But that's where you're wrong, Wilhelm, and precisely my point. We don't need Director Omar's approval. Think of the big picture. Those androids are what keep our quarry in operation. Buying *more* androids will take me a year or more, and at that rate, we'll never rebuild the mine to get back on track. We'll be fighting desertion, apathy, and depression from our workers. The Republic will replace us if we don't continue to produce results," Scales explained.

Wilhelm held up his index finger and shook it slowly. "You need to understand your place, Scales. You're not even an official member of the quarry's hierarchy."

"No, I'm not, but you trusted me enough to leave me in charge of this tank, didn't you?" Scales asked.

"Huh?" Wilhelm demanded.

"At this point, you've failed at convincing them to surrender. And the only way to salvage anything is to take it by force," Scales replied. Harcan's eyes widened as he stared down the barrel of the tank gun turret. The dark barrel pulsed red-orange as the tank rocked backward.

"Get down!" Harcan yelled, shoving Ellie away as the tank round slammed into the dump truck to his left, blowing it in half. The force of the blast knocked him down. "Aaargh!" Harcan growled and rolled on the sand, putting out the flames on his coat and his neck.

The scent of singed fur filled his nostrils and his ears popped. His vision blurred as he regained his hearing, panning around in confusion. The first thing he saw was Orchid returning fire, launching a rocket at Scales's convoy. Orchid's rocket narrowly missed the tank, striking a truck behind it. Soldiers sailed out of the back of the vehicle as it exploded in flames. "Kill them all!" she yelled.

Androids from the top of the diner unleashed a hail of gunfire that whizzed over Harcan's head.

Ellie ran over and helped him to his feet. "Are you alright?" she asked, patting out the smoke on his coat.

He looked down, noticing the pocket that held his cigarettes was burnt to a crisp. "I'll be damned," he muttered.

"What's wrong?" she asked.

"Nothing. Get my ship in the air!" he ordered, pointing at the dock.

"On it," she said.

Harcan watched as dust swirled from beneath his ship, powering up the engines. The Roland-class freighter ascended quickly, leaning to one side as the motors screamed under maximum throttle. "Concentrate on the tank first!" he shouted over the gunfire. He watched as Orchid reloaded her rocket launcher and fired it again.

"Don't stop shooting!" Orchid shouted, full of rage. She snarled as one of the androids on the roof fell lifelessly from a well-placed gunshot.

As Harcan's ship ascended near the convoy, the tank's turret raised and fired, narrowly missing his freighter. Ellie took evasive maneuvers.

"Ellie, higher! Gain altitude!" Harcan shouted. But it was too late. The tank fired again, scoring a direct hit on his Roland-class ship.

Harcan's mouth dropped as the fireball of wreckage came crashing down in the middle of Scales's convoy, nearly hitting one of the military vehicles.

"Oh no," Ellie said, glancing at Harcan in disbelief.

Harcan snarled, firing his shotgun around one of the dump trucks. Scales's convoy of vehicles pushed forward, returning fire as an intercom blared:

"DROP YOUR WEAPONS IMMEDIATELY AND WE WILL CEASE FIRE."

A tank round landed near the east side of the restaurant, blowing a half dozen androids away. The blast sent arms, legs, and torsos sailing through the air. Orchid rushed toward Harcan and Ellie. "We need to retreat underground!" she shouted, pointing at her diner. "Go!"

But another blast blew a hole in the diner's roof, collapsing the front entrance and stopping them in their tracks. Debris rained down on them as they covered their heads. A few androids tried to flee into the dunes but were ran down by Scales's smaller vehicles. Hundreds of androids corralled around Orchid, but there was nowhere to run with the diner in flames.

They turned, facing the tank as it veered around the dump trucks at full speed. It stopped twenty meters from them, aiming its turret directly at Orchid.

Harcan panted as he looked left and right, looking for an option. Both sides had ceased firing. The intercom from the tank chirped:

"IT'S OVER. THIS IS YOUR LAST CHANCE. LAY DOWN YOUR WEAPONS."

Harcan glanced back at the army of androids behind Orchid. They clung to their weapons firmly. She looked at Harcan. "I never thought you and I would die like this, in defiance of the Republic that created us," she said.

"Me either." Harcan looked around him. The situation was clear. They were beaten.

Orchid lugged the rocket launcher on her shoulder. "I say we banzai charge the bastards. They can't kill us all," she estimated.

"Actually, they probably can," Harcan commented.

Solus turned and faced her androids. "Not before we take control of that tank. It'll be a cold day in hell before we go back to the mines. On my command, I want *every* android to rush that tank."

"Hold on. What are we doing?" Ellie asked, looking up at Harcan as the androids began to chant, almost like a war cry.

Harcan pushed Ellie behind him with his paw.

Orchid snarled and held her hand in the air. "On my mark," she said.

"Wait!" Ellie spoke up. There was a ruckus coming from inside the tank. Ellie pointed ahead as the tank's hatch flung open. Wilhelm crawled out with a bloody nose and fell over the side, scrambling to his feet. He took off in a mad dash toward the quarry.

"What the hell happened?" Orchid leaned forward, arching an eyebrow.

Harcan narrowed his eyes as the tank's turret swiveled away from them. To his surprise, Wes emerged from it, the old android cowboy from the landing dock. Harcan noticed his coat, and much of his fake skin was charred black as he aimed a six-shooter down inside the tank. "Now, come on outta there, you big scaly fella, or I'll have to make a mess of things. We don't want that, do we?" he warned with a smirk.

"*Wes?*" Orchid asked.

"Howdy, Orchid." Wes put his foot on the hatch as Scales emerged with his hands up. The androids cheered loudly as he held the pistol to Scales's head.

Wes tipped his hat. "When Harcan's ship took off, I figured I'd hitch a ride and get closer to the action. It was a bit bumpier than I hoped, but I was able to crawl under this here tank to an access port."

The few trucks remaining from Scales's convoy tried to flee, but Ellie remotely blocked off their escape path with the dump trucks. Over a hundred androids swarmed them, overtaking the vehicles with their weapons drawn.

Orchid chased down a jeep as the driver attempted to steer around the obstacles in a panic. She leaped onto the hood and shoved her hand through the window, ripping out the driver's throat as blood sprayed the glass.

Several androids chased Wilhelm down as he limped back toward the quarry, calling for help. He fell face-first, reaching out for the mine.

Ellie smiled from ear to ear as she marched beside Harcan toward the tank. She jumped and clapped Harcan on the shoulder. "We did it."

He laughed as she skipped around the tank like a young girl. Her newly acquired adult chassis seemed poorly suited for her antics, her breasts nearly spilling out of her top as she jumped up on the tank and turned toward Scales.

"Excuse me," Ellie said. She punched him in the face, knocking him off the tank.

His massive frame plopped onto the sand face-first as Wes jumped down, holding his aim at the amphibian.

Scales stared at Wes for a moment, shaking his head. "After all those years of tracking down androids for me, you disappeared, only to show up *now*?" he muttered, picking himself up out of the sand.

Wes arched an eyebrow at Scales. "Let's get something straight, partner. You lied to me by giving the impression that these androids were criminals. When I found out the truth, I quit. Then I bought my own freighter and planned rescue missions out of the quarry. But in those days, no one knew about the proximity bombs you planted inside them. I watched my ship blown to hell, full of innocent lives," he recalled.

Wes pointed to the partially destroyed dock beside Orchid's diner. "And I ain't left that same spot, not 'til today," he added, digging his pistol barrel into Scales's forehead as he grimaced in pain.

Harcan noticed Scales's leg was burned from his shotgun blast at the nightclub shootout. He wondered where Scales had hidden his offspring. Harcan observed a pair of androids dragging Wilhelm by his arms. He was kicking and screaming as they dumped him beside Scales.

A large crowd of androids began to surround the captives.

Solus approached Ellie and Harcan. "We've commandeered the remaining vehicles from Scales's convoy and have taken prisoners. Additionally, we set up a perimeter," she said, looking up at Harcan.

"Good. Any chance we need to worry about additional security from the quarry?" Harcan asked.

The powerful android flipped her wavy blonde hair behind her. "Not anytime soon. I would wager most of the security forces perished in the collapse of level six. Along with the soldiers we've captured, my guess is they would need to send backup from another facility," Solus replied.

Ellie looked at Solus. "Whatever judgment we're going to deal, we don't need to take our time. The diner has been destroyed, and we can't stay here," she estimated.

"Agreed. Then let us begin." Solus marched ahead of them and glared down at Scales.

"Rrrr-aaagh!" Enraged, Solus lunged forward and kicked Scales in the jaw. The impact caused his head to smack against the tank. His big oval eyes rolled back in his head as he lost consciousness for a moment, slumping over in the sand.

Solus leaned toward Scales as he snapped out of it. "My only hope now is to see you *beg* for your life. My pleas were never heard as your miners tortured and raped me, and neither will yours."

Five androids stood Scales up. They escorted him and Wilhelm about twenty paces from the tank to a flat spot in the sand.

"On your knees!" an android yelled. The angry mob of androids formed a circle around the two criminals, jostling for position so they could see.

Solus jumped atop Wilhelm. "This one first! I want Scales to see what's going to happen to him!" she shouted.

Wilhelm shook his head. "I tried to stop this attack! I wasn't in command! *He* was!" he pleaded, pointing at Scales as the bloodthirsty androids chanted and yelled obscenities at them.

Solus held Wilhelm down at the shoulders as the androids began tugging at his legs and arms. His left arm gave way first, ripping off at the shoulder joint as a large glob of blood splattered on Scales's face. He turned away, spitting out the blood.

Harcan noticed Ellie cringe at the gruesome display. "You don't *have* to watch this," he said.

"I know. We androids don't get much in the form of justice, so when it does happen, I don't want to miss a moment of it," she mumbled with wide eyes.

Solus kneeled, staring into Scales's eyes as Wilhelm was torn limb from limb, slowly. "You're next," she taunted.

Scales closed his eyes as Wilhelm screamed in pain, falling in and out of consciousness as his tendons and ligaments stretched and snapped.

"Open your eyes!" Solus shouted, forcing his eyelids open with her fingers. She turned Scales's head toward Wilhelm.

Harcan grimaced at the brutal display. He'd inflicted his fair share of pain, but most of his kills were quick. This agonizing display was another level of torture. The androids seemingly prolonged the pace, slowly removing Wilhelm's limbs while they basked in Scales's fear.

Scales's body shook from the stress. Now four androids were forcing him to watch, holding his body and head while they laughed and taunted him. As Wilhelm's eyes faded, Orchid parted the crowd and stood over Wilhelm.

Her body cast a dark shadow on his face. She stared at him for a few moments, and bent down, ripping into his throat with her fangs. She drained what was left of him dry, turning him into a bag of bones with only a thin layer of skin over it.

Orchid stood up and wiped her chin, licking the blood from her hand.

Solus pointed at Scales. "Now it's your turn. And we're going to make this last as long as possible," she said. Solus straddled him as the androids cheered. They grabbed each of his limbs, tugging at them as he shook his head in horror.

206206206206206206

206206206206206

206206206206206

"Wait!" Harcan roared. His deep powerful voice echoed throughout the sand scape.

Silenced ensued as Orchid and every android stopped, staring at Harcan. He met eyes with several of them.

"Is there a problem?" Orchid asked as a droplet of blood fell from her chin, dotting the sand.

Harcan stared into Scales's large eyes full of terror. His mouth was wide open, exposing his parched pink tongue. Harcan could see his rapid, panicked breaths pumping air through his mouth at a high rate, drying up all his saliva.

"*Please,*" Scales panted.

"Shut up!" an android screamed, holding Scales's arm.

Harcan waded through the crowd of androids and stood over Scales. "This isn't the right course of action. Not yet," he said plainly, gesturing toward Scales.

"Are you sympathizing with this piece of trash?" an android demanded, gritting her teeth in anger.

"No," Harcan replied.

Solus looked Harcan up and down. "You must not be thinking clearly; you were injured in one of the explosions. Perhaps you need rest?" she asked. She nodded Harcan away with her head discreetly, seemingly warning him that his outburst could be detrimental to his own safety.

Ellie walked next to Harcan and nudged him with her elbow, tugging at his paw to back away from Scales.

"Wait." Harcan panned back and forth. "Have any of you considered what happens next? After we kill Scales? We have no starship. We'll be on the open road, on the run. Why not keep Scales as a hostage in case we run into more trouble with the Republic?" he challenged.

Harcan gestured toward the quarry. "Not just that, but Scales is just part of the problem. We all know he's not the *end* of this. Director

Omar runs the quarry, and he understands that in order to keep his mine running efficiently, android sex slaves are part of the equation to keep the miners content. He'll just find another slaveowner like Scales to fill the void, and the cycle will continue."

"But he's too dangerous to spare!" Orchid yelled, stabbing her index finger at Scales.

"He could also be worth more to us alive if we can get him to testify against his associates in the quarry," Harcan argued, glancing at Ellie.

"Testify to who?" Solus demanded.

"Before we arrived here, I noticed a Republic district outpost on the map. It's just under two hundred kilometers from this location. As a bounty hunter, I know that each district office is required to have a sheriff and a social services office," he stated.

Orchid raised an eyebrow. "Harcan, it's called a *Republic* district for a reason. That means it's owned and operated by the Republic. I don't know if you got the memo, but they also own the quarry. The only positive in going there is the social services office. They can help relocate refugees to safe zones, but that sheriff is probably no help to us," she responded.

Harcan held his stare at Orchid. "I would wager that Ellie and I have more experience dealing with district lawmen than anyone in this group. They tend to be fair, and even hold Republic employees accountable for their crimes. We've brought several of them to justice, and I've personally seen them executed for their crimes. With Scales's confession, I don't see how the district sheriff could ignore this," he explained.

"And if he does?" an android demanded. The crowd stirred as Solus approached Harcan, covered in Wilhelm's blood. "What guarantee do we have that Scales can help shut down the quarry?" Solus asked.

Harcan showed the androids his palms. "Look, I'm not making guarantees here. What I'm saying is if we execute Scales *now*, we lose the potential advantage of his testimony. Scales is a well-known

Republic contractor, and if he incriminates his associates in the quarry, it could be enough to shut it down. I don't see the harm in trying. Worst-case scenario, they don't help us, and we execute Scales anyway," he said.

Solus looked away in deep thought. It was apparent that Harcan's plan wasn't what she wanted to hear, but it seemed she was considering his strategy's advantages. She began discussing it with a small group of androids off to the side.

Wes stepped forward and tipped his hat at Harcan. "Sorry, partner, but I gotta ask ya—how the heck do you plan on getting a confession out of Scales? This fella isn't known to be the most *honest* character if you get my drift," he said.

"I'll give him an incentive to help us," Harcan stated, looking at Scales. The amphibian turned his head away.

"Which is?" Wes asked.

Harcan pointed at the armored vehicle. "Wes, I need you to go back inside Scales's tank and take a better look for any hidden compartments. Tell me if you see anything unusual," Harcan hinted.

Wes looked around, seemingly aware that the androids' patience was running thin. Wes glanced at Harcan before turning toward the tank. "I sure hope you know what you're doing, partner, for your own sake."

Harcan's heart raced as Wes slowly climbed aboard the tank.

Scales leaned up, following Wes with his eyes as he neared the hatch. "What's the meaning of this?" he asked. One of the androids backhanded him across the mouth, knocking one of his teeth out. The dynamic seemed to shift after Scales's outburst. Instead of impatience, the crowd of androids seemed curious about Harcan's assertion. Every set of optics was focused on the tank as Wes rummaged around inside.

Ellie stepped close to Harcan, leaning in. "I'm guessing there's *something* you're not telling me?" she muttered.

"You'll see," he replied, scratching under his chin.

After several minutes, Wes remerged from the tank without his cowboy hat. He climbed out and shook his head, placing his hat back on.

"*Well?*" Orchid asked with her hands on her hips.

"What did you find?" Solus followed up.

Wes looked around. "It's the darndest thing. There's an escape pod of some sort in there. It's well hidden but big enough for Scales to fit inside. The damn thing is heavily armored too, and shaped like a gigantic egg," he revealed.

Harcan's eyes perked up. "But did you see anything *inside* it?" he asked.

Wes wiped his brow. "Yeah, I did. We're all used to seeing Scales wear that liquid suit full of little critters. Believe it or not, those creatures are *inside* that escape pod, swimming around. But the strangest part 'bout all this is that escape pod is connected to a heart monitor of some sort. Best I can tell, if Scales dies, the escape pod ejects from the tank and travels to an unknown location," Wes estimated.

Everyone's eyes shifted toward Scales as Harcan sighed in relief. The androids began to discuss the matter among themselves. "That's Scales's incentive to do the right thing." Harcan raised his voice.

Suddenly, Scales grabbed the closest android and began shaking its neck with all his might. The other androids began beating Scales senseless, but not before he snapped off her head.

"Don't kill him! That's exactly what he wants!" Ellie shouted.

A dozen androids held Scales down as Orchid's head whipped toward Harcan. "How the hell did you know the contents of that tank?" she demanded.

"It was a hunch. Without knowing my identity, Scales wanted to hire me as a bodyguard. Not just for himself, but for the creatures inside the escape pod. Those are *his* offspring, the last of his species, killed off by machines that turned against his race years ago," Harcan explained, gesturing toward the tank. "My guess was that he'd never let them out of his sight. And I was right," he added.

"Looks that way, partner," Wes commented.

Ellie leaned close to Harcan. "Now you've got me thinking. Did you purposely miss that kill shot on Scales in the nightclub? Was it because you were worried about the genocidal repercussions?" she whispered.

"Ellie, can we talk about that later? I need you to get inside that tank and disable the escape pod's ability to eject or travel autonomously. If Scales *is* killed, I don't want to chase that thing down," he requested.

Ellie glared at him before walking toward the tank.

Her look said it all—Harcan should have told her the truth about Scales. Harcan gritted his teeth as the army of androids seemed to be discussing the matter with Orchid and Solus. They began to take a vote on the matter, and after several minutes, it appeared the votes had been tallied.

Orchid and Solus approached Harcan.

"Well?" he asked.

"Sixty-two percent of our androids are in favor of your plan. If Scales testifies, we will postpone his execution. Another advantage is that Scales could be valuable as a hostage until we're able to relocate our androids to safe zones," Solus said.

Harcan nodded. "Fair enough. Can you give me a moment with Scales alone? I think saving him from a gruesome, agonizing death helped me build some trust. Probably best that I do the talking," he replied.

"Just make him understand the risk if he doesn't cooperate," Solus replied. Orchid turned and nodded as the androids bound Scales's feet and arms. They walked away, allowing Harcan privacy with the amphibian kingpin.

"Hurry it up. We can't stay here long," Orchid said. As Harcan stepped toward Scales, Orchid grabbed his arm. "I want you to understand something first. If Scales tries to slither his way out of this, you'll be held responsible. No matter how far we go back, I won't be able to help you."

Harcan moved her hand away and marched off without a response.

He stood over Scales. The ancient amphibian looked up at him. His eyes were swollen, and his jaw and lip were bloodied. "Well, look who it is." Scales coughed. "The mutant *smuggler* with a soft spot for machines," he said.

Harcan cleared his throat. "Look, it's real simple. You testify the truth at the local outpost or your children will die, along with any hope of your species' future," Harcan threatened. Deep down, he hoped it wouldn't come to that.

"Hm. What assurance do I have that my offspring will be taken care of once I've admitted these crimes?" Scales asked.

Harcan kneeled beside him. "There's no such thing as assurance for someone in your position. But there is a science division in every district outpost. If you cooperate, I'll turn your offspring over for preservation. Refuse, and these androids will rip you limb from limb, then tear apart that escape pod. They'll kill each and every last one of your brood in the sand."

Scales stared at the tank for several seconds. He looked at Harcan. "You've done nothing but lie to me since the first time I laid eyes on you. But I don't have much of a choice, do I?" he asked Harcan.

"Nope."

Scales sighed as blood trickled out of his mouth and onto his chest. The scorching heat dried it almost instantly. He panted, looking at Harcan. "The Republic science division you speak of was always my backup plan. The escape pod's coordinates were preprogrammed to rendezvous there. Those scientists could at least freeze my offspring until arrangements could be made to find a more suitable world for my people," he said hesitantly.

"So, you agree to the terms?" Harcan clarified.

"I'll testify against the quarry and confess to my crimes in the hope that you and the androids hold up your end of the bargain. The way I see it, it's my only option," Scales grumbled, slumping his head.

"What? Are we letting him live? *Solus? Orchid?* I do not believe this!" an outraged android demanded.

Orchid approached the distressed android, attempting to calm her. "I don't like it either, but if it helps future generations of androids, it's worth a shot," she comforted. The android held her stare at Harcan for a moment before storming off.

Solus leaned close to Harcan. "Be honest. What do you wager our chances are of making it to the Republic outpost? The trek could be full of danger."

Harcan looked around him. "No way to know, but we have to take our chances. Staying here makes no sense. We've got a high-profile hostage, a convoy of working vehicles, a small army of androids, and two of the deadliest mutants in the galaxy."

Solus looked back at her androids before returning her gaze to Harcan. "We androids don't have much experience in the wild. We've been slaves most of our lives, confined to the quarry. Orchid tells me you and Ellie are quite versed in alien worlds and perilous situations. We're placing our trust in you two, relying on your skill to get us to the district outpost."

Harcan took in a deep breath. "We're up to the task."

She nodded and narrowed her eyes at Harcan. "But I want you to understand something before we go."

"What?" he asked.

"No matter how dangerous the trip to the outpost might be, it won't compare to the anarchy that will follow if that outpost sheriff doesn't make things right. These androids will get their revenge on

Scales, lawfully or unlawfully. Just a word of caution, stay out of our way if the time comes," she said plainly.

Harcan held his stare at her and nodded. He looked around. "All I know is, we need to move out. Before we know it, the Republic will send forces to investigate the destruction of the quarry."

Solus narrowed her eyes at Harcan. She turned toward her androids. "Ready yourselves for deployment! We depart immediately!" she shouted.

To be continued...

Thank you for reading! I hope you enjoyed my little tale. I'm incredibly humbled that you ventured into part 1 of Harcan's story.

• • • •

The sequel Remy's Rejects is now available across all major ebook platforms.

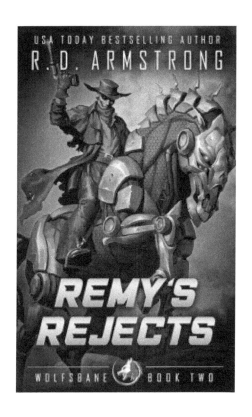

9 798223 200550